Going All In (Samantha Summers – Book One)

By

R. G. Peterson

Going All In

Trey Williams: basketball all-star, husband, millionaire, murderer.

Well-respected three-time all-star professional basketball player Trey Williams has a beautiful, intelligent, loving wife, a gorgeous home, an idyllic life, and was voted People Magazine's Sexiest Man of the Year. But when his housekeeper, Anita Sanchez – a woman who accused him of fathering her unborn child – is murdered, it all comes crashing down.

On the verge of losing everything, he reaches out to Samantha Summers, a smart-ass private investigator, ex-cop, and disbarred lawyer, who knows how to solve mysteries. What she doesn't know is the seamy side of professional sports. Sam invites her housemate and best friend, professional gambler Chancy Evans, to assist her with the case.

With every clue, and despite a host of viable suspects, the evidence against Trey is overwhelming. Sam and Chancy's investigation takes them to the dark underbelly of professional sports and the sinister characters who operate behind the scenes.

Who is the person who's so keen to see Trey's life ruined? And how far will that person go to make sure Sam and Chancy don't solve the mystery?

GNM Books

Cover Illustration by James A. Peterson

www.GNMBooks.com

Find us on Facebook @ GNM Books

Prologue

Anita Sanchez was cleaning up in the kitchen when she heard a knock on her front door. She waddled the length of the hallway cradling her belly and the unborn baby within. Thinking it was her twin sister returning to their house, she unlocked the door, twisted the knob, and asked, "Did you forget your key again?"

When Anita saw who was standing on her porch, she staggered back. After a moment of indecision, she said, "Come inside." She opened the door wider and motioned the man in. He wiped his feet on the mat and entered the hallway.

Annoyed that the man had shown up uninvited, she asked, "What do you want?"

"I came to see if I can get you to change your mind. Come to some sort of agreement."

"Why would I do that?"

"Money," the man said. "Lots of it." He explained just how much.

Anita laughed derisively. "You can't be serious. You think that will make me change my mind?"

Raising his voice, the man asked, "Why are you doing this?"

"Because it is the right thing to do."

"The right thing to do? For who?"

"For me. And for my baby."

"Your baby? You've got to be kidding. You've never given any thought to anyone but yourself."

"Get the hell out of my house," the woman spat through clenched teeth as she pointed toward the door. "Or do I have to call the police?"

The man didn't move.

"Now!" she screamed.

The color rose in the man's face. He let out a guttural, feral growl. He reached out, grabbed a trophy sitting on the flower stand less than a foot away, and swung it at Anita. The point of the base sunk into her skull with a dull thud.

She fell to the floor, unmoving.

The man dropped the statue. He hesitated then leaned over to feel if she had a pulse. Not finding one, he pulled the collar of his coat up to cover his face and hurried from the house. He rushed down the stairs, threw open the door of his dark-colored SUV, and drove away.

Anita regained consciousness long enough to call 911. The last words anyone would ever hear her speak were, "Trey Williams…"

ONE

My life as a professional gambler – I don't always win, but I seldom lose – had become boring and predictable, until my housemate, Samantha Summers, asked me to tag along on a murder she was hired to investigate. Sam, unknown to her, is the love of my life. Unfortunately, she sees me as her best friend and treats me like the brother she'd always wanted. Which makes my life interesting. And lacking.

It started at 5:52, the morning of February 11th as I stood before the door of my apartment engaged in a near-death or sure-death debate, knock on the door, wake Sam and subject myself to her wrath, or retrieve my keys from the front seat of my car parked five flights below, and, most likely, perish re-climbing the stairs.

As I raised my fist to knock, the door to our loft swung open. The woman standing before me was not the woman I'd expected to see. Her dark-brown eyes widened, and the color in her cheeks rose. She retreated a step and looked at my housemate, tilting her head in my direction.

"Just Ace," Sam said. "He's harmless."

The raven-haired beauty glanced my way, then offered Sam a tentative nod. Sam pulled her paramour inside and motioned for me to enter. To set the embarrassed woman at ease, I gave her my warmest, most sincere smile, which only served to make her

7

more uncomfortable. I held out my hand. "I'm Chancy Evans," I said, "and you are?"

"None of your business," Sam said, as the woman shrank farther from me, refusing to make eye contact.

She wasn't the first woman I'd seen saying goodbye to Sam at that hour. And she certainly wouldn't be the last. But she certainly was the most stunning.

Sam placed her hand on the small of the woman's back and ushered her into the sanctuary of our hallway, leaving the door open a crack. As your average, immature, red-blooded, American male, I inched closer to the door to eavesdrop.

The raven-haired woman said something about the media finding out, but Sam reassured her I could be trusted, and there was no need for concern. Once Sam had allayed the woman's fears, they said their goodbyes. "I enjoyed our night together," the raven-haired beauty said. "But we can't do it again. You understand?"

I looked through the security peephole. The woman leaned into Sam and gave her a long, soft, wet kiss. They separated in slow motion, staring with such lust into each other's eyes, I thought they might head to Sam's room once more.

Before Sam had agreed to move in, she'd asked me how I viewed lesbian relationships.

With a double eyebrow lift, I'd said, "Preferably in 4K high definition," which caused Sam's eyes to narrow, cutting laser beams through my skull. I think I misunderstood her question.

As I continued to watch the women share a second, more platonic kiss, I ran through the last four minutes in my head, the woman *had* looked familiar. I opened the door wider in hopes of jogging my memory. When the mystery woman reached the elevator, she turned to wave goodbye. Seeing me, she raised her fingers to her temple, blocking my view of her face, and showed me her back.

I called out to her, "The elevator's not work..."

The lift's doors parted, and the woman stepped inside. Without turning around, she leaned over, pressed a button on the panel, and closed the doors.

I threw my hands up in mock exasperation. I smiled at my housemate, who wore her usual morning attire, which consisted solely of a ratty old sweatshirt hanging from one shoulder, barely covering her ass.

"Hi, Sam," I said.

She didn't reply. I couldn't tell if Sam was annoyed or *annoyed*.

I looked once more toward the elevator. "She's something else."

In a tone belying her demeanor, Sam said, "Yeah, Ace. Your team lost one there."

I continued to stare at the closed elevator doors. "Man, I wanna watch."

"Buy a Rolex," Sam said as she stepped back inside our loft.

Before she could slam the door, I leaned back, moving my head out of the way, and asked, "Where'd you meet *her*?" It sounded as if I was insinuating the raven-haired woman was out of Sam's league. Not a chance. A former University of Wisconsin volleyball player, Sam stands six-foot-one, with eyes so dark they double as black holes. I've lost count of the number of women, and men, who'd drawn too close to Sam and became captured by those eyes. She's olive complected, with pitch-black hair. At least it was when I first met her. Since she'd become a private eye, Sam changes its color more frequently than most men change their underwear. That morning's version was white-hot blonde.

"I like your hair, by the way," I said. "Much better than the shocking fuchsia you started the day with."

She shrugged one shoulder, suggesting she couldn't care less what I thought before answering my earlier question: "I met her at Lie to Me Lounge. I was on a job. A client thought his wife might be cheating on him with another guy. I followed her to the bar."

"And?" I asked

Sam raised one eyebrow.

"Oh!" I said. "She's both. As in the husband's 'her' and her 'her.' "

"She hit on me as soon as my ass touched the barstool." And, because Sam's about as subtle as a brick thrown through a window, she added: "You look like shit."

The raven-haired beauty wasn't the only major loss for my side. Sam's got an athlete's body, with legs that stretch to heaven – the kind they display in ESPN's annual "Body Issue." It's her voice, however, that makes my knees shake like a newborn colt's. It has the same smoky quality as the room where I'd spent the night playing cards. Emotionally, however, Sam has more issues than Time magazine.

"Rough night?" Sam asked, watching me

slump in my recliner as I tried to recall where I'd seen the raven-haired beauty.

"Yeah," I answered, distracted.

"It's really put you off your game," Sam said with a laugh.

I shook my head.

"Seeing us kiss." When my blank expression remained unchanged, she added, "Usually, you'd have some stupid, if mildly amusing comeback, but the best you can come up with is, 'Yeah.' "

I gave up trying to remember where I'd seen Sam's latest lover. I leaned forward and said, "You'll never guess who I played poker with last night."

As if I'd asked Sam how to spell "A," she said, "If I had to surmise, I'd say they were wealthy, and at least one of them was some sort of celebrity."

She lost interest in our conversation and began to search for something. I scrunched my face like a petulant five-year-old and whispered, "If I had to surmise..."

Sam gave me a dismissive wave of her hand. "You asked. And stop acting like a four-year-old." ... Close enough.

Sam steadfastly believes I have Peter Pan syndrome. The first time she mentioned it to me, I asked, "So, does that make you Wendy?"

"No," Sam said. "That makes me a masochist."

Over the years, I've seen Sam, time and again, take a minimal amount of information and come to the correct conclusion. Like her knowing I'd been watching them through the peephole. "Man," I said, "it's freaky the way you do that."

"Not really," she said and returned to her search. "You wouldn't be this disappointed if they'd been regular Joes with little or no money. You'd have taken the attitude that it was more a waste of time than anything else. As for one or more of them being celebrities, your tone and body language suggested I'd be excited to hear who one of them was."

I thought back to my less than lucrative night. More to myself than Sam, I said. "I couldn't get a handle on the guy, and I ended up grinding the whole night. It drove me insane."

"Then, you should feel right at home," Sam said.

"This from someone whose family crest is a straight jacket."

Sam momentarily stopped her search, thought about what I'd said, and shrugged in agreement.

When she didn't chastise me, I said, "There were two marks who were Dick and Jane. You know…"

"Yeah, yeah. Easy to read."

"I had the celeb pegged as a mark. But every time I thought I'd picked up on his tell… I missed something obvious. I was sure he'd be the easiest to read…"

"Perhaps it's time you tried something more challenging than picture books." Sam found the remote – hidden under a stack of week-old newspapers – and pointed it at the TV.

I smoothed my eyebrows with my middle fingers, causing the corners of Sam's mouth to curl.

"We – me and the celebrity – ended up chopping the money." I added, "I'll give you three guesses who the guy is."

Sam had become locked on the morning news program and ignored me.

I took note of what she was watching and sat bolt upright. "Hey," I said, "that's..."

"Shush, Ace." She turned up the volume.

"National Basketball League player and Milwaukee Muskie all-star, Treymon Williams – better known to his fans as Trey – has been arrested for the murder of his housekeeper, Anita Sanchez. Again, breaking news, Milwaukee Muskie star, Treymon Williams, has been arrested for murder. We'll bring you more later as the story unfolds."

"You won't believe this, Chancy," Sam said. "That's my client."

I continued to gawk at the screen. "Really? Because that's my poker celeb."

TWO

Although they'd gone to commercial, Sam continued to stare at the TV.

"Trey's your client?" I asked. "I thought you said the wife plays for your side?"

"She did last night. Besides, I can't tell you all the gory details, no matter how boring your so-called life is."

I yawned.

"I rest my case."

"Hold on a second, counselor. I do all right."

"If by 'all right,' you mean having no social life, no real friends...besides me." Sam shivered as if somebody had walked on her grave. She often questioned why I'd chosen to be her one and only friend. Sam knew few people were able to tolerate her caustic wit and inept social skills. As if she'd never stopped, Sam said, "When's the last time you were in any kind of relationship, even one that lasted an hour? Sorry, I'm giving you way too much credit. Fifteen minutes. And when are you going to get your degree? You must have a gazillion credits." She gave some thought to what she'd said and smiled. "You know so much useless trivia, you could write the answers for Jeopardy."

"You can stop anytime, mom," I said. "And why do I need a piece of paper?" I swept my arm as if showing a prospective buyer my 2,400 square foot loft overlooking the Milwaukee River, the downtown skyline, and a sliver of Lake Michigan, paid for in full with my winnings from various World Series of Poker tournaments. "And where have your Criminal Justice, and Law degrees gotten you?" I asked. I didn't wait for Sam's response and answered my own question, "Stuck here with me."

I'd met Samantha Octavia Summers, the woman I share my trendy Eastside loft in Milwaukee's third ward, during our sophomore year at the University of Wisconsin. I'd accompanied some of my football buddies to a frat party. Sam was there with a couple of her teammates from the U's volleyball team.

Despite her intimidating beauty, I'd enough to drink that I decided to hit on her. "Hi, there," I remember saying. "I'm Chancy Evans. I hear you've been looking for me."

"Yeah, I wanted to say goodnight," Sam said, "because it's time you left me alone."

At that moment, one of Sam's teammates came up behind her and gently spun her around. They kissed. Not the chaste kiss of friends. Or the buss-on-the-cheek-to-say-hello kiss. But one of those trying to see who could touch the other person's tonsils first kind of kiss. Having never seen two women embrace that passionately – at least in person – I was determined to commit each detail to memory.

As I watched every straight guy's fantasy spring to life, Jean-Baptiste "JB" Lafayette, a six-foot-five, three-hundred-ten-pound, fourth-string offensive lineman from Louisiana, walked up behind me, reached around and grabbed Sam's ass.

Sam shot me an icy glare. I recoiled at her cold, take-no-prisoners scowl, and threw my thumb over my shoulder, pointing it in JB's direction. He reached around me once more, this time to grab her breast. I stopped him. "Come on, JB," I said. "Let's leave the women alone."

"Uh-uh," JB said, "God doesn't believe in that shit. It's a sin against nature. It's...it's... it's...a dom-somethin'."

"An abomination?" I asked.

"That's it. It's a domination, man."

"I could say the same thing about you, you Neanderthal," Sam said.

"Who you talkin' to, bitch?" JB shouted.

"Obviously, someone who doesn't understand multi-syllable words."

"Come on," I said to JB, "let's go find someone else for you to play with."

"Uh-uh. I want *her*." JB's eyes drifted to Sam's partner. "But she can bring her friend if she wants."

JB tried to step past me. I placed my hand on his chest. "Hey, Buddy..." Before I could finish my sentence, JB had rearranged my nose, making it point in a direction, which, if I followed it, would have me walking around in circles.

When I came to, I had an ice pack on my face and was seeing double. Which wasn't all that bad as it meant seeing two of Sam as she and her friend, Carly McCabe, attended to me. When Sam left to get more ice, I asked Carly what had happened.

"Your pal's on his way to the hospital. Sam made short work of him." Her smile turned mischievous as she thought of Sam whopping JB's fat ass. "His knee will never be the same," Carly said. "Sam choked him out. He was out for three minutes before he came around. Your friends had a bet going as to who'd wake up first. When he came to, crying like a baby, your teammates decided to cart him off."

Carly paused and got a mischievous grin. "Oh, and don't piss her off. She can hold a grudge."

She went on to tell me, when Sam was a freshman in high school, four guys, who didn't appreciate losing the on-going-put-down battles to a girl, assaulted her. So she learned how to take care of herself. Sam holds black belts in Jujitsu and Karate, and is proficient in Jeet Kun Do. Three years later, after the four guys graduated, Sam caught the leader of the group alone. Carly put a period on the end of her story. "He ended up in the same place your fat friend was sent."

Fourteen years later, after stints as a police officer in Madison, and as a high-profile criminal lawyer in Milwaukee, Sam found herself unemployed, in need of a place to stay. I have an affinity for lost puppies and perceive myself, rightly or wrongly, as someone who can repair damaged or broken people. I suggested she move in with me until her nascent PI business was up and running. That was three years ago. Despite her business' moderate success, we'd grown so comfortable living together neither of us suggested she get her own place.

Over the course of our seventeen-year relationship, we've been there for one another through thick and thin, good times and bad, for better or worse, fat and... You get the picture. We're like an old married couple. We take delight in giving each other a hard time, and, on rare occasions, we fight. And, like with most long-married couples, there's no sex. Sam refers to us as "Besibends" – best friends who are closer than the closest of siblings.

Speaking of sex, it wasn't the first time Sam had slept with someone she shouldn't have. Which brings us back to Treymon "Trey" Williams.

"Trey hired you to see if his wife was cheating on him, and, naturally, it led to you going to bed with her."

Sam turned away and mumbled, "After hearing her story and a few drinks."

"What's her story?"

Sam refused to look at me, but said, "I'm sure it'll come out now, so I suppose it can't hurt to tell you. Treymon impregnated his housekeeper, Anita Sanchez. When Shannon, aka, Mrs. Treymon Williams, heard the news, she acted on some deep, dark, revenge motive and fulfilled a longtime fantasy. Which happened to be me."

"She fantasized about you?"

"Not me specifically," Sam said. "I just fit the bill. There was an instant attraction...on both our parts. I don't know if either one of us could have stopped, even if we'd wanted to. She came on strong. I knew I shouldn't, but..."

"Isn't that a conflict of interest?" I asked. "You sleeping with your client's wife."

Sam shifted in her chair and stared out the living room window. "It's a gray area."

"A gray area?"

"When she told me what had happened, I decided to drop Treymon as my client. I just hadn't told him yet."

"So, what happened? Allegedly."

"No allegedly about it. She said the paternity test came back yesterday. The baby is his."

"Trey Williams'?" The reason I was having trouble believing what Sam had told me was because Trey was the poster boy for the NBL. He'd received the Citizen of the Year Award an unprecedented four times.

"I know you've been up all night,' Sam said, "but try to stay focused."

"There's no doubt?"

"No doubt whatsoever. At least, according to the test results. She brought a copy with her and showed it to me. Of course, he denied it. Gave her the old, that's-my-story-and-I'm-sticking-to-it defense."

I slowly wagged my head. "He didn't say anything last night when we were playing poker."

"You mean like, 'I raise you a thousand, and by the way, the paternity test came back positive. Congratulate me, boys, I'm going to be a dad.' "

"I didn't mean that. I studied him all night. He didn't give off any kind of vibe as if he was distracted or upset."

"Maybe he's just a cold-hearted S.O.B."

It didn't fit. Yeah, I know, I'd only played poker with the guy. But he seemed like someone who didn't have a care in the world. I have this sixth sense about people. It's more than mere intuition. It's knowing. Trey didn't have any sign of hiding a deep, dark secret. I saw him as someone who had life by the short hairs.

Sam watched me try to wrap my head around Trey doing something like that and remaining so calm. "Maybe he was so relaxed," she said, "because he knew Anita Sanchez was dead?"

"Possibly," I said, without conviction. "You'd have to be some cold-hearted bastard to kill someone before going about your day, or night as if nothing happened."

Sam's cell phone rang. She glanced at the display and held up a finger telling me to wait. She answered and spent the next two minutes listening. Finally, she said, "We'll meet you there in a couple of hours."

I might have been tired, but I did pick up on the "we" part of her answer.

"That was Shannon," she said. "I'm on the case. I'd appreciate it if you'd come along."

THREE

Greendale – Shannon Williams and Dr. Foucher – Trey's Agent

Sam gave me the address where we were to meet Shannon. I punched it into my GPS. The police had sealed off the Williamses' house while they scoured the premises in search of evidence. Shannon's sister lived on the Southside, in the suburb of Greendale, on a street called Serene Court. We wound our way through the subdivision until we found her sister's home: a massive, two-story, yellow and white, two-family, side-by-side, wood structure. I pulled into the driveway and parked alongside a Cadillac Escalade.

We were bundled in our winter coats to protect ourselves from the subzero temperatures that'd hung around Southeast Wisconsin for the past few weeks. My vanity didn't allow for a hat, so the short trip to Shannon's sister's front door stung my ears. As I walked past the Escalade, I noticed the color of the SUV changed with the light from forest green to purple and back again.

"Pretty cool. Right, Sam?"

"Boys and their toys," Sam said with a dismissive wave.

I saw the living room curtain fall back into place. We were five steps away when Shannon opened the front door. "Thank you for coming so soon," she said.

"No problem," Sam said with a hint of formality, showing none of the closeness the two had shared mere hours before.

Shannon had changed into black jeans, a royal blue V-neck sweater, and black flats. Without the heels, she was four inches shorter than me. "Please come in," she said. "My sister won't be back for at least an hour or two. We should have plenty of privacy. Trey suggested his agent join us. He's waiting in the family room."

We handed Shannon our winter gear, and she placed our coats on the rack stationed in the entryway. She led us down a twelve-foot-long hallway, stopped before an open archway, and motioned for us to enter.

The room was twenty-by-fifteen feet. Photos adorned most of the wall space, including a family portrait hanging above the fireplace. A floral patterned couch and two matching chairs were positioned before the large-screen TV resting in one corner of the room.

Sam gave the pictures a cursory inspection before she assessed the light-skinned, portly, African-American gentleman slouched in one of the chairs. I estimated him to be in his mid-fifties. As we stepped farther into the room, he rose and moved toward the three of us, holding out his hand to Sam.

"Samantha Summers," Shannon said, "this is Dr. Charles Foucher, Trey's agent. Dr. Foucher, Samantha Summers and …"

He gave Sam a guarded, knowing smile. "Yes," he said. "I know all about Ms. Summers." His eyes slid toward Shannon. It was apparent he knew the women had slept together. Sam extracted her hand from his, narrowed her eyes, retreated behind her impenetrable wall, and offered him her best reproachful glare. He took a step back and stumbled. To cover his less than macho retreat, he offered me his hand. "I can't say it's good to see you once more, Chancy, after you cleaned me out last night. You and Trey." He grunted a mirthless laugh, still sore about losing the night before.

"It's always nice to get together with a fellow poker aficionado," I said. "I'm more than happy to have you try to win it back."

"I'll take you up on that someday."

With the not so pleasantries out of the way, Shannon gestured for Sam and me to sit on the large couch as Dr. Foucher retreated to reclaim his chair. Once the rest of us settled in, Shannon moved to the lone remaining seat and moved it to face us so as not to be in Dr. Foucher's direct line of sight.

"I know why Ms. Summers is here," Dr. Foucher said to me, "but why're you here?"

I stole a glance at Sam and Shannon. "To bring the beautiful people quotient down to human level?" When no one smiled, I added, "I guess Sam thought with my knowledge of sports and having played poker with Trey, I might be of some use."

Sam cleared her throat. "I know you have a law degree," she said to Dr. Foucher, "but what exactly do you have your doctorate in? Education? Psychology? Math? Business? What?"

"None of those," Dr. Foucher said as if any of the degrees Sam mentioned were beneath him.

"Let me take another guess," Sam said. "African-American Studies. Couldn't you have found a college closer to home, in Michigan, than moving all the way out to Connecticut?"

Foucher's eyes widened a millimeter, astonished to find Sam knew his background. It was the same tell which allowed Trey and me to relieve him of his money, in what I suspected was one of his shorter nights of gambling.

When Sam had successfully unsettled the good doctor, she turned to Shannon. Sam rolled her neck and let her shoulders drop as she fought her nature, straining to change her mindset, and her tone. Her physical and mental transformation appeared quite painful as if she were dancing "The Tennessee Waltz" with a Sumo wrestler who had two left feet. Once the conversion had taken place, Sam said in a compassionate voice, "I assume you thought I could help. What is it I can do for Treymon?"

Shannon stole a quick glance at Foucher. "Actually, Dr. Foucher was the one who *suggested* Trey hire you in the first place. To check up on me."

Dr. Foucher shifted uncomfortably and stared out the patio doors.

"When they found Anita and accused Trey of killing her," Shannon said to Sam, "his lawyer mentioned he'd have his private investigator dig into it. I thought we should hire our own. Trey suggested we keep you on."

Shannon took a deep breath before continuing. "Despite what we've gone through the last few months, I know Trey couldn't possibly have done this. Killed anyone, I mean." She saw Sam's skeptical expression. "You know how many fights he's been in since playing in the NBL?" She didn't wait for Sam to answer. "Not one. Not even close. When guys knock him around, trying to intimidate him, he bounces back up and smiles. That stuff doesn't upset him. It makes him more focused."

"But this is different," Sam said. "This affects his reputation and his livelihood."

"I know Trey," Shannon said. "This didn't bother him. He knows he's innocent, that the kid couldn't possibly be his. When the lab results came back, he was shocked. Certain it was a mistake. He believes someone paid off the lab technician..."

When Shannon stopped, Sam asked, "Yes?"

Shannon gave Foucher one more accusatory glance. "I don't know. When we got the lab results, I lost it. I know ninety-five percent of the guys in the NBL, white and black, American or foreign-born, coaches and personnel, have groupies in every city. Before we were married, Trey was one of those guys, but a wife knows. Most NBL wives are in denial. They don't want to mess up the chance of losing their wealthy lifestyle. But Trey is different."

Sam made no effort to hide her skepticism.

"You think I'm one of those wives?" Shannon asked, offended. She slid forward in her chair, rested her forearms on her thighs, and spoke with unabashed vehemence. "Let me tell you, I could give up this lifestyle in a heartbeat. This is not what I wanted out of life. I married Trey because he's a kind, decent human being. Gentle. Thoughtful. Caring and benevolent. Not because of his celebrity status or his money. We give thousands and thousands of dollars to charities every year. I'm on the board of a half-dozen of those groups. I speak out on inequality, both civil and economic. Trey is with me every step of the way. He's very supportive. He lends his name to every cause the NBL gets behind. And he doesn't give it lip service like many of the others do. He knows we're blessed, the majority of the people are not anywhere near as fortunate as we are."

Sam held up her hands, signaling for Shannon to stop. In a reassuring voice, Sam said, "That's all well and good, but my job is to examine everything with a clear mind. I don't need to know he's Mother Teresa. Just like I don't care if he has the reputation of Vlad the Impaler. I'm only interested in the facts." Sam waited until she held Shannon's undivided attention. "If the facts prove he's guilty, I won't sweep them under the rug. On the other hand, if I determine he's innocent, you won't find a stronger or fiercer advocate in his defense." Sam waited until Shannon acknowledged her statement. When Shannon offered a tentative nod, Sam said, "Let's start from the beginning. When were you made aware of Anita Sanchez's claim Trey had gotten her pregnant?"

Shannon leaned back in her chair. "It was four, almost five months ago. October. The start of training camp. Dr. Foucher brought it to Trey's attention. Trey told me as soon as he knew."

Sam regarded Dr. Foucher, waiting for him to corroborate Shannon's statement.

"That sounds 'bout right," he said.

"Do either of you remember the exact date?"

Shannon shrugged her shoulders. "October 5th, 6th, 7th…some time around there."

Sam glanced at Dr. Foucher for confirmation. "I remember it was a Tuesday," he said, "because I drove up from Chicago to meet with the Muskies' officials earlier in the day to talk about a possible contract extension for Trey. That was…" He pulled out his smartphone, hit the calendar icon, and scrolled back four months. "October 7th."

"How far along was Anita at the time?"

"Two and a half to three months," Foucher said.

"The fetus was…?" Sam did the calculation in her head. "Around twenty-eight to thirty weeks…" Her voice trailed off, troubled by the murder of a pregnant woman with an unborn child ten to twelve weeks from term.

"There's something you should know," Shannon said with a catch in her voice, tears welling in her eyes. "When they found Anita, she was clinging to life. They gave her oxygen and did CPR to keep her heart going. The paramedics' kept her alive long enough for them to perform a C-section at the hospital. The baby has a less than 50-50 chance."

FOUR

*Attorney John Anthony Thomas' Offices –Trey's
Lawyer*

We left Shannon's sister's place before 3:00 p.m. We
were driving back to my loft when Sam's cell phone
rang. She glanced at the caller ID. It was from the law
office of John Anthony Thomas and Associates. She
answered the phone with a simple, "Yes?" listened for
a few minutes and said, "We'll be there as soon as we
can." She hit the end button. "That was Trey's lawyer.
The secretary, actually. Trey's out on bail. They want
us to meet them at his office in the US Bank
building."

I drove to what is the tallest of Milwaukee's
thirty-two skyscrapers and into the parking ramp
across the street. We took the elevator to the thirty-
third floor of the forty-two-story building and entered
the plush law offices of Attorney Thomas and
associates.

Treymon had been released earlier on five
million dollars bail, when Attorney Thomas argued
Trey wasn't a flight risk, and the crime did not appear
to be premeditated. As one of the most recognizable
people in the world, let alone the U.S., the judge
ordered him released pending the relinquishing of his
passport.

We waited in the outer office for over an hour.
The wait seemed interminable, mainly because Sam
had become uncharacteristically quiet.

"Tell me, Ms. Summers," I said, "what's going
on in that brilliant head of yours?" Sam refused to

acknowledge me. "Come on, Sam. I can tell something's bothering you."

In a little more than a whisper, she said, "I shouldn't have taken this case. Me having been with Shannon may influence the way I approach everything. I can still feel an attraction between us." I thought Sam had finished. I started to say something, only to have her add, "Plus, Foucher was so judgmental. It reminded me of Rainey." I watched Sam's eyes narrow and her lips purse as she withdrew into her memories of her hypercritical mother.

At that moment, John Anthony Thomas' secretary, Rose Marie McGuire, came out to get us. "Mr. Thomas can see you both now."

"He can see through walls?" I asked. My comment was lost on her.

The secretary ushered us into a large office with a panoramic view of Lake Michigan and the War Memorial Center. In the distance, through the bare trees lining Lincoln Memorial Blvd, we could make out the Milwaukee Yacht Club.

A vertically challenged gentleman, wearing a toupee that didn't quite match the graying hair beneath it, and clothed in what appeared to be an expensive suit, walked around his aircraft carrier sized desk and offered his hand. "Hi. I am Attorney John Anthony Thomas. We appreciate you meeting us on such short notice."

Sam didn't respond. I knew she didn't appreciate being left to her thoughts for the past hour.

"You have a great waiting room," I said. "The magazines proved to be of great historical reference. I found the 1989 issue of Life Magazine's pictorial on

Reagan leaving office especially enlightening. And thanks for the refreshments. You sure know how to treat a guest."

"I apologize," Mr. Thomas said, without sincerity. "Mr. Williams and I had some details to discuss and, because it's after hours, we no longer had anything to offer."

"That's understandable," I said. "I know how long it can take to make a Starbucks' run."

He ignored my censure and looked at Trey for help. With a broad smile, Trey stepped forward to greet us.

John Anthony Thomas muttered, "Obviously, you three have met. Shannon called and told me to let you talk to Treymon. She thought you might be able to help," he directed his statement at Sam. "I usually use my own private investigator, but Shannon and Trey insisted. Trey says he hired you for another matter. He holds you in high regard."

Treymon reached to shake her hand. "I'm pleased to see you again," he said. "Shannon tells me she's a huge fan of yours." The way he smiled at Sam, it was evident Shannon had kissed and told. He hugged Sam as if he were John the Baptist, washing away her sins in the waters of forgiveness.

Treymon stood 6'5". Even through his athletic-tailored, handmade, Italian, dark-gray suit, it was evident he was chiseled. He wore handmade Italian shoes, and a gleaming white shirt, which should have come with a label warning to avoid looking at it directly or go blind. His tie was candy apple red, and he had a handkerchief tucked inside his breast pocket cut from the same swatch of material.

Mr. Thomas motioned for us to sit so we could discuss Trey's case. He directed his remarks at Sam. "As I said, Trey and Shannon believe you can help clear Trey of this injustice. I'm aware of your excellent work with the police and sheriff's offices." Thomas left it hang in the air that he was also aware of Sam's disbarment for having an affair with a married female judge presiding over one of her cases. After a long moment, Thomas swiveled his chair, leveling me with a penetrating glare. "But how did you come to be here?"

"I have a Tesla Model S," I said. "Which reminds me, can you validate my parking ticket?"

Before John Anthony Thomas could call security and have me removed from his office, Sam said, "Mr. Evans can help. He's emotionally over-excitable."

Attorney Thomas couldn't decide if it was a good or bad trait – I'm sure he thought it explained my obnoxious, immature behavior.

"It allows him to read people," Sam said. "He's exceptionally sensitive to other's emotions. He can read someone's body language and tone of voice. He's a human bullshit detector. Plus, he's familiar with Mr. Williams, having spent a night playing poker with him. He also knows the ins and outs of professional sports, and an exceptional judge of character. He's been a huge help to me."

I'd never worked a case with Sam. The last part of her statement was as close as she'd ever come to thanking me for coaching her on how to overcome her social ineptitude – something, as you might have noticed, continues to be a work in progress.

"What can you tell me about me?" Thomas said, challenging Sam's statement.

"Someone have a deck of cards?" I asked.

Before I could offer my take on Attorney Thomas, Sam said, "You choose to give the appearance of being affluent, but you're not. You're well off, your watch, which is a knock-off, would have cost $214,000 minimum. That's out of your price range. You'd have to take out a loan for something that expensive. You're wearing it because you believe image is a large part of what you do. Your suit, although expensive, is four years old. It's a Norton and Sons knockoff. It didn't cost you the $4,000 plus price tag, but it had to set you back two grand. I suspect you wear it on days when you need to appear in court or impress a wealthy client. Your shirt, which *is* the latest style, has been dry-cleaned a number of times. Your suit has not. Even the best dry-cleaning slightly dulls the fabric and leaves a subtle residue and smell, which only a small percentage of the population can detect. Your suit appears too new to have been repeatedly dry cleaned over that time. You don't wear it often. Same with your shoes. They're Testoni knockoffs. Or they're seconds. The stitching is off, near the toe. The soles appear brand new, the creases in the leather show you haven't worn them much. I'd say they were purchased at the same time as your suit.

"You care for your family, but more for your reputation as the top criminal law attorney in town. You have one picture of your son and one of you and your wife," Sam said, pointing to the pictures on Thomas' desk. "But none of the three of you together.

No family vacation photos. What you do have are numerous pictures of you with well-known people. Most of the pictures are meet and greets. I can tell by the background in the pictures. Their posture suggests a staged, forced, happy attitude on the part of the celebrities. Something in their smiles isn't genuine. Their eyes?" Sam glanced at me, and I nodded. She went on. "You, on the other hand, are leaning toward them as if to suggest you have a more personal connection. The exception is the picture of you with the governor. It's different, somehow."

Sam looked beseechingly in my direction, her way of telling me I was up to bat. I cleared my throat. "The Governor's body language depicts a relationship where he knows, you know, way too much about him. Perhaps where the political bodies are buried."

I stopped and waited until Thomas finished scrutinizing the picture, and I held his full and undivided attention. "He doesn't like you. He sees you as a threat. Be careful. If he ever finds a way to screw you over, he will. In a heartbeat."

John Anthony Thomas shifted his shoulders then tugged at his already straightened tie.

"Aren't you glad you asked?" I said. "Stop me if you've heard this."

"I've heard this," Thomas murmured.

I ignored him and addressed Trey. "What do you get when you cross the Godfather with a lawyer?"

"I've heard this," Thomas said again.

"An offer you can't understand."

Trey released the stress from the day's events, laughing so hard, tears filled his eyes. Sam glared and gave me yet another dismissive shake of her head.

John Anthony Thomas acted as if I was opposing counsel and had submitted a piece of evidence destroying his case. I thought he might leap out of his chair and object, but when he saw Trey's reaction, he smiled.

Sam brought us back. "Mr. Thomas," she said, "you're considered the best criminal lawyer around, but you practice in Milwaukee. It's not the same as New York or LA or Chicago with a population of wealthy clients. Appearance *is* critical. I'm sure Treymon doesn't care about any of what I said. His only concern is whether you're talented and smart enough to save his ass."

Thomas shifted his attention to Trey to determine if Sam's statement was correct. Trey bobbed his head in thoughtful agreement.

"Now that we have that out of the way," Sam said, "might we move on to more essential matters?"

"Speaking of which, here's my parking stub." I slid the ticket across Thomas's desk.

He regarded it as if I'd used it to blow my nose. He gave me a condescending stink eye, hit an intercom button, and asked Rose Marie McGuire to come into the room.

"Actually, Mr. Thomas," Sam said, "what I need from you are the police report and their preliminary findings. We'd appreciate it if you have another room where we can talk to Mr. Williams alone."

Thomas protested, but Sam held up her hand and gave him a reassuring smile. "Give me a dollar. That way, you've hired me, and I'm part of your team, and we maintain attorney/client confidentiality."

"Ms. Summers, it is essential…"

Trey stopped him. "That's okay, Mr. Thomas, it'll be fine. None of these things the police are accusing me of are true. Besides, she works for us now."

Treymon handed John Anthony Thomas a dollar. He gave it to Sam. I got it next. Sam said, "You work for me now." She smiled mischievously as if I'd made a deal with the devil.

I snapped the dollar a couple of times to hear it pop, folded it, and placed it in my shirt pocket. "I'm going to have this framed and put up on the wall." I winked at Sam. She shook her head dismissively once more. If she kept it up, she was going to have brain damage.

We moved to a small conference room and sat around a six-seat table. Sam sat next to Trey. I took the chair across from him. She'd told me on the way, she didn't want John Anthony Thomas in the room when we talked to Trey. She knew as a defense attorney he'd prove incapable of not interjecting himself into the interview.

"Before we start," Sam said, back to business, "let's address the person who's *not* in the room." She hesitated then dove in. "You seem to be aware of Shannon and…" She took a deep breath, held it, then slowly let it go. "Knowing what happened between us, why would you agree to hire me?"

Trey considered Sam for a long time as he gathered his thoughts. As if giving a well-rehearsed motivational speech, he said, "I like being the best at everything I do. I take great pride in being the best three-point shooter in the league. In the world. I like being around the best. I like associating with the best." He paused once more. "I *need* the best. Whenever possible, I hire the best. That's why we decided to hire Attorney Thomas. It's also why I hired Dr. Foucher as my agent. Other players don't necessarily like him, but for me, he's been great. One of the best decisions I've ever made. Despite what happened between you and Shannon, everyone I spoke to said *you* are the best – not just in Milwaukee or even in Wisconsin. They stressed my best chance of getting out from under this is to have you on my team. Maybe my only chance."

He deliberated once more before adding, "In some weird way, I understand what happened between the two of you. It was Shannon's way of getting even with me for what she thought I'd done."

He gave further consideration to what he was going to say next. "I know this might sound strange, but with all that's happened, in some ways, it's a relief. Even though I know I'm innocent of all of the things I've been accused of, a large part of me still feels guilty. What happened with you and Shannon has helped to ease that. Shannon has assured me it will never happen again. I believe her. More importantly, I trust her. I trust her more now than ever. So…" He stopped and shrugged his shoulders, as a way of expressing he hoped his explanation made sense.

Sam shifted in her chair and remained silent as though she was giving what he'd said deep thought. "Fine," she said. "Let's start. Shannon showed me the results of the paternity test. It concludes you're the father of Anita's baby. How do you explain that?"

"I can't," he said. "I never touched her. Not in that way. A hug once in a while first thing in the morning and, again, before I left for the arena or practice. Nothing more than that. She became a member of our family, always smiling and pleasant, willing to do whatever we asked her, without complaining. She was a welcome relief from our last housekeeper. I swear I never touched her. "

Sam grew skeptical.

"You have to believe me."

"I don't have to. I'd *like* to," she assured him. "What do *you* think happened?"

"You should check out the guy who did the test. Somebody must've paid him off."

"It'd have to have been a substantial bribe," Sam said, "to convince someone to falsify a report. One, which could be easily checked. Did Anita have that kind of money?"

"I've got no idea. We paid her pretty well, a few dollars above the going rate, but..."

"But nothing that allowed her to move up socially."

Trey showed signs of irritation for the first time since we'd been there. "For god's sake," he said, "she's a maid." He stopped and amended his statement. "Was." He dropped his head a couple of inches before he raised it again. "We – Shannon and me – believe in economic equality, but that doesn't mean we pay someone triple the going rate."

"What did you pay her?"

"I'm not sure. Shannon handles that stuff for the house. I heard her say we were paying over $3,000 a month."

"Over $36,000 a year?" I said.

"I guess so."

"What did she do?"

"What did she do? She was our housekeeper."

"I know," Sam said. "What were her housekeeping duties?"

"The usual, I guess. She cleaned the place. Did our laundry. Made dinner once in a while, although, Shannon and I eat out most of the time when I'm not on the road with the team. Stuff like that."

"Did she have access to any of your personal items?"

He shrugged. "We don't lock anything up, if that's what you're asking."

"When did you learn she'd been murdered?"

Trey flinched. "The police were waiting for me at my house when I arrived from the poker game, a little before six this morning. They asked me when was the last time I saw Anita. I told them I hadn't seen her since she accused me of sleeping with her. I'd never even been to her sister's house. Everything was done through our lawyers."

"What happened next?"

"The police told me she'd been killed and wanted to know where I'd been around seven yesterday evening. I told them I was out for a drive because we'd received the official results of the test, and I knew Shannon was pissed. I was avoiding her until she cooled off. They asked me if anyone could substantiate that. I said I wasn't sure because I was locked onto the paternity results, I wasn't paying attention to anyone around me."

"Is that why you were late to the poker game?" I asked. Sam's eyes narrowed. Her body language screamed, don't interrupt again. I slid my chair farther from the table, determined not to disrupt anymore.

"I was trying to clear my head," Trey said. "I was worried 'bout Shannon. I'd never seen her react that way. Never. We'd had our fights and disagreements like every married couple, but this was a whole 'nother level."

"After they questioned you," Sam asked, "what happened?"

"The lead detective, Callas – I think that's his name – was asking me questions, but then got a phone call. When he hung up, he told me I was under arrest for Anita's murder."

"Did he tell you what they'd found to make you their number one suspect?"

"Uh-uh," Trey said with a shake of his head. "Not a word. They cuffed me and took me downtown. I didn't even get inside my house. They questioned me for two hours before Thomas showed up, ordering them to stop."

"Did you say anything to incriminate yourself while you were there?" Sam asked.

"I don't believe so. I told them the truth. That's all."

"How'd Thomas know where you were?"

"Shannon called him. Said she'd heard it on the radio. She called my lawyer, Mitch Jablonski – he does my contracts and the handling of the paternity suit. Mitch told her Mr. Thomas has the reputation of being the best criminal lawyer in town."

Sam pointed to the bandage on the side of Trey's left hand. "How'd you cut yourself?"

Trey moved his hand so he could see the bandage and shrugged. "I don't know. At practice the other day, I glanced down and saw I had blood on my jersey. At first, I thought it was somebody else's, because I didn't remember anything happening. Then I realized it was mine." He shrugged once more to indicate he had no idea.

"Is there anything else you can tell us about any of this?" Sam asked. "While they were questioning you, did they let something slip? How she was murdered? Anything along those lines?"

Trey scrunched up his face trying to recall anything that might help but gave up after a minute. "I've got nothing."

"Here's what I need from you and Shannon," Sam said. "Make a list of anybody who might have a motive to hurt you in any way. Someone you've screwed in a business deal. A teammate…"

"Whoa." Trey held up both hands to stop Sam. "They're my teammates. Teammates don't do shit like that. We may not like one 'nother, but… no way. Uh-uh."

"Men!" Sam said to me. "You can be such boys. So naïve. You won't trust your girlfriend or your wife, but some guy with whom you're in competition for a job leading to insider trading level money, you trust with your life."

She focused on Trey once more. "A. Complete. List. That means everyone. Coaches, teammates, your GM, the scouts, the dance team, your mascot. Any letters from disgruntled fans. Anyone you've had even the slightest disagreement with. Someone you remember not giving an autograph to, who cursed you out for blowing them off. Your mailman, if you didn't give him a big enough Christmas bonus. This is no time for you to see everyone in a positive light. If I knew you'd played poker with Ace before all this happened, I'd have you put him on the list."

"What?" I asked, sitting straighter.

"Do I have to remind you," Sam said to me, "that you were none too pleased with not being able to take Trey for every cent he had?"

I smiled at Trey. "Nothing personal," I said. "I hate to lose."

Trey returned the smile. "But you didn't lose. Remember? We split it."

"When it comes to poker, I'm with Freddy Mercury, I want it all. No offense."

"No problem. I get it. It's your living. If I score forty, and we lose, I'm pissed. The best nights are when I score forty *and* hit the game-winner."

Sam scowled at me, letting me know I'd driven the conversation off-road. I thought of reminding her she was the one who'd brought up the poker game, but after her menacing glare, I decided to live and fight another day. "Sorry," I mumbled as I sank deeper into my chair.

"Trey," Sam said, "I need that list. You two have to do it together. It might help trigger memories of someone who might hold a grudge. In the meantime, I'll get the police report and see how soon we can get access to the murder scene. Have your other lawyer set up another paternity test to verify the results of the first one, and I'll investigate the lab where it was done. Have any questions?"

"No questions, but I'd like to say, first of all, thanks for agreeing to help. I also apologize for having you spy on Shannon. I couldn't stand the thought of her with another guy."

"But it's okay with another woman," I said.

Sam shut me up with a you-are-beyond-hopeless look.

Trey didn't react to my comment, but when he saw Sam's discomfort, he repeated his earlier absolution. "I don't blame either of you for what happened. It's been crazy since Anita accused me of sleeping with her."

Trey gathered his thoughts before continuing. "When Shannon saw the paternity results, she lost it. As a professional athlete, you have women throwing themselves at you all the time. They'll slip me their room keys and phone numbers. The higher a player's profile, the higher up the food chain the women are."

He paused once more, deliberating if he wanted to add to what he'd already told us, then said, "There've been times when we've been on those five cities in seven days road trips, and it's tough to turn it down. What makes me stop, is knowing what it'd do to Shannon if she ever found out."

FIVE

When Sam and I left John Anthony Thomas' offices, it was past 7:00 p.m. Rose Marie McGuire had given us a copy of the police report. The file was thin because the results of the forensic and lab work had yet to come back. It contained the initial police findings, but no pictures or lab results. The sun had set. I knew Sam was eager to get back home to read the report. We walked up the five flights. I opened the door, Sam headed straight for the chair near the window, sat down, pulled her long legs up under her, and read.

The city behind her was lit, but the lakefront along Lincoln Memorial Drive faded to black as you looked out on frozen Lake Michigan. Never having seen a police report, I was surprised at how few pages it held. It would, I supposed, grow much thicker as they added evidence over the coming weeks, if not months.

Sam motioned for me to sit. "I want your impressions on everyone we've talked to."

"Shannon included?"

"Particularly Shannon."

"What?" I said. "A woman scorned?"

"I don't rule out anything."

Sam signaled for me to start.

"I read her as someone genuinely hurt and upset about the situation. She doesn't appear to be holding anything back. What guilt she feels, stems from acting out her revenge through a one-night-stand. She deeply regrets it, but there's a part of her that found it exciting. She likes you but is uncomfortable because she's not sure how you feel about her. She doesn't want any complications. The closeness she feels with you is why she trusts you, and why she agreed to have you on the case." I paused to let it sink in. The conflict Sam experienced was evident in her body language. I knew she felt much the same way as Shannon. I finished by saying, "Do I believe she could have killed Anita? I'd have to say, no. Unless she's a great actress."

"How about Trey?" Sam asked.

"I'm not finished," I said. "Did I mention she really likes me? She really, really likes me. If she weren't with Trey, she'd be all over me like flies on an ape."

"It's shit or ugly," Sam said. "And you're making that last part up."

"A guy can fantasize," I said as I summoned my best lascivious smile. "As for Trey," I said, "despite his effusive style – the hug, the handshakes, the openness – he's adept at hiding his true feelings and emotions. He shows you what he wants you to see. He comes off as non-violent, but there's a hidden volcano beneath the surface. That quick flash of anger he showed when you asked him how much they paid Anita was out of line for such a mundane question. He feels guilty about something. It's either, he doesn't want to come across as an oppressor, or he harbors some deep resentment toward Anita. Which, if she *did* lie about the paternity test, is understandable. Or – I just had another thought – he's upset he got Anita pregnant, and it came out when you mentioned her name."

"If you had to guess?"

"I'd say, he sees himself as this crusader for equality, and you questioned him about it. I have to agree with Shannon, he doesn't appear to be the violent kind. At least the kind who'd kill. But neither did OJ."

Sam gave thought to what I'd said. A few moments later, she asked, "Dr. *Foucher*?"

"I didn't pick up much from Dr. *Foucher* today," I said, "other than his righteous indignation about you two sleeping together. I suspect Trey told him. He spent the entire time trying to determine if the two of you might still be involved. Or might want to be involved. Or how deeply you're involved."

"Can we evolve from the involved part?"

Before Sam resolved to dissolve me with her revolver, I moved on from my Doctor Seuss moment. "Foucher didn't approve of you and Shannon knowing each other in the Biblical sense. More accurately, he very much disapproved. He was repulsed by what happened. I noticed last night while we were playing poker that he's protective of Trey. Losing to him didn't upset him half as much as losing to me. He became a real asshole."

"Like the rest of your kind." Sam's eyes narrowed, her body language spoke volumes. She resented Foucher for being quick to judge their one-night-stand. I also knew Sam felt guilty for sleeping with Shannon, betraying her client's trust.

"Whether Foucher's an asshole because he grew up being shit on and discriminated against," I said, "or because it's his nature, I'd have to spend more time with him to know. I've heard the rumors.

Being around him, I sensed Foucher has rivers of insecurity running through his veins. I do know if he were a bridge, I'd never ride or walk across it." When Sam didn't respond, I added, "If he were a plane, I'd never fly in it. If he were a house, I'd never live in it. If he were…"

"I get it," Sam said. "Move on."

"Okay. I'd say, despite having a law degree and his doctorate in African-American Studies, on top of being a high-profile agent, Dr. Foucher still feels intimidated in the presence of white people. Even Shannon makes him uncomfortable."

"How so?"

"He hesitated to make eye contact with her at any point of our conversation. Though it could also have been from him knowing the two of you slept together. Although no one mentioned it, that little dynamic threw everybody. Including you. Which was fun to watch. I've never seen you behave like that."

Embarrassed, Sam shifted her eyes downward, proving my point. I pretended to give the situation deep thought. "If you're asking me who did this," I said, "I'm going with the lawyer." Sam gave me a blank stare. As justification, I said. "He didn't laugh at my joke."

"If that's the criteria," Sam said, "than 99.99% of the free world is a suspect. Including me."

I ignored Sam's comment and added, "Besides, did you notice he kept referring to himself by his full name, John Anthony Thomas?"

"I'm sure that's because in England, John Thomas, is their way of referring to their dicks."

"I rest my case," I said.

I received another subtle shake of her head before returning her attention to the report sitting in her lap. She frowned. "This is bad." She flipped the folder as if it were a fan. She went on to note there was no forced entry, and, likely, Anita knew her killer. The police believed the cause of death was a deep head wound. They found Trey and Anita's fingerprints on the murder weapon, no one else's. There was also dried blood on her clothes, which wasn't Anita's. The police were waiting on the DNA report to see if it was a match for Trey.

The police had pinpointed the time of her attack at 7:10 p.m. because her watch had stopped when she fell, smashing it against the hardwood floor, gouging it twice, and breaking the crystal. She'd called 9-1-1 at 7:12 p.m. When the paramedics arrived, she was unconscious, barely breathing. She died at 9:36 p.m., never having regained consciousness. The neighbor who lived above her stated she'd heard arguing, but couldn't make out what they said because she speaks little English. She did say one of the voices was a male, and the other voice, Anita's, screamed Trey's name. The upstairs neighbor had gone into the kitchen and noted the clock on her microwave read 6:56 p.m. Furthermore, the neighbor across the street saw a late-model black Suburban parked in front of her house, but didn't see the person who drove it, nor was she aware how long it had sat outside Anita's place.

When Sam finished, I went wide-eyed. Sam gave me a what's-up shrug.

"I noticed a black suburban when I left the club where we played cards," I said. "It was Trey's."

SIX

Mequon – Shannon, Trey, and Dr. Foucher

I woke up sprawled in my recliner. The sun came through my living room window, forcing me to turn away as I opened my eyes. Voices reached my ear from the foyer. Through my haze, I watched Sam, in her favorite sweatshirt, talking to a petite blonde with a ponytail. The young lady seemed so peppy and bouncy, she reminded me of a college cheerleader. I thought she might do back handsprings down the hall.

Sam said something that made the young lady giggle. I tried my best to make it appear I wasn't watching, but Sam sensed I was. She gave me a mind-your-own-business squint. I kept watching.

They pressed their lips lightly together and bid their farewells. After Sam watched her latest lover walk toward the elevator, she closed the door.

"Did you enjoy that?" she asked.

"Not as much as I will later, in my imagination."

"I'm happy to have obliged. But you need to get a love life of your own."

I pushed myself into a more upright sitting position, stating the obvious, "I guess I fell asleep."

"I was telling you about the police report. When I looked up, you were out."

"Sorry. My all-nighter caught up with me. Why didn't you wake me and send me off to bed?"

"What? Now I'm your babysitter?"

"Obviously not," I said. "Any decent babysitter would've at least covered me with a blanket."

Sam pointed to a pair lying near my feet on the floor.

"Why'd you put 'em there?"

Sam ignored my attempt at humor and said, "You were snoring so loudly, I left. I went to Hooligans. I was minding my own business when Beth hit on me."

"Her name's not Bambi? She looked so young. Did you ask her for ID?"

"If she passed the Remi test, I wasn't going to question it."

Remi was one of the bouncers/doormen at Hooligans – a bar near the University of Wisconsin-Milwaukee – employed to make sure the underage students didn't cost them their liquor license, an enormous fine, or both.

I opened my mouth to say something, but Sam cut me off. "You'd have been disappointed. She was merely bi-curious, not bi-serious. We didn't do much. I pulled an Ace and fell asleep while she was talking. Hurry up and get dressed."

"Sure. Why?" I asked.

"We're meeting with Shannon and Trey to go over their list."

I took a quick shower, threw on some jeans, a V-neck navy blue sweater over a gray T-shirt, and slipped into some loafers. I wrapped a wool scarf around my neck and slid into my Canadian Goose jacket, leaving it unzipped to stop feeling as if I was walking in a sauna. I held the door for Sam, who was dressed similarly. The longer we lived together, the scarier it became. What next? I'd become as big a smart-ass as Sam? On the plus side, maybe I'd be more successful picking up women?

We jumped into my car and drove to the City of Mequon on Milwaukee's North Shore, where most of the Muskies' players own houses, although, describing million dollar plus homes that can comfortably accommodate a migrant family of thirty, as simply a house seems less than adequate. We pulled into the paved driveway of Trey Williams's massive, five-bedroom, fieldstone English Country home. Sam threw her shoulders back and became righteously pissed when she saw the purple and green Cadillac Escalade once more.

We parked on the drive. Sam marched along the winding cobblestone path to the front door, looking every step of the way like Yosemite Sam getting ready to duel Bugs Bunny.

When I stepped up onto the concrete slab at the Williamses' front door, I was awestruck. Their door alone would have cost close to what I'd spent on my loft. It was made of light oak, with half-moon stained-glass windows two-thirds of the way up, separated by a three-inch vertical strip of wood. If you put the two halves together, they formed a basketball – NBL logo, lettering, seams, and all. The rectangular glass framing the doorway, when merged, depicted the basketball court the Milwaukee Muskies called home.

Shannon must have been watching for us on one of the dozen hidden cameras surrounding the six-acre compound, because she opened the door before we had a chance to ring the bell.

She greeted us with a guarded smile. I sensed she was uncomfortable with the prospect of Trey and me with her in the same room. Okay, maybe Trey and Sam and her. But as I said, a guy can fantasize.

Shannon took our coats and led us down a twenty-five-foot hallway to a huge den. I checked out the rooms we passed to see if I could spot any of the residue left behind by yesterday's police search of their premises, but the house had been cleaned and put back together.

The den, the size of most homes' living rooms, was stacked floor to ceiling with awards and trophies from Trey's years of community work, as well as with his basketball memorabilia. He had framed pictures of every team he'd been a part of from AAU and high school ball to his years at U Conn, and then his seven years in the NBL as one of the great three-point shooters of all-time. There were also pictures of him with various dignitaries and celebrities. Two, in particular, drew my attention: one of Trey with President Obama, the other of him with BB King.

When Sam saw Dr. Foucher sitting in the room across from Trey, she didn't bother to hide her displeasure. "I didn't expect to see you here today," she said to Foucher. "I thought it was clear. This was supposed to be between the four of us." The edge on Sam's comment was so sharp, it could have easily sliced through an overly ripe tomato.

Foucher shifted in his chair. "Trey asked me to join you," he said. "He felt I could offer some perspective on their list." Sam and I swung our attention to Trey, who'd become interested in some imaginary spot on his desk.

Shannon motioned for us to sit in a tan leather love seat situated in front of a large picture window, overlooking an expansive backyard covered with two feet of untouched snow. We took our places, and Shannon sat next to Trey in a second leather chair, matching the one Dr. Foucher occupied.

Foucher glowered at Sam. Sam returned his dark look, causing him to squirm and do his best to avoid further eye contact. Despite his turning away, Sam continued to scowl his way, hoping to make him so uncomfortable he'd leave of his own volition.

"How about this?" I said to help bring Sam back to the moment. "We'll go through the list once, with Dr. Foucher offering any insight he might have. After that, he'll go to Starbucks while the four of us go over it once more. Then Sam and I can ask any follow-up questions we might have."

It was as if everyone had donned industrial-grade ear protectors and hadn't heard a word I said. "Good, now that that's settled." I clapped my hands and addressed Trey. "So how many?"

Trey didn't understand my question, so Shannon answered for the two of them. "We have seven people on the list. Trey feels most of them shouldn't be on it, but I told him we needed to think of potential motives, no matter how inconsequential we think they are." She handed the pack of letters across the desk. "Here are some thirty letters from people who have written Trey nasty notes over the past couple of years."

I rose and took them from her.

Dr. Foucher made a slight coughing noise, indicating he had something to share. He glanced at Sam, asking for permission. She continued to give him a fierce look. He said to me, "I've seen the list. I can understand why Shannon wanted some of the people on it. One of Trey's faults is he's much too trusting."

Sam mumbled, "You can say that again," as she stared at Foucher.

Shannon spoke over her. "We didn't prioritize them because we couldn't agree who should go where. The first person is Elijah Zacharias." It was Trey's turn to shift in his chair. Shannon sensed his ill ease, and said, "Come on, Trey. He resents you big time."

Shannon aimed her explanation at Sam. "EZ was supposed to be the star of the team, but since the Muskies drafted him, he's had to play second fiddle. First to VT Barker – who they let go to free agency because of his salary demands. Then they drafted Trey, who, after two years, surpassed EZ as the face of the franchise. They told EZ during his last contract negotiations, that when VT was off the books, they'd take care of him. Now Trey is scheduled to hit it big, and EZ believes Trey is going to get the money they promised him. Over 12 million dollars per year."

I said for Sam's benefit: "Ronald Landrace has allowed his star players to bolt and not pay them."

Sam nodded and asked, "Who else?"

"There's Sonny Stokes," Shannon said.

"Sonny?" I asked bewildered. Sonny Stokes was the Muskies' point guard and came off as easy going, a bit childlike in his behavior.

"He's in the same boat as EZ," Shannon said. "He'd love to get the max, but with Trey around, and Landrace and Andres Rosario controlling the purse strings, there's no way they're going to give him much of a bump in salary. Especially if Trey gets the maximum offer."

"I don't agree with having Sonny on the list," Dr. Foucher said. "He's a con man, but I don't see him being behind this. He's a pretty decent guy, just manipulative. Besides, point guards like him are in high demand around the league. If Landrace doesn't pay him, he'll go someplace else and still be paid handsomely."

"But not the max," I said. "The Muskies are the only ones who can pay him that. This will be his last huge contract. With his years in the NBL, it means forty million dollars or fourteen million more than anyone else." My statement made everyone's head spin and get cartoon eyes. Sam, once again, was the exception. Shannon went wide-eyed, her mouth agape. I wanted to reach out and give her chin a gentle nudge. I settled for a knowing smile.

Shannon quickly looked away, cleared her throat, and said, "Then there's Tim Howard."

"Who's Tim Howard?" Sam asked.

"He's our game-day operations guy," Trey said.

"Your game-day operations guy?" I repeated. "What? He resents having to organize your bobblehead nights."

"He's a miserable guy," Trey said. "Bitter, mean, two-faced,"

"How so?" Sam asked.

"He tries to make you feel like he's your best friend, but when the players aren't around, I've heard he tells whoever will listen, we're a bunch of prima donnas. That he can't stand any of us. He expects to be the team's COO someday. He's been with the team since the franchise started. What I hear is, he's gone as far as he's going in the organization. He's dead-ended, but doesn't know it."

"I don't see the motive," Sam said. "There're a lot of bitter people in this world. I'm sure there're a few running around your league."

Dr. Foucher cleared his throat again. "Trey went and spoke to the Muskies' GM, about Tim's attitude. The GM talked to Tim. Now Tim believes Trey is trying to get him fired. With the influence Trey has with Landrace…"

Shannon regained her composure and her voice. "Landrace is on the list. Of course, there's no way he did this directly. He'd pay someone. He's known to have a payroll of enforcers, primarily for his inner-city houses and apartments."

Foucher added, "If he can besmirch Trey's name, it'd mean he could offer him much less or let him go because of the scandal. Then he'd be off the hook with the sponsors and the fans. There's nothing he loves more than money. He believes the rest of the owners are fools, especially those who have to pay the luxury tax."

"Good word," I said. Everyone but Sam looked at me uncomprehending. "Besmirch. It bemuses me."

"Amuses," Sam corrected. "It doesn't confuse you, it amuses you."

"Huh?" I said. I received you're-such-a-child squint from Sam. The other adults in the room were bemused by my behavior.

"There's also Andres Rosario," Trey said.

Sam looked confused, so Shannon added, "He's the Muskies' CFO."

"Why is he on the list?" I asked.

Dr. Foucher explained. "Rosario's bonus is based on how much money he saves Landrace. We hear it's anywhere from five to ten percent for every dollar he stays under the salary cap. Once Trey signs his new contract, the huge bonus Rosario gets will evaporate. Rosario has been fighting us the whole way. But that's not uncommon. He fights every agent. He's the toughest guy in the league to negotiate with. He and Landrace prefer to let their players walk than have to pay them their market value and go over the cap. But with Trey, it's a losing battle. He's the most popular player in the history of the franchise. Even Landrace isn't dumb enough to allow the face of the organization walk away. He'd not only lose fans in one of the smaller markets in the league, but some of the sponsors, too. There's a rumor going around the Muskies' next TV contract, is in part, tied to the team bringing Trey back."

"I don't know," Trey said. "I hear Rosario's well paid by Landrace because he's made him so much money. Close to a half-million a year. I don't see it."

"Good," Sam said. "Anyone else?"

"One more, I guess," Trey said. "Our trainer. Miles Phillips."

Dr. Foucher noted our confusion, and said, "He came to Trey with a business proposition. Trey brought it to me. It was a bad deal. He wanted Trey to put up virtually all the money for the project. He asked Trey for thirteen million, with Miles being the working partner. It had to do with an orthotic insole he claimed was revolutionary. The trouble is, it's been tried already in Australia and proved to be little better than existing technologies. I told him we were going to take a pass. He didn't talk to Trey for the rest of the season. Even now, it's superficial interaction at best."

Trey added, "I hear he's lost a ton of money investing in some get-rich-quick schemes and on the verge of having to declare bankruptcy. When we turned him down, it got pretty ugly. He begged me to reconsider. Said I was his last, best chance to get out from under. Somehow his idea, or one similar, ended up with one of the insole companies. He blamed me for selling the blueprints to them. He threatened me. Told me he'd destroy me. He later apologized, saying he was under a lot of pressure, and he didn't mean any of it."

"Did you believe him?" Sam asked.

"He sounded sincere," Trey said, "but as Dr. Foucher mentioned, things have been pretty frosty between us ever since. I usually go to one of the assistant trainers for treatment and taping."

"Could you see him doing this?"

Trey shrugged. "He's a bit off. And he lies a lot."

"Like what?"

"Little things. After a while, they add up. Joe Carroll has caught him lying on quite a few occasions."

"Speaking of your head coach," Sam said, "we heard rumors you two don't get along," Something I'd shared with her during our car ride.

Trey once more shifted in his seat. Dr. Foucher offered his take on the situation. "Carroll believes Trey is 'too pretty.' Meaning he's not tough enough. Carroll's old-school. When he played, he made his living with scrappy play, taking charges, diving for loose balls, making the hard foul. Carroll feels when he's knocked down, Trey needs to jump up and fight the guy. He felt so strongly about it, he went to Landrace and told him he wanted Trey gone. Landrace ignored him."

"Is it something we need to investigate?" Sam asked.

Trey refused to answer, instead deferring to Shannon, who said, "As long as you're examining everybody else."

"Please be discreet," Trey said. "When this is over, I'll have to live with these people. It's hard enough to win when everyone's on the same page, but something like this, accusing people in the organization, especially teammates, would kill..." Trey was about to say, "kill any chances of winning," but knew he'd chosen a poor way to express it.

"No problem," Sam said. "We'll approach it as doing background checks. That we're interested in finding character witnesses for the trial."

Trey gave her a grateful smile. "Thanks."

"Anything else?" Sam asked. Trey, Shannon, and Foucher regarded one another and shook their heads. Sam said to Foucher, "Time for a coffee break." Dr. Foucher was either slow on the uptake or conveniently forgot what he'd tacitly agreed to.

"Can you get me a triple, venti, soy, no-whip mocha, please?" I asked as I made a show of reaching into my pocket for some money.

Dr. Foucher smiled, yet I caught a flash of irritation in his eyes. A millisecond later, he recovered, getting himself under control. "I'd be happy to. Anybody else? Trey, Shannon, your usual?"

He grabbed the twenty from my hand, letting me know it wasn't enough. I handed him a second bill. He inspected it. I knew he was trying to determine if it was part of the money I'd taken from him last night. I confirmed his suspicions. "At one time, those belonged to you."

"They do again." He said with a half-smile. Something I'm sure Sam thought matched his wit.

"That'd be great," Shannon asked, "How about you? Do you want anything?" It wasn't lost on the rest of us Foucher hadn't offered to buy Sam anything.

"No, thanks," Sam said. "I'd hate to put Dr. *Foucher* out." When Sam said his name, it came as close to the "F" word as possible without her saying it. I knew Sam could hold a grudge, but since Dr. Foucher had entered the picture, it had moved from level yellow straight past orange to red.

SEVEN

Sam waited until we heard the front door close, leaned forward in her seat, rested her forearms on her thighs, gave Shannon and Trey that hard, incredulous scowl usually reserved for me, and asked. "Have you considered putting that man on the list?"

Trey and Shannon were taken aback. "What?" Trey said. "He's my agent. I'm one of the few clients he has left. Most people think he's incompetent, which is why he's lost so many other players. The truth is, he spends most of his time taking care of me. And my best interests. The other guys resent that. They complain the only time he had left for them was after he tucked me in and read me a bedtime story."

A thought hit me. "Should any of those guys who left Foucher be on the list?"

"No," Trey said, "They've gone with other agents and are doing fine."

"Did any of them hold a grudge against Dr. Foucher?" Sam asked. "Could this be their way to get back at him through you?"

I could see that thought hadn't occurred to Trey. He glanced at Shannon for help. "Ahmad Salaam was the most upset," Shannon said. "He claimed Dr. Foucher failed to capitalize on Ahmad's name, and it cost him over a million dollars in endorsement money and deals."

"He's doing okay in LA," I said. "He's all over TV for Sprint."

"Exactly," Shannon said. "Ahmad believes the deal should have been made sooner. His new agent secured it for Ahmad within weeks of signing. He's still upset about it and says something to Trey every time they play each other."

"So, in some ways," Sam said, "the criticism is warranted?" Her newfound distaste for Dr. Foucher evident in every word.

"Sam, Sam, Sam." I sang the last one, capturing her attention. "Let it go."

She sat a bit straighter, rolling her neck to relieve some of the tension. "Sorry." She rolled her neck once more. "Let's move on. I have a couple of questions, and you're not going to like them, but I need you to answer me truthfully." She stared at Trey and Shannon until they nodded. "Shannon, where were you when Anita Sanchez was killed?"

Shannon moved away from Trey and stared at a spot halfway between Sam and me. "I was with you." It came out as a whisper.

"I don't mean then," Sam said. "The assault happened around seven at night. You drove into the subdivision at 7:48 p.m. You left the house an hour later at 8:48 and drove to Milwaukee."

It took Shannon a moment to grasp Sam's implication. "You think I could have done this?"

"I don't rule anything out. Where were you?" Sam's voice was far from accusatory. It was filled with the hope of hearing a solid, credible alibi.

Trey defended Shannon. "Come on now, you…"

Sam held up her hand. "We need to establish where Shannon was in case their accusation of you falls through. They'll turn to her as the next most logical suspect."

Shannon became flustered. I could see her searching her memory for where she'd been, what she'd been doing…or to come up with a cover story. It came to her. "I went over to East Towne Square."

"Did you go into any stores?"

Shannon gave a quick shake of her head. "I did some window shopping. Luci Boutique, the Last Detail, Faye's. I skipped Allure. I remember looking at some of the jewelry at East Towne Jewelers and shoes at Goody 2 Shoes, but I went to walk around and think, not shop."

"How long were you there?"

"I'm not sure. An hour, possibly a bit more. You have to understand, we'd just received the paternity results. I felt my whole world coming apart."

Trey slid his chair closer to Shannon. He raised his arm to put it around her shoulders, but Shannon pulled away and said, "I believed you. Then…"

"Then?" Sam asked.

Shannon stared accusingly at Trey. The temperature in the room dropped sixty degrees in one second, prompting me to wonder if I was in Spearfish, S.D. Sorry, you'll have to Google it. Trey moved back to his original spot, then past it, putting him out of Shannon's reach.

"Trey has always told me he doesn't want kids. We've discussed it time and again. He said it was because of the bad memories of his childhood. Then to hold the paper in my hand, stating he was the father of some other…" Shannon teared up.

"But, you're well off now…" I said to Trey.

Trey stopped me with a cold look. "It's more than that," he said in a harsh tone. "You don't know what it was like. I was so big for my age, the other kids constantly teased me. They called me dummy and stupid. They made fun of my feet. I was bullied and teased for as long as I can remember."

He glared at Shannon as if she'd betrayed him, and the dark secret from his past. "I don't like kids much," he said. "I know you see me signing autographs. Everyone has a part of their job they don't like. That's mine. I have to take myself to another place inside my head before I walk out to see those kids. It sometimes takes me hours to get over it. It's why I don't do personal appearances unless a sponsor asks, and why this is so outrageous."

Sam waited for Shannon to compose herself before asking her follow-up questions. "Do you remember seeing anyone you knew at the mall? Anyone come up to you and say hello? Did you catch the eye of a store clerk or security guard?"

At each question, Shannon shook her head. "I didn't notice anyone or anything," she said. "I couldn't even tell you what was in the stores' windows. My thoughts were on the paternity test, and how I could have been so wrong about Trey. That's when it really hit me. I decided to get even. I went home. I changed into something more alluring before driving into Milwaukee. As I drove, I realized I couldn't go to one of the more upscale places, because most people know who I am. I went to Lie to Me Lounge. I'd heard it was small and dark. Less chance of seeing someone I knew."

Sam focused on Trey. "How about you?"

"As I said, I was upset about the test results. I knew I hadn't done anything. Shannon was beyond talking to. I did what I always do when it comes to confrontation. I went for a drive. I drove to Port Washington and parked in the Coal Dock lot, looked out at the lake, and thought. I came to the conclusion the test results were wrong, or somebody paid off the lab tech."

"Same question," Sam said. "Did anybody see you? Did you talk to anyone? Get out of the car, walk around? Buy something? Gas, coffee, anything?"

Just as Shannon had, with each question, Trey shook his head.

Sam leaned forward. "Why'd you wait so long to have the test done, if Anita approached you in September?"

Trey shifted his focus to the floor before answering. "Dr. Foucher thought we should have the tests done outside Milwaukee. We agreed I should wait until I was back in Connecticut. We had a short road trip to the East Coast. When we had a night off in Boston, we, Dr. Foucher and I, drove over to Storrs and asked my old team doctor, Dr. Evans, to do the blood work. Dr. Foucher came up to Milwaukee the day before and took Anita to a clinic in Kenosha to have some blood drawn. I'm not sure how it works. They sent the blood to the clinic in Connecticut. We didn't want the possibility someone here might leak it. I know it's supposed to be anonymous but..."

"I thought they had to take it from the baby," I said. "At least they did when I was in pre-med."

Sam saw my confusion. "They bled people, too. In this century, they draw blood from the mother. They don't need to do an invasive procedure, taking the fluid from the amniocenteses or a CVS."

"You can buy blood from a pharmacy?"

"The local drug store sells it by the pint," Sam said. She offered me another shake of her head, before returning her attention to Trey. "When was that?"

"About two weeks before we got the results. I don't remember the exact date, but it was the night before we played Boston."

"I'll check the date," Sam said.

"You don't have to," I said. "That was January 23rd, a Friday. The Muskies played the Shamrocks on Saturday, the 24th."

Trey looked my way, stunned. Why do I get that from so many people...and so often?

I went on to explain. "I still bet on an occasional NBL game, or two."

He made tiny circles with his hands begging me to tell him more. "I bet against you guys," I said, "and the nine and a half point spread. You had two games against Brooklyn and Atlanta after playing one game at home. Before that, you'd played five games in seven nights on a Western swing. It was like you were finishing a nine-game road trip. The last game on any trip, especially one like that, teams seldom cover the spread. I made six large."

Trey gave me a weary smile. "We lost by twenty-one."

Sam stood. "Thank you. I appreciate you answering our questions. I'll let you know when we uncover anything. If you think of anybody else you might want to add to the list, let me know."

I remained seated on the couch.

"Come on, Ace, let's go." It wasn't a request but an order.

"What about my coffee? … And my change?"

"Starbucks' coffee sucks," Sam said. "I'll buy you one at Alterra's Lakefront Café."

We took a few steps toward the door. I knew what was coming. Sam stopped and asked another question. I watched Trey to gauge his reaction.

"One last thing," Sam said. "The police have determined the murder weapon was a dark gray trophy, a foot tall with a globe at the top. Do you recognize that?"

Trey recoiled. Shannon stared at him in disbelief. "Sounds like my Walker I. Kelly Citizenship Award." We waited for further explanation. Trey glanced at Shannon before turning to survey the corner of the room and his trophies. He walked over to them. "It's missing," he said. "The one I won last year. The other three are here but…"

Sam stepped up behind him. "Where should it be?"

"Right here in the front. It's gone. The one behind it has been moved to the front instead."

The shelf they looked at was more than five and a half feet off the ground. Sam needed to stand on her tiptoes to be able to see what it held. Stacked behind one another were trophies and awards. Unless you were searching for something in particular, especially something relegated to a spot in the back, it was easy to see how no one missed it.

"How did it end up at Anita's place?" Sam asked.

"I'm not sure. She could have taken it when she left, I suppose. I'm not sure."

Sam inspected the shelf. "You say she stopped living here in October when she accused you of fathering her baby."

"Yes?" Trey said, trying to grasp Sam's implication.

"The trophy was taken more recently," Sam said. "Based on the amount of dust where the other trophy sat, I'd say within the last month and a half. Unless she's been back here since then, she didn't take it."

Shannon and Trey exchanged questioning looks. "That doesn't make any sense," Shannon said.

"Who's been here? Inside your house during that time?"

"The two of us, of course," Trey said. "We did hold a New Year's Eve party here after our game that day."

Shannon grew excited. "That's right. We invited whoever wanted to come to join us."

"Who showed up?" Sam asked.

"Most of the team," Trey said, "coaches and front office higher-ups. Some of our neighbors and friends from my charity work. There were sixty people, at least."

"How about the people on your list. Were they here?"

They looked at one another and ticked off the names. "Rosario was here," Shannon said. "So was

Howard. I remember because I was a little surprised he showed."

"Sonny was here, because he brought some porn star with him," Trey added.

I perked up. "Which one?"

Trey started to answer, but Sam shut him down. "Don't encourage him. Who else?"

"Coach Carroll was here along with the rest of the staff. EZ was here for about two seconds," Trey said. "Even Phillips showed up. So everyone on the list, except Landrace."

"Dr. Foucher?" Sam asked with renewed hope.

"No. He didn't make it," Shannon said. "He was at a fundraiser for Chicago's Boys and Girls Clubs."

Sam didn't attempt to hide her disappointment.

"Was he here at any time around then?" I asked, hoping to raise her spirits.

"I don't think so," Trey said. "I don't remember him being here since this began. Until today. We'd always meet at our practice facility. Not here."

Sam checked out one of the lower shelves. "Who cleans your place?"

"We hired a cleaning service called The Merry Maids of Mequon."

"You may want to ask them to clean all the shelves, not just the ones they can easily reach."

Sam walked away. I nudged her, motioning toward Trey and Shannon with my head. With a bit of reluctance, Sam said, "Thanks for the list."

EIGHT

I took the scenic route along the lakefront. The day was crisp but warmer than it'd been, with the temperature in the mid-teens. I pulled into Altera's, which I noticed had changed its name. It was now Colectivo Coffee Café. I hoped they hadn't changed the coffee, as well. It had been voted the best in the city. The cafe was nestled in the base of a steep hill, covered with decade-old trees running the length of its slope, situated on the west side of Lake Michigan's shoreline. I enjoyed coming here during the summer to sit and contemplate life. I thought of the place as a first step in Milwaukee's attempt to transition from one of the largest manufacturing cities in the world, to a more cosmopolitan one, its diversity seen in the endless ethnic festivals held every weekend from Memorial Day through Labor Day.

We ordered our drinks – an extra-large mocha for me, a medium-sized Chai Tea for Sam. I waited for Sam to pull out her wallet, but I'd still be standing there at the end of summer if I hadn't extracted mine.

We headed upstairs and found an empty table overlooking the lake. We were an hour early for the lunch crowd and had the upstairs to ourselves.

"A thanks would be nice," I said.

"You're welcome."

"No. ... Oh, never mind."

I'd loosened my scarf and draped my coat over the chair. Sam asked me to tell her my impressions. I took a sip. "It doesn't appear to be much different than I remember. The coffee tastes the same, but I'm not in love with the new name."

That received a dramatic sigh from Sam. "It means 'collective' in Spanish." She said and waited.

"What the heck do the Spanish know about coffee?"

"It's Latin-American."

"Oh!" I said. "Okay. Here goes. Trey is sincere. He believes he's innocent of everything. I can see the confusion in his eyes every time the paternity test gets mentioned. It's as if he's watching Jar Jar Binks' scenes in Episode One on continuous loop. The one thing that struck me, though, was his unwavering dislike of kids. It goes against everything we've seen from him when he's in public. He'd make a great actor. Probably why I'd had so much trouble reading him the night we played." I went silent, getting lost in my thoughts.

Sam barked out a laugh, which brought me out of my reverie.

"What?" I wiped my mouth, thinking I'd left foam perched on my lip.

Sam pointed to a place near the side of her mouth. I imitated her. She gave a quick shake of her head and pointed to the other side, I switched and wiped that side. Another quick shake from Sam as she moved her finger a little higher on her face. I mirrored her move. She pointed even higher, this time next to her nose. I realized she was jerking me around, causing her to laugh even harder.

"Did you hear they've decided to take the word gullible out of the dictionary?" she said.

"When did they do that!?" I asked, trying my best to appear shocked.

"I can't get over how much it still bothers you. You walked away with, what? $15,000. And you're still obsessing over not winning it all."

"$15,500," I said. "It's not about the money. It's what I do for a living. How do you think Trey'd feel if I beat him in a game of one-on-one? Besides, I'm more bothered I couldn't get a better handle on him."

"Do you think it's still a possibility? That he did do it, and you're just having trouble reading him?"

I thought about it for a few seconds and shrugged. "Maybe."

"How did you read his reaction to the mention of the trophy being the murder weapon?" Sam asked.

"He was genuinely bewildered. Your statement came out of thin air. He didn't see the high, inside heat coming, pulling the rug out from under him."

Sam drummed her fingers on the table.

It encouraged me to continue, "When he went over to see if one of the trophies was missing, it was impossible to see his reaction because his back was to me, but his tone suggested he was shocked. Stunned, actually. That's hard to fake."

"How about Shannon?" Sam asked.

"Her, I have absolutely no trouble reading. She's devastated by what Trey is putting her through. The whole, somebody else having Trey's baby, hit her like a tsunami. She's caught in a firestorm, and now she's come to the fork in the road."

"Maybe she should take it to escape your crappy metaphors."

I smiled and added, "Is she capable of killing someone, especially someone having the baby she desperately wants? Sure, I guess anything is possible. But..."

"It doesn't compute."

"I can't see it."

"Is it possible, as with most guys, you're having trouble believing someone so beautiful could do something so ugly?"

"Trust me. *You* cured me of that a long, long...long...long..." Sam gave me her patented death stare. "Long time ago. Besides, I'm past it now."

"Yeah," Sam said, "and I'm straight."

"I knew it," I said. "When do you want to go out on a date?"

"Just analyze her, please."

I offered her a sly smile, making her turn away.

"Although this has thrown her, she believes Trey. Or at least she believes Trey believes he's innocent. Is that too many believes? The baby thing bothers her, but it's tempered by the fact she's convinced herself that Trey's telling the truth. You were with her. Did you sense she'd committed murder? Maybe hiding something?"

"No. I knew she was upset. But when she told me about the paternity results, it was as if she'd stepped into a confessional and unburdened her sins. She still wanted revenge, but in the morning, I could tell she'd moved past everything and decided to stand by her husband."

I agreed with Sam's observation. "Dr. Foucher is not one of your biggest fans. He resents you sleeping with Shannon. The resentment skyrockets every time he sees you and Shannon in the same room. Not because he has some morally superior objection to it, but because he's protective of Trey."

I let it sink in before I continued my evaluation. "The night we played poker, I noticed when he's upset, he scratches the side of his left hand. The one time he stopped, was when we talked about Sonny Stokes, Ron Landrace, Andres Rosario, and Coach Carroll. And the times he looked at you."

Sam didn't appreciate being the object of Foucher's scorn and censure. I attempted to reassure her. "The longer he's around you, though, the more awkward he feels."

"That's disappointing. I'd love to make him feel as uncomfortable as he makes me."

"Don't get me wrong," I said, "you make him uncomfortable. But on a whole other level. He experiences physical pain when you're around. I suspect he'd like nothing better than to leave the room. I sense whenever you and Shannon are together, he's reminded of what happened, and it bothers the shit out of him. It borders on righteous condemnation. When you add Trey to the mix... Foucher was relieved when we sent him for coffee. It's why a twelve-minute coffee run took much longer than it should have."

Sam was pleased with what I'd said. "I was hoping he was in their house at some point before today. It'd be great to see him on the list. It's a bit hypocritical on his part, don't you think? Especially after all the rumors regarding him sleeping with Trey's mother."

"Hey, Elsa of Arendelle. Let it go."

"You're probably right for once, Hans."

"Kristoff, you mean. Hans was the asshole."

"So, Hans, what time was the poker game supposed to start?"

"7:00. Why?"

She ignored my question and asked a follow-up. "What time did you arrive?"

"Fashionably late. A minute or two after 7:00."

"Dr. Foucher?"

"He beat me there. I'm not sure what time he showed up, but when I got there, he was standing at the bar drinking a vodka martini." I added with a hint of provocation, and in my best British accent, "Shaken, not stirred. As if he were auditioning for the part of the first black James Bond."

"And Trey. What time did he arrive?"

"About 7:45."

"Hmm," was her terse, undecipherable response. Sam considered the various suspects and their possible motives as she continued to drum her fingers on the table. She stayed silent for all of the next five minutes. When Sam broke free, she noticed I was watching her. She gave me an enigmatic smile. "There's no better place to start than the top," she said as she picked up her phone and called Trey. When he answered, she asked him if he could call Landrace to set up a meeting with the two of us. Trey called back ten minutes later and told us we could meet Landrace at 8:00 in the morning for breakfast.

NINE

Pfister Hotel – Donald Landrace – Muskies' Owner

Ronald Landrace lived in the penthouse of the Pfister Hotel. Every morning at 8:00 sharp, he ate breakfast downstairs in the hotel's elegant restaurant.

We valeted the car and made our way to the restaurant fronting Jackson Street. We identified ourselves, and the hostess showed us to Landrace's table. When we approached, Landrace raised his head, but didn't bother to stand or shake our hands. When I offered mine, he became Howard Hughes-esque and appeared repulsed as if he suspected my hand carried billions of deadly germs. When he saw Sam, his expression changed. He evaluated Sam from bow to stern and every point in between. A lascivious grin spread across his face. It pissed me off, so I told him, "You're an even bigger asshole than I'd heard." I didn't say it out loud, but I sure hoped he could read minds.

He didn't invite us to take a seat and returned to eating his food. We sat anyway. Sam began the interview. "Thank you for seeing us, Mr. Landrace. We won't take much of your time."

Landrace kept eating as he shifted his focus to Sam. Not Sam so much as Sam's lady parts. I knew if I asked him the color of Sam's eyes, he'd be hard-pressed to answer, but he could have given an educated guess about her bra size.

If Landrace hadn't been rich, he'd have been considered a dirty old man instead of an eccentric billionaire. He was old enough to be Sam's grandfather. Hell, he was old enough to be everybody's grandfather. The bags under his eyes gave the impression he'd packed for a long trip, and his belly stuck out so far over his belt he needed to sit a foot from the table. He had to reach close to arm's length to cut his food. In between bites, he rested his hands on his stomach as if he were eight months pregnant.

"We hoped you could tell us where you were in negotiations with Trey before this happened," Sam said.

Landrace shrugged and kept staring at Sam's chest. He spoke with his mouth full. "That's Rosario's department. He doesn't come to me with that shit 'til he needs final approval. You'd have to ask him." Bits of food sprayed as he spoke. He didn't apologize.

"We plan to," Sam assured him.

"I find it hard to believe you have no idea," I said.

He glanced my way, ignored my statement, scooped up another helping of eggs Benedict, shoved it into his mouth, and returned to eyeing Sam.

Not to be deterred, Sam asked, "Can you describe your relationship with Trey?"

"What do you mean...relationship?" Landrace asked. "I'm not queer or nothing. He's one of my boys. Like the rest of them. I pay them well. Sometimes I think I pay them a little too well. But the league has rules."

"Boys?" I asked.

Landrace offered me a lingering scowl. "Who the fuck are you?"

I reached out my hand once more. "I'm Chancy Evans. An associate of Sam's."

Still refusing to shake, he asked, "You fucking her?"

"Not at the present time."

He returned his attention to Sam, grabbed his napkin, and wiped his mouth. "Who are you fucking?" he asked. "Would you like it to be me?"

"Thanks, that's very generous of you," Sam said, "but no thanks. When you say 'boys' is it because you're sooooo much older than them, and that's how you see them?"

Landrace missed, or, more likely, chose to ignore, Sam's insult. He waved his fork airily as if hers was a dumb question. "Sure, why not." He brightened. "If you're interested, I can take you into the locker room after a game. You should see the bodies of those young bucks."

"Again, very generous, but I'd like to discuss Trey."

"That's too bad," Landrace said. "I like that boy. Not like the rest of them. He speaks English, not that crap from the ghetto."

I could see Sam getting worked up. Before she exploded, I said, "With all the money you pay them for playing a silly kids' game, you'd think they'd at least hire a speech coach."

He swung his attention to me to see if I was screwing with him. When I gave him my most sincere smile, he concurred. "That's not a bad idea. I might suggest it to some of their agents."

I watched Landrace cut into the meat on his plate like he was a lumberjack. I added, "Perhaps some etiquette lessons, too. You know how crude they can be."

He attempted to speak with his cheeks bulging, but gave up and simply nodded.

Sam leaned back in her chair, folded her arms, and glared at Landrace in disgust. He must have seen her reaction hundreds of times, because he behaved as if everything between them was proceeding down the path of debauchery. He addressed Sam once more. "I'm having a little party upstairs tonight. Just a few close friends and my wife. Perhaps you'd like to join us. I can show you my etchings."

"Sorry," Sam said, "I have other plans. I'm getting deloused. Can we get back on track? We heard you weren't happy with what you were going to have to pay Trey in his new contract, and the sponsors were forcing your hand."

"Yeah, I'm not happy the sponsors are blackmailing me... Hey, wait. Do you think I had something to do with this Mexican broad being whacked, and then, what? I planted evidence to make it seem like Trey did it?"

When Sam continued to give Landrace an accusatory look, he said, "That makes no sense. Yeah, I may 've been pissed at the sponsors. But it's because I don't like ultimatums. Especially when it comes to my club and my money. I worked hard for that money, and I'm supposed to just give it away to some young colored kids because they can play basketball?"

"If you feel that way," I asked," why do you own a team?"

Landrace never stopped leering at Sam. "I like being able to impress my friends. I bring them to games. I let them sit in the owner's box while I sit courtside so I can watch the virile, young studs run up and down the court. I especially like to be able to take those friends into the locker room afterward. It turns on the young ladies I invite to the game with me, if you get my meaning. But what I like most, is at the end of the season, when all the money's counted, and I've made a few more million, every other owner in the league, 'cept the one who wins the championship, wishes they were me."

He waited, before adding, "Am I upset with what's going on with Trey? Sure. It's bad publicity for my club, which affects ticket sales and revenue. Am I upset I won't have to go over the cap to pay him? Not in the least. But to suggest I'd have something to do with any of this is absurd. Every time someone hears about Sonny and his porn stars, or EZ smoking dope, it takes away from my bottom line. This whole thing is costing me a shitload of money. I'd have to be crazy to frame my best player for murder."

Sam jumped back into the fray. "What kind of car do you drive?"

The sudden change of topic threw him. He squinted and said, "A Buick Skylark '98. A classic."

"Isn't it the last year they made those?" I asked.

He looked at me with contempt. "As I said, a classic. They don't make them like they used to. Modern stuff falls apart soon as you leave the freakin' showroom." He gazed at Sam. "How'd you like to go for a ride with me sometime?"

"No thanks," I said.

"What? Are you her social secretary?" He focused on Sam. "Whaddaya say? You and me, goin' for a long drive, maybe up to Door County for a weekend? We could leave right now."

Sam's eyes narrowed. "No thanks. I'm on my way to church to see if they have some holy water for sale. I'm feeling a need to bathe and gargle."

Landrace shrugged as if what Sam had said had no effect on him. "Suit yourself. Now I'd like to eat my breakfast in peace."

He lowered his head and dug into his food once more. Landrace jammed a huge hunk of meat into his jaws and chewed it with an open mouth.

As we got up to leave, Sam said, "There's never been a better example of the old Jewish proverb – it's obvious God shows His contempt for wealth by the kind of people He selects to receive it."

Landrace ignored Sam and kept shoveling food into his mouth.

When we were back in my car, I said, "Man, I wish I had the money to buy his team."

Sam rounded on me, startled. "Why would you want the headache of owning a team?"

"I don't. I'd just like to have all that money."

TEN

Vegas – Elijah Zacharias "EZ" Jackson – Muskies' Small Forward

The next morning Sam and I jumped on a plane to Vegas. It was All-Star Weekend in the NBL. Three of the players on "the list" were there. Better yet, Trey and Shannon were paying our expenses, which meant I'd get a free plane ride. And when we weren't chasing down and interviewing suspects, I could make a few dollars. It was as if I was a five-year-old, and Christmas had come early. Sam would tell you I *am* a five-year-old. Remind me to pull her pigtails.

We checked into the Bellagio on The Strip. Trey had called the concierge and told him to put us in one of the suites reserved for high rollers. While Sam unpacked, I went to play a little blackjack. I found a 3:2 table using a five-deck shoe and parked myself next to an older gentleman who resented the intrusion. I said, "Hey." He inched farther away. "You don't mind me sitting here, do you?"

He grimaced as if I carried mad cow disease and had foam dripping from my mouth. He grunted. I couldn't tell whether it was his way of saying yes or no. I remained seated.

I was at the $25 minimum table. I played conservatively, at first, until I developed a feel for the way the cards were falling. The first hand I busted: I was hit with a queen playing off twelve. My cantankerous friend hit on eleven and was dealt a six. He stayed and lost when the dealer added a four to the house's fifteen. It garnered me a pissed off glare from my next-door neighbor. I was going to have to build a fence.

The next hand, I stayed on nineteen, and the dealer busted. My buddy busted, as well, when he hit on sixteen because the dealer was showing a king. Somehow, that too was my fault.

I hit blackjack, while my new pal lost again, hitting on sixteen because the dealer had an ace showing. He scooped up his remaining chips and moved on.

"It was nice talkin' to you," I said. He showed me his backside and marched away. I smiled at the dealer. "What's up with him?"

"He thinks you're a cooler."

"Me?" I said. "If I'm a cooler, how come I'm going to take this place for thousands?"

I won four of the next five hands and had a nice little stack of chips growing. When I won six of the next seven, the dealer's eyes darted skyward toward the security camera. It was a subtle sign, but one I knew too well.

"I'm not counting," I said. No reply from the dealer.

I won the next four hands, and I sensed someone move up behind me. "Hi, Eddie," I said without turning around. "Trust me. I'm not counting. Just calculating the odds."

"That's a new one," Eddie said. "Never heard that before. Didn't we tell you, you're backed off?"

I spun my chair to face him. "I thought there was a statute of limitations."

"Same old wise guy, I see. Leave the chips and come with me."

I gathered my original stack and tossed the dealer a couple of twenty-five dollar chips. I followed Eddie. "How's it hangin', Pepper?" I asked to his broad back. Eddie had been a defensive lineman at Michigan. It was a good thing he was as huge as a doublewide so they could fit his name, Saltalamacchia, on his jersey. Nobody could spell it much less pronounce it, so everyone called him Pepper.

When we were away from the table, he spun on me. "Goddamnit, Chancy. You trying to get me in trouble, coming back here again? I told you last time what'd happen. A good thing I was up in the nest when you walked up to the table. On top of that, you scared away one of our best customers. Shit! Do you know who that was?"

"Some guy from Jersey."

"Anthony Giordano."

I gave him an I-still-don't-know-who-the-hell-you're-talking-about shrug.

"I can see not much has changed," Pepper said. "The pizza king of Chicago?"

"*That's* why I smelled oregano."

At that moment, Sam walked up and joined us. Pepper stood a little taller and made sure his tie was snug and straight as if it would clinch the deal and get him laid. See my perfectly tied tie? Your place or mine?

"Sorry, slugger," Sam said. "I'm after the same thing you are."

Pepper, due to a few too many blows to the head, didn't catch Sam's drift. He laid on his best charm, "I've been searching my whole life for someone like you."

"My point exactly," Sam said.

It dawned on Pepper. "Oh! Oh." Our language needs to come up with a punctuation mark expressing someone's utter disappointment. Pepper reminded me of my time on the Badger practice field, repeatedly getting run over by our All-American linebacker at scout practice.

After Pepper picked his ego off the floor, while still checking out Sam, he said to me, "I take it there's a purpose to your little visit?"

Pepper isn't as dumb as he appears. Close, but not all his brain cells have been concussed. "I need to know where the game is tonight," I said.

"The game?"

"Pepper. You forget I can read you like *The Cat In The Hat*. You know exactly what I'm talking about. The one where the NBL guys will be. The place with the big, easy money."

Pepper scanned the room to make sure we weren't overheard. He leaned in. "They're over at the Palms." He glanced at his watch. "It's not scheduled to start until one this morning."

"How do I get a place at the table?"

"You have to know someone."

He didn't seem to understand what I was asking. I made it clear. "Pepper," I said, "I know you."

He raised one eyebrow.

"How much?" I asked.

"Ten will do."

Sam reached into her clutch and pulled out a ten-dollar bill. Pepper and I didn't bother to stifle our laughter. I pulled out my money clip and counted off ten one hundred dollar bills. Pepper swept them from my hand. "Go in through the east door," he said. "A guy will be there – a black guy. Built like the pyramids. His name is Squeaky. Tell him I sent you." He smiled at Sam. "He'll hit you up for another ten."

"Squeaky?" I asked.

"Yeah."

"Do I have to use your full name? Or does he know you by Pepper?"

He laughed. "Hell, I have trouble pronouncing Saltalamacchia," he said. "Good luck." He pocketed my money and walked away.

I opened my cellphone to see what time it was.

"What do you want to do until then?" I asked.

"I'm starving," Sam said, "Let's go get a steak." Another reason I love Samantha Summers. She eats like she's still in training.

We grabbed a cab to take us over to The Mirage. At Tom Colicchio's Heritage Steak Restaurant, we asked for a table for two. The headwaiter peered down his nose at me before examining his reservation list. Though the lobby was empty, he said, "I'm sorry, sir…" I leaned in as if to read the list, placing the tented end of a folded hundred-dollar bill on the podium. He didn't miss a beat, pulling the money from my fingers. "One should be available shortly," he said. I placed a second one on top of the podium. "Good news," he said. "One just opened." If this continued, I'd be lucky to break even before I left town.

The steaks were terrific. Sam ordered the Porterhouse along with a side of mushrooms. I ordered the New York Strip. Sam ordered white wine.

I asked for sparkling water, because I don't drink if I'm going to gamble. The bill came to a little over $300. I left a $100 tip. I suggested the waiter write a thank you note to Trey and Shannon.

We took our time and walked the point-two miles to the Palms. It took us half an hour to make our way. Sam had decided to accentuate her skintight, blue, fuck-me dress with five-inch heels. Every guy, and half the women along the way slowed down and stared. If we'd been strolling along the Mississippi River, it would have stopped to take a look. I'm sure everyone we passed thought I was the luckiest guy in the world. Not wanting to spoil the illusion, I walked arm-in-arm with Sam.

We found the east entrance to the Palms. I made a show of searching for Squeaky. Sam punched me in the arm and pointed at a substantial human being standing ten feet away. I didn't know sequoias were ambulatory.

"Excuse me," I said, "Pepper told me to introduce myself to Squeaky." I held out my hand. He checked my palm, noting the folded bills.

"That'd be me," he said in a voice belying his physical breadth. I'd expected "Squeaky" to be one of those ironic names. Hearing the voice of a three-year-old girl coming out of a man the size of Godzilla threw me.

Sensing I was going to laugh and blow the whole thing, Sam stepped into his line of sight and placed a hand on his arm. "Aren't you a big fellow? My name's Samantha."

He glared at Sam's hand as if she'd taken off her shoe and wiped dog shit from its sole onto his jacket sleeve. When Sam removed her hand, he said to me, "Walk this way."

I'd always hoped someone would say that to me.

Squeaky led the way. I mimicked his big man waddle, his thighs too massive to move straight past each other, he swayed side to side. Sam dug her fingernails into my arm to stop me in case Tiny looked back.

After we entered the poker room, and my eyes had adjusted to the light, I spotted my mark. "Yahtzee," I whispered to Sam.

It was too dark to see her reaction, but I sensed an eye roll. She confirmed my suspicions when she whispered, "You're such a dork."

Trey had told us EZ, aka Elijah Zacharias Jackson – small forward for the Muskies – liked to play Texas Hold 'Em. The All-Star coach, Denny Harrison, had selected EZ for the game as Trey's replacement.

Elijah's tell, courtesy of Trey, was the way he leaned on his forearms, which he rested on the edge of the table. When EZ felt he held a winning hand, he put a bit more weight on his left forearm. A bit more on his right when he bluffed. It took me a minute to see it because it was so subtle. But just as Trey had assured me, it was there.

I let the NBL guys win a few hands. I even stayed in on one when I knew I had better odds of having a threesome with Sofia Vergara and Selma Hayek. As EZ pulled in the pot, I threw my cards toward the middle, the leading edge up, causing the cards to flip. Every NBL player at the table believed he'd just spotted the easiest mark he'd ever hoped to play poker with.

"You're pretty good at this," I said to EZ.

"Uh-huh."

"What is that?" I said. "The fourth hand you've won already?"

His eyes narrowed. "What're you, my accountant? If I wanted to talk, I'd 've called my mom."

"Sorry," I said. "It's just, I've never played with anyone this good before."

He softened. I sensed he was beginning to like me. Not a lot, but then every journey begins…never mind.

When he won the next round, I said, "I'm going to have to call your accountant and ask for a loan." He smiled. It was a rough smile, but a smile, nonetheless.

When I noticed he was bluffing and couldn't help myself, I won the next pot with a pair of kings. I smiled at EZ. He returned it with a glare.

Sam came up from behind and leaned in between EZ and me. She whispered, so I alone could hear. "You make a living doing this?" She kissed my cheek, letting her lips linger.

EZ ogled Sam as she walked away and was drawn back into the action only after the dealer said, "Mr. Jackson, we need your ante."

He watched Sam lower herself back into her chair, not bothering to adjust her skirt, which slid so high you could see heaven. EZ felt for his chips and tossed them toward the middle of the table.

"Man, she's hot," EZ said.

"She's alright. I guess."

EZ was incredulous. He appraised Sam once more. She gave him her best coy smile. "You don' want her, man, I take her," EZ said. "What's she see in you?"

"I have big hands and feet."

"Then she'd love me," EZ said as he placed his hand alongside mine, dwarfing it in the process.

"Aren't you Elijah Jackson?" I asked. "You play for the…ah, ah…"

"Muskies."

"Yeah, them," I said. "What brings *you* to Vegas?"

It was apparent he thought I was the dumbest person he'd ever encountered in his short, wealthy life, but didn't say anything.

"Oh, that's right," I said. "You guys have your All-Star game here this weekend. Are you playing?"

"Yeah, man." His answer was filled with so much indignation I thought he might ask if he could sit at another spot like my Chicago pizza buddy.

Before he could, I hit him with what I hoped might set him off. "I thought Treymon Williams was representing your team."

"Fuck you, man. He ain't fit to carry my jock. I'm here because I deserve to be. Besides, the motherfucker's in jail for killin' his maid. Shit."

Our conversation had drawn everyone's attention.

"Really?" I feigned shock. "He killed someone."

"Yeah. He offed some bitch. She was his maid *and* his baby mama."

"How'd he do it?"

"What, now you want me to tell you 'bout the birds and bees?" he said with a laugh.

"No. I mean, yes. I mean, how'd he kill her?

"How the fuck I know? Do I look like Sherwood Homes?"

"I guess not."

"Shut the fuck up and play cards, motherfucker."

I walked away from the table with *everyone's* money, $80,000.

I tipped the dealer two thousand and went and found Squeaky. I handed him the cash. "Can you have this delivered to the concierge at The Bellagio?" He nodded. "Keep five for yourself, give five to Pepper."

ELEVEN

Vegas – Sonny Stokes – Muskies' Point Guard

We left the Palm as the sun lit up the horizon. It'd been a long day's journey into night and back again. We grabbed a taxi for the short ride to the Bellagio. Once inside our suite, I said to Sam, "Slick."

"I thought my little move might distract him," Sam said. "I heard what he said about Trey. Maybe he was trying to throw you off."

"Uh-uh. He didn't know who I was. He thought I was some ordinary asshole with a beautiful girlfriend."

"So, he's not a complete and total imbecile."

"I guess, but I hear his dog has to teach him new tricks."

"I gather it's a no-go with EZ?" she said.

"As soon as he said it, I knew by his body language and tone, he had no clue about what happened. What's more disturbing, he regrets not being the one behind it. To say he dislikes our client is akin to saying the Hatfields and McCoys had a minor disagreement."

"I'm beat," Sam said. "Good night."

"Good night, sleep tight, don't let..." Sam offered me hooded eyes. I smiled and gave her a finger wave.

Sam had commandeered the master suite – something about the Williamses being *her* client, not mine. It mattered little. I went into my room, hung my clothes over the mahogany chair valet, and crawled under the two-thousand-thread-count sheets and the goose-down comforter.

The next thing I knew, Sam was not too gently dragging me out of bed. She stopped when she saw I was naked. She took a quick peek before turning away.

I searched for the clock. It was 8:00. "What the hell? Why'd you wake me so early? I just got to bed."

Sam glanced at the clock's readout. "It's eight in the evening. You've been in a coma for the last eleven hours."

"Really?"

"Get up," she said. "I want something to eat before tonight's activities. I'm going to need a full belly to stomach it."

"Really?"

"You're a great conversationalist," she said. "Especially when you first wake up."

I threw back the sheets. Sam spun and headed out of my room. I took a two-minute shower, brushed my teeth, shaved, and fixed my hair. I slipped into my For All Mankind $1,000 jeans, my John Varvatos, $180, black, V-neck T-shirt, and my Paul Smith, $1,100, black velvet jacket. What can I say? I appreciate the finer things in life.

I struggled to wedge my feet into my Lucchese Heritage Chocolate Matte Ostrich boots. I thought of calling Sam to help, but I wanted to see her reaction to my complete ensemble. I fell over twice, hopping around the room wrestling to pull on my boots.

After the second fall, when I crashed into the valet chair, knocking it over, Sam yelled, "Are you okay?"

"I'm fine," I called back.

"Get your ass out here," she said. "As a pervert, I want your opinion on this."

"One more minute," I said, but it took me another five – four to get the second boot on, one to catch my breath.

I opened the bedroom door with a flourish, certain I'd stun Sam into silence with my sartorial splendor. Instead, I could have easily been mistaken as Wile E Coyote's stunt double smashing into yet another mountainside.

Sam wore a red sequined dress, leaving little to the imagination. If she hadn't pulled me out of bed a half-hour ago, I'd have sworn it would have taken her all day and five chambermaids to squeeze into the little – hardly the adequate word – number, which appeared painted on. Her body was trying to escape the dress, and her breasts were playing the role of Houdini.

She saw my reaction. "This works?"

I nodded.

"You look nice, too," she said. It was far from the reaction I'd hoped for. "Let's go. I'm starving. I haven't had anything since last night. I called and got a reservation at Picasso's. We have just enough time to get there and eat before the show."

I slipped the maître d' another hundred to seat us on time for the reservation Sam had made. They gave us a table near the window where we could view the Bellagio fountains.

The fare was French haute cuisine, not my favorite, but Piccaso's was in the hotel, and we were pressed if we wanted to be on time for the 10:00 p.m. show.

Sam ordered the Maine lobster salad and chardonnay at $120 a glass. Trey and Shannon were going to flip when they saw the bill. The dinner and tip were even more expensive than the night before, leaving me – more accurately, the Williamses – $500 lighter. The hotel comped us our tickets for the show, saving Trey $350.

We – by we, I mean every person attending the performance – were mesmerized by the acrobats and divers launching themselves from great heights into a watery stage, which a moment before appeared solid.

When it was over, we – this time, I mean Sam and me – made our way out of the theater. "Want to head outside and catch a taxi?" I asked.

"Unless the hotel has started sending them to the guests' rooms."

I gave the driver the address and sat back for the fifteen-minute cab ride. "That was outstanding." Sam didn't acknowledge my succinct review of Cirque Du Soleil's "O." "Don't you think?"

"Sorry," she said. "I guess I'm a little on edge. I've been to a lot of places of questionable activity, but nothing like where we're going." More to herself than to me, she added, "I can't believe I let you talk me into this."

"I thought we'd agreed. We don't have much time in Vegas, and getting these guys to talk to us in their everyday life will be next to impossible. We have to get what we need without them suspecting

Trey hired us." When Sam didn't respond, I added, "Relax. You'll do fine. Just let him come to you."

She offered me a tentative nod.

The cabbie pulled up to an old warehouse. The two of us stared out the passenger-side window, certain he'd taken us to the wrong place.

"Are you sure?" I rechecked the address Kenny Miller – Muskies' head of security and a friend of Sam's from her days as a police officer in Madison – had given us.

"This is my third run here tonight," the driver said. "This is the place." I handed him a fifty and told him to keep the change.

We knocked on the steel door. A shadow covered the peephole. A huge guy, a shade smaller than Squeaky, stuck his head out. "What can I do for..." he started to ask, but catching sight of Sam, he couldn't open the door fast enough.

"Kenny Miller sent us," I said.

"Yeah, yeah," he said as he waved us in, staring at Sam the whole time. "They've already started. Don't make no noise when you go in."

We walked along a short hallway to a room from which we heard screams and moans emanating. We waited outside the closed door for a minute before a second security guy, sporting an earbud, opened the door, put his finger to his lips, and motioned us to enter.

Sam took one step into the room and froze. Before us were three naked bodies, two women, and a guy who could double as the skewer at a pig roast. I nudged Sam, motioning for her to move to the far side of the room and closer to Sonny Stokes, who was engrossed in watching the threesome on the king-sized bed.

As we made our way around the set, most of the men, and all the women, including the two involved in making the flick, gave Sam admiring glances. I was the invisible man, or woman, or dog. We stopped at a spot leaving three people between Sonny and Sam. As the action in the scene began again, Sonny weaved his way toward us. Despite her numerous trysts over the years, Sam wasn't much of a voyeur. I caught her trying not to watch. She surreptitiously followed Sonny.

When there was a break in the action, Sonny said, "Hey there," doing his best Samuel L Jackson impression. "How you doin', sweet thang?"

"I'm doing fine," I said.

Undaunted, Sonny asked, "You a connoisseur of the arts?"

"Yeah," I replied.

"I was talkin' to the lady."

"Sorry," I said.

Sam smiled sweetly at Sonny. "This is the first time I've ever been to something like this. Ramsey here has taken me to a couple of live shows, but never to an actual movie set." Sam made it sound as if I'd gained access to the filming of "Star Wars."

I reached around Sam. "Ramsey Hardin," I said. "I'm in the business."

Sonny ignored me. "How 'bout you?" he said to Sam. "You in the business?"

Sam let a shy, embarrassed smile play across her face. "I'm thinking about it."

"I can help you out. I know some people."

"So do I," I reminded him.

Sonny ignored me once more. "How 'bout we go someplace so we can talk?"

"I don't know," Sam said. "I'd hate to leave Ramsey all by his lonesome."

"He'll be alright. My name's Sonny Stokes. I'll be starrin' in the NBL game Sunday. You need tickets? I'll get you some. I'm stayin' at the Wynn."

"NBL?" Sam asked. "What's that stand for?"

"National Basketball League. I'm the point guard for the Muskies."

"What's a Musty?" Sam asked.

"Muskie. A kinda fish. Strong and long. Like me."

Sam, wearing her stilettos from the previous night, peered down at Sonny. "You're kind of short for a basketball player."

"Not where it counts," Sonny said.

The action started up behind us. I was having trouble staying focused, reading Sonny, while hearing the moans and groans twenty feet away.

"Say," Sam said in her best I-just-remembered-something voice, "didn't I see on the TV, I think it was TMZ, where somebody from the Musties..."

"Muskies," Sonny said.

"Whatever." Sam waved her hand. "Where a player from the Muskies," – Sam said "Muskies" as if it was the most difficult word she'd ever had to pronounce – "killed his old lady?"

"He's been arrested for murder," Sonny said, "but it wasn't his old lady. It was his maid."

"Really? I thought it was his old lady?"

Sonny shook his head. "Let's not talk 'bout that. Let's talk 'bout you and me."

"And Ramsey," Sam said.

Sonny glared at me in disgust.

Sam smiled, touched Sonny in the middle of his chest, and let her finger drift to his belt.

"I guess, just as long as we don't cross swords," he said, then suggested, "Let's go back to my place."

"Sure," Sam said, as she offered him a coy smile.

Sonny motioned to a guy who could have been Squeaky's big brother. The giant pulled a cell phone out of his pocket the size of a hardcover book and hit a number on the contacts' list. By the time we walked outside, a stretch limo waited by the door.

Sonny's bodyguard rode in front while the three of us sat in the back. Sonny insisted I sit across from him and Sam, which was fine because I wanted to get a better read.

"What do you like?" Sonny asked Sam, trying to get a head start on the next few hours.

"I'd like to know more about this murder thing," Sam said. "I'm a huge SUV fan."

"You mean, SVU?"

"Whatever. Do you know what happened?"

Sonny decided it'd be best to get this whole old lady/maid story out of the way. "I hear, Trey – that's the dude's name – Trey knocked up his maid. When he found out 'bout it, he offed her."

"How'd he do it?" Sam asked.

Sonny shrugged. "Dunno. They didn' say."

"Maybe he shot her," Sam said.

"Dunno. Could be. I didn't hear nothin' 'bout Trey havin' no gun. I have three myself," he said with great pride. "I could show them to you."

Sonny moved his hand to reach for Sam. She blocked it and said, "Not here. I'm kinda shy. I don't like other people watching."

"We can drop him off at the corner," Sonny said, motioning toward me.

"Not him, silly. The two guys up front."

"They can't see," Sonny said. "The window's tinted. Besides, they've seen it all before."

Sam blushed.

Sonny reached for her once more.

Sam caught hold of his hand and placed it back in his lap. With a little more force, she said, "Not here. Behave yourself, or you won't be opening your present."

In an attempt to draw Sonny's attention back to her face, Sam asked, "What else can you tell me about this murder? It kinda turns me on. Ramsey and me are kinda into M&M."

"You mean S&M?" Sonny asked.

"Whatever."

I didn't think it was possible, but Sonny's interest in Sam had gone from low earth orbit to mission to Mars. "It seems Trey just found out 'bout the daddy test. I hear it was his. The funny thing, it didn' bother him. A couple of days later, she was dead."

"Oh, my," Sam said. "Do you think he did it?"

"Trey? Dunno," Sonny said. "The dude's a pussy. Shit, he'd go outta his way to avoid bumpin' into the wind. Ya know what I'm sayin'? Can' remember the last time he took a charge much less fouled somebody hard. We call him 'rabbit' because he's like the Easter candy shaped like a chocolate bunny with all the gooey stuff in the middle."

"Marshmallow?" I asked.

"Whatever," Sam and Sonny said together.

Sam moved a little closer to Sonny. "How'd you've done it? Kill someone, I mean."

Sonny's eyes lit up like an octogenarian's birthday cake. "I'd 've capped the bitch. Get me a throwaway. Bust a couple in the girl, then drop it like in *The Godfather*. 'Leave the gun, take the cannoli.' "

Sam gave him a blank stare, pretending she didn't have a clue.

"It's quick and fast," Sonny said. "But it makes no sense. Hell, Trey's richer than 50 Cent." Sam was genuinely confused. "The rapper?" Sonny said. When Sam still showed no recognition, Sonny said, "Why'd he wanna kill her over a baby? Most of the guys in the league are payin' support to someone. I've got two of my own out there. It don' 'mount to much, unless you got seven or eight. One? Shit." Shit came out as a ten-second word.

We pulled up to the Wynn and exited. Sonny closed the taxi door on my leg. It caught me on the shin. I hopped around on one foot as I waited for an apology. Sonny smirked and caught up with Sam.

She slid her arm through Sonny's, and said, "I'm looking forward to this. I'm glad it doesn't bother you that I have my friend." Sonny glanced over his shoulder. I thought he might just bust a cap in *me*. Sam came to my rescue. "Oh, not him. My friend. Aunt Flow? ... That time of the month?"

Sonny's step faltered. Sam walked past him, pulled up short, and gave Sonny a blank stare. Sonny was conducting a massive internal struggle. "I just remembered I have practice in the morning," he said. "Give me a rain check."

"Are you sure?" Sam regretted it the moment the consonants and vowels left her mouth. Before Sonny could reconsider, she added, "Here's my number. Call me some time."

Sonny watched with heightened excitement as Sam wrote the number. When she'd finished, he grabbed it out of her hand. "I will."

We watched Sonny disappear inside the hotel before we hailed a cab to take us to the Bellagio.

"For a guy who's probably been with hundreds of women," I said, "and more than a handful of porn stars, Sonny acted as if you'd be his first."

Sam gave me a withering glare.

"Woman," I said. "Not the other."

Mollified, Sam leaned toward the window and peered up at the neon lights illuminating The Strip. "I seem to have that effect on people," she said, sounding mystified.

I asked, "What number did you give him?"

"The STD hotline."

TWELVE

Vegas – Ahmad Salaam – Former Client of Dr. Foucher

We slept in. I woke a little before noon. Sam was still asleep. Playing the tease must have worn her out. To start my juices flowing, I went to the casino. I stopped at the roulette table and soon found myself a thousand down. That's what I get for drifting out of my lane.

I headed to the poker room, where one quick peek told me I'd be wasting my time. The heavy hitters never show up until the sun is down, and the heat has dissipated. I wandered over to the craps table and watched a young couple ride a winning streak. They thought, like most, their streak would last forever. They lost it all on one roll. One of the reasons I'd been successful in the gambling business, I don't get greedy. I keep my head and play the odds, even when I feel unbeatable.

I walked out onto The Strip and to Margaritaville. I ordered – what else? – the cheeseburger and fries, and an Arnold Palmer with unsweetened tea. Halfway through, I ordered another cheeseburger and fries to go. I paid the waitress, left a generous tip, and walked back to the Bellagio.

I placed the burger on the table near Sam's room and waited. A minute later, she opened her door. Her hair was askew, and she had one of the two-thousand-thread-count sheets wrapped around her. She stumbled out of the room toward the bag of food as if sleepwalking.

"That smells good," she said. Her eyes opened a bit, raising them to half-mast. "Are you going to share?"

"All yours," I said. "I already ate."

"I love you," she said.

"Welcome to the club."

"Would that be the club for the desperately desperate?"

Feeling she'd adequately chastised me, she sank her teeth into the burger and moaned. When she dug into the take-out bag, her eyes lit up. "Fries. Almost makes me want to sleep with you." She tossed a handful into her mouth. Her eyes twinkled. "Too bad, you're not the girl your mom always wanted."

She devoured the meal in record time. When she finished, I thought she might lick the bottom of the bag. When nothing was left, she slumped back in the chair, her disappointment evident.

"Would you like me to order something from room service?" I asked.

Sam gave her head a definitive shake. She asked, "Are we set for this afternoon?"

"Yup. The word is Ahmad will show up at the Butch Harmon Golf Center at 4:00. He has a private lesson scheduled for 5:00, but he likes to loosen up on the range beforehand. Make sure you wear your most flattering golf outfit."

We leased a car for the day and drove the twenty-five miles to Henderson. We hit the pro shop and rented two sets of clubs. The guy brought out a set of women's clubs for Sam. She raised her eyebrows and folded her arms. He exchanged them for a set of men's Callaway's.

We made our way to the range where we found Ahmad loosening up, hitting balls. Sam walked past his station and positioned herself two places away. I took the one behind him, so I could hear what he had to say when Ms. Summers drew his attention.

Ahmad smelled her perfume, raised his head, and caught sight of Sam. She leaned her golf bag against a bag stand, pulled out her driver, and placed it behind her back. She hooked her elbows around the shaft and swung her shoulders back and forth. When she bent over to stretch her hamstrings, her gorgeous ass pointed at him. He stood ramrod straight.

Sam took an easy swing with a wedge and sent a high arching shot, stopping it near the flag at the 100-yard mark. She raked a second ball, repeated the swing, and the results.

Ahmad timed his swings so he could watch Sam take hers in between his. Sam worked her way up through the bag, hitting one beautiful shot after the other. Ahmad was mesmerized.

When Sam hit the driver, she sliced her first shot thirty yards right. "Shit," she muttered. She teed up another ball and hit it even farther right. "Damn." Ahmad watched her while leaning on his three-iron. When she sliced her next drive one more time, she swore. "Fuck!" She spun around, embarrassed. "I'm sorry."

"Don't worry about it." Ahmad turned on his best charm. "Do you know why they call it golf?" Sam shook her head, encouraging him. "Because all the best four-letter words had already been taken."

Sam laughed as if it was the funniest thing she'd heard in months. "That's a good one. I'll have to tell it to my friends."

"Would you like some help with fixing your slice?"

"Would I?" Sam said. "I've been working on it for months, but I can't seem to straighten it out."

Ahmad looked like a kid who'd been promised if he was good, he was going to get a puppy or some other furry pet. He walked over to Sam. In the interest of being accurate, he floated. "Take your stance," he said.

Sam gripped her club and addressed the ball. She gave her rear a little waggle. "Now what?"

Ahmad had to clear his throat. "Move the ball back in your stance a few inches."

Sam giggled. She was way too skilled at this. I knew she was working *him*, but *I* was getting turned on.

"Now, make sure you lead with the handle on the downswing."

Sam swung, and the ball sliced, but not as much as it had earlier. "Ooh, that felt much better."

"Do you mind?" He didn't wait for Sam to answer. He came up behind her and reached around, placing his hands on top of hers. "We'll do this slow." Ahmad was finding it harder to talk as the seconds ticked by. "Address the ball," he said.

Sam bent slightly at the waist and went through her pre-shot routine. When Ahmad paused and, to move the lesson forward, Sam asked, "Shouldn't we be doing something else?"

He pulled her arms up and back, pausing once more. He cleared his throat. "Start the downswing by bumping your hips toward the target." When Sam didn't move, he placed his hands on her hips and moved them for her. Sam's shoulders stiffened. She started her downswing, letting her hands brush Ahmad's jaw. "Oh, I'm sorry."

It snapped Ahmad out of his daydream. "No problem." He failed to notice Sam's apology was a bit less than sincere. With considerable reluctance, he let go and stepped to the side.

"When you bring the club back down, aim for the inside quarter of the ball."

He stepped farther away from her and watched her make a perfect swing, sending the ball on a line with a slight draw. It stopped 270 yards out.

Sam smiled at Ahmad. "That felt great." She said, "I don't know how to thank you."

"You could let me buy you a drink later. My name's Ahmad."

"Tracy Adams. I'd like that."

I rolled my eyes. Sam scratched her nose with her middle finger.

"I have a lesson in five minutes," Ahmad said. "Wait for me in the bar. Tell Tony to put it on my tab. I won't take long."

"That's encouraging," she said. Sam gave him an impish smile. "And disappointing at the same time."

I knew Ahmad was about to pay $2,000 for his lesson. I also knew he was going to ask to have it cut short. He picked up his clubs and hurried to the private hitting bays.

Sam waited until he was gone, teed up a ball, and hit it farther than her last. She sent five more just like it screaming down the driving range before jamming the driver back in the bag. With an enormous amount of revulsion, she said, "Men! I hoped he enjoyed that. God, I need a shower." She stared hard and long at me, before adding, "I can't believe I let you talk me into this. Or at least doing it this way. ... You'll pay for this." To make certain, I understood what she meant, she added, "Having me act like some trollop."

"Calm down," I said. You'd think after thirty-seven years on this planet, spending a majority of the time dealing with acerbic women, I'd have known better.

"Don't tell me to calm down," Sam said in a cold, menacing voice.

But I've learned how to handle such situations. I added something to take her mind off my previous comment. "We only had a couple of days to do this. Besides, you catch more flies with sugar than honey."

"You mean vinegar."

"You catch more flies with vinegar than honey?" I said, sounding perplexed. "I don't think so?"

She shot me a look of utter disgust. "You guys are all pigs. ... I swear."

"I believe that's what got his attention." Sam looked at me, uncomprehending. "You saying fuck," I clarified. "On the driving range?"

"Screw you, Ace. I had him at hello."

"You had him as you walked past. He didn't hit one decent shot after you went through your stretching."

"How about my pre-shot routine?"

"I liked it," I said with a smile, knowing she was calming down, her attention back on discovering what Ahmad knew.

We returned our clubs to the pro shop and took adjoining seats at the bar. I ordered a vodka tonic, Sam, a Chardonnay. We talked about what we'd discovered, which wasn't much. Sam was eager to see the lab results from the autopsy and crime scene reports. What she wanted most was a chance to examine the murder scene. At 5:45 p.m., I moved to a nearby table, so Ahmad could have Lady Summers to his lonesome.

He came in and made a beeline for Sam. He removed his hat as he swooped down on her like a hawk with its sights on some poor field mouse. As he approached, Sam's eyes grew wide. "Now that you don't have your hat on," she said, "you look familiar. I know you from someplace."

He pulled out his cell phone and flashed the back cover. It carried a picture of him holding up a phone, smiling. Beneath it was the word, "Sprint."

"That's right," she said. "That's where I've seen you before. You're the Sprint guy. I have AT&T, but I might have to switch." It made Ahmad beam. Little did he know, he was about to become one very disappointed spokesperson. "You play for the LA Steamers? That's what they say in the commercials." Further enlightenment hit Sam. "The All-Star game is this weekend."

"I was the second-leading vote-getter in the West."

"How exciting," Sam said. "I've never met a professional basketball player before."

Ahmad's ego was ready to pop. Sam put a pinprick in it. "I remember you now. You came out of Cal Berkley. Fifth in the 2011 draft. With your numbers, how come it took so long for a guy like you to pull in a national sponsorship deal? I'd have thought you'd be doing Subway or All State commercials way before now?"

For the first time since he'd laid eyes on Sam, Ahmad saw something he didn't like. "Yeah." It came out as a grumble.

"What's the story?"

When Ahmad hesitated, Sam motioned to the bartender that she wanted another drink. Ahmad's focus drifted to her chest then slid to her micro-golf shorts. When the bartender placed another glass of wine in front of her, Ahmad said, "Give me my usual."

"Right away, sir." The bartender hurried off.

Ahmad still hadn't responded to Sam's question. She gave him an I-have-all-day shrug, and he laid it out for her. "I had this agent. His name is Dr. Foucher, but everyone calls him Dr. Fucker, because he's such a fuck-up. He promised me he'd get me all kinds of sweet deals, but he spent so much time taking care of Treymon Williams..." Ahmad stopped to see if Sam knew who Trey was. She nodded. Ahmad continued. "He spent so much time taking care of Trey, there wasn't any time left for the rest of us. Trey was doing State Farm and Verizon and Pepsi and

Gatorade. He did so many commercials they needed to let him leave early from practice."

Sam offered him a look of disbelief.

"Hyperbole," he said with a shrug. "I'm surprised he'd time to take a dump. The first chance I got, I bolted and got me a new agent. Within a week, he landed me Sprint."

"You sound upset."

"Fucker cost me a small fortune," Ahmad said. "Ten million at least."

Sam raised her eyebrows.

"Not ten million, but it was seven-figures."

"I'd bet you'd love to retaliate somehow?"

"For sure. But there's justice in this world after all."

"How's that?"

"Trey was arrested for murder."

"Wow!" Sam said. "What do you think happened?"

"Supposedly, he got his housekeeper pregnant. The next thing we heard, she'd been murdered."

"Do you know Trey?"

"Sure."

"Do you think he did it?"

Ahmad thought about it. "Nah, I guess not. A lot of guys don't like him. Especially the brothas. They think he's not blackish adequate. They're a little suspicious of the way he talks, not ghetto enough."

"But you're eloquent," Sam said.

"I speak two languages. When I'm with the brothas, I revert to my inner-city days. When I'm around the sponsors and people like you, the ghetto is a million miles away."

"If Trey Williams didn't do it, who do you think did?"

"I have no idea," Ahmad said. "We were preparing to play Phoenix when we heard about it. At first, everyone thought it was a mistake. Somebody trying to punk us."

"Perhaps someone was getting even with Dr. what's his name and did it through this Treymon person."

Ahmad sat up straight. "Who are you? You some kind of reporter or something? Wait a minute. Do you think I had something to do with this?" He didn't wait for an answer. "Let me tell you, Dr. Fucker is a world-class screw-up. He cost me a shit load of cash. But I can't make it up if I'm in prison. Besides, he's his own worst enemy. After he fucked over so many of his clients, ain't no one going to sign with him again. Trey's it. Fucker's already screwed himself. He'll more than likely end up coaching some YBA team if he's even in basketball after Trey's gone."

I walked up at the end of Ahmad's tirade. "There you are, Tracy. Our ride is leaving. We've been searching everywhere for you. It's time we get you back to the sanitarium."

Ahmad's hard stare never left Sam. He knew something was amiss, but he'd been so enamored with Sam, he was having trouble seeing his golf tip wasn't going to be repaid with a few hours with her in the bedroom, or the backseat of his limo.

Sam offered him her hand. "Thanks for the lesson."

THIRTEEN

Anita and Juanita Sanchez's Home

We caught the 12:42 red-eye out of Vegas, landing in Milwaukee fifteen minutes ahead of schedule at 8:17 in the morning. A cab brought us back to the loft, where we tossed our belongings into our respective rooms. Sam had read and reread the letters Shannon and Trey had put together, but after reading them for a third time, Sam felt they held no significance.

"These are from your kind," she said.

"Smart, intelligent, handsome, heterosexual males?"

"Only, if you leave off the adjectives."

I knew Sam was still upset over having to use her feminine wiles to make guys talk, so I didn't poke the bear. Perhaps it was the fact she ended up touching two of them. And kissed me on my cheek. Every time I thought about it, I touched my face and got a warm feeling inside.

"Most of these are from guys blaming Trey for the team not beating the point spread," Sam said. "There's also a few pissed at Trey for not stopping during the middle of his meal for people who thought he owed them more respect because, in essence, they helped pay his salary."

Attorney John Anthony Thomas had telephoned to say we'd be able to get into Anita Sanchez's flat Monday morning. We drove to the Near Southside, Milwaukee's equivalent of Spanish Harlem. Detective Dominic Callas of the Homicide Squad met us there. He was one of the few Detectives in the Milwaukee Police Department Sam hadn't worked with before. The crime scene tape had been removed. We were told that after the police spent five days taking a fine-toothed comb to the place, Anita's sister was allowed to move back in.

"Ms. Summers," Detective Callas said, greeting Sam. He looked at me and said, "And who the fuck are you?"

Sam had reached out to shake Callas' hand but withdrew it when he made his rude remark. "This is my associate, Chancy Evans."

Callas studied me, trying to determine if I was gay. I'm pretty sure he knew Sam was gay from the police office scuttlebutt, and probably assumed her partner was, too. I'm sure Chancy sounded gay to him. Like, Iffy or Dodgy or Dicey. Either way, I could tell he felt I was trouble. Maybe not trouble so much as a pain in the ass. It was easy to see why he had the reputation as a skilled detective.

Callas addressed Sam. "In a way, I'd hoped we'd got this wrong. I like Trey-Man. He appeared like a nice enough guy, but..." He left the rest of his disappointment go unsaid.

"We're hoping," Sam said in a conversational tone, "to prove beyond a shadow of a doubt he didn't do this,"

Callas' body language gave off an uncomfortable vibe as if by letting his guard down and expressing any affinity for Trey, he'd betrayed some unspoken police code. He raised his head high, threw back his shoulders, and put a snarl on his lips. "That ain't gonna happen, Summers. We have him pretty much dead to rights." Something in his tone suggested the police possessed definitive proof, but he stopped short of telling us what it was.

Sam left Callas' remark hang in the air. She asked, "Can we see the place?"

We walked up the ten stairs to the front porch. Detective Callas knocked on the door. He surveyed the neighborhood while we waited. His expression showed how much contempt he felt for that part of the city as if the conditions the people contended with were of their own doing. When no one answered, Callas knocked a little louder a second time. He leaned in to hear if he could discern any movement coming from inside. He pulled a key out of his pocket and reached to unlock the door. "She said she'd be home. I guess there was someplace else she had to be…" He grabbed the doorknob to test it. The handle turned, and he pushed open the door. "Hello," he shouted. "Ms. Sanchez, are you home?"

He glanced our way, shrugged, and stepped inside. Sam followed. A subtle transformation in her demeanor took place. I felt like I was watching a documentary on a lioness, her senses sprung to life, stalking her prey.

We moved into a small foyer. Sam focused on the area described in the crime scene report where Anita Sanchez had fallen the night she was murdered. The hallway led past two bedrooms on the right, a living room, dining room, and a bathroom on the left and into the kitchen. A third, smaller bedroom was off to the side in the back. A few pictures hung on the wall. A dozen feet away rested a bare flower stand. Sam glanced over her shoulder at me. Her wide eyes and the infinitesimal shake of her head told me something was wrong.

Callas held up his hand, ordering us to stop. He pulled out his MP 40 Smith and Wesson service revolver. "Don't move," he said to us over his shoulder. Sam drew her gun.

The feet of a woman stuck out from behind a half-wall that set off the living room from the hallway. Detective Callas stepped around the corner into the room, where he dropped to one knee. He checked whoever lay on the floor for signs of life. He removed his cell phone from inside his jacket pocket, hit a number on his contacts' list, and scanned the rest of the house as best he could from his kneeling position.

"This is Detective Callas, badge number 8750. I need backup, immediately." He rattled off the address and asked them to send the ME van, as well. The person lying on the floor was dead.

FOURTEEN

We were ordered to not go anywhere. Callas, more specifically, told us not to move, while he cleared the house. As we waited for his partner and the forensic team, he said under his breath, "Damn back door was unlocked too." We heard the sirens' wails. The vehicles came to a screeching stop outside. A young detective, in a wrinkled, off-the-rack, slept-in, blue suit, led the parade of police and CSI people and headed straight for Callas. The two moved out of earshot. Or so they thought. Callas explained to his partner what he'd found and gestured, numerous times, toward the body and the back door.

Sam surveyed the flat from the edge of the foyer, paying particular attention to the empty flower stand. She was at such ease, she appeared as if she was at the lakefront, on a beautiful summer day, watching the sunbathers and the sailboats.

I looked like the kid who'd swam too far out and was drowning. My first murder scene. I felt as if any minute one of the detectives might pounce, stick an accusing finger in my face, and order me to confess to killing whoever lay on the floor. At that moment, I would have.

Sam surveyed the area. I knew I was the only thing she didn't notice. When Detective Callas was through talking to his partner, he motioned toward us. The young detective studied Sam before turning his attention to me.

Callas' partner ambled our way doing his best Dirty Harry imitation and introduced himself. "I'm

Detective Markus Nunn, Detective Callas' partner. Please step outside with me. I have a few questions I'd like to ask you." Detective Nunn and I took two steps before he realized Sam hadn't moved. "Ma'am, please come along," he said. "I want to ask you some questions. Ma'am? Ma'am? Hey, lady."

Sam woke from her trance and turned to see who was calling her. "Yeah?"

"You and your boyfriend need to come with me."

"He's not my boyfriend, he's my associate."

The young detective looked me over. To clarify, I said, "Besibends, actually. She's not my type."

He leaned away, once more, studying me. On top of trying to decipher what "besibends" meant, I'm sure he jumped to the same conclusion as Callas. I must be gay because Nunn thought Sam must be every guy's type. He stepped back, allowing Sam and me to walk past him to the outside, where a crowd had gathered. When I saw the makeup of the ever-increasing mass of people, a majority of them children, my first thought was, *shouldn't those kids be in school learning the odds of filling an inside straight?* It's 11:1, by the way.

Descending the stairs, Sam surreptitiously asked me a question out of left field, or so it appeared at the time. "Are you 100% sure about Trey's reaction to his missing trophy?" It took a second to search my data banks to understand what she'd asked. When it finally came to me, I nodded.

Officer Nunn led us out to his squad car. We stood alongside it, and he asked us some questions.

With most people rubbernecking to get a glimpse of us, I was sure everyone in the crowd thought: those have to be the killers. It was thrilling. I felt like Bonnie and Clyde. Not both of them, of course. Just Clyde. Then I thought of how he ended up and searched my memory for a murderer with a much longer shelf life. There's a rumor Butch Cassidy might still be alive. Probably hanging out with Elvis.

"Why did you two insist on coming here today?" His tone conveyed a haughty, superior attitude, one I'd heard all too often from my mom.

It evoked an even stronger reaction in Sam, reminding her of Rainey. "Insist?" Sam asked with a bit of steel in her voice. "Tell Callas we didn't *insist* on anything. We asked to be granted a viewing of the crime scene at your department's earliest convenience. It took six days. Six. Days. Before we received a phone call this morning informing us, we'd finally be allowed in."

Nunn shifted his attention to the house. I'm sure, in most cases, the people he talked to were more like me, scared shitless, willing to say anything to exonerate themselves. He wasn't accustomed to somebody like Samantha Summers. Welcome to my world, pal.

I started to say something but remembered Sam had whispered to me to let her do the talking. When Sam sensed I might speak, she turned her head a smidgeon, shutting me down as effectively as if she'd put a roll of duct tape over my mouth.

Sam's eyes narrowed to slits, causing Nunn to squirm as if *he* were the main suspect. His superior attitude vanished quicker than dessert in a fat guy's lunch box. He glanced at the house a second time and decided to change the tone of future questions.

"I was told you guys, ah, gals, um, ah, the two of you, kind of, wanted to see the house today."

Sam didn't let him off the hook. "Detective Callas knows we're the private investigators hired by John Anthony Thomas to look into who killed Anita Sanchez." Nunn started to say, "Trey...," but Sam gave him a malevolent glare, and he swallowed his words as he glanced toward the house one more time.

"We requested to see it before it became too degradated from so many people being inside." Sam waved at the house. "Good luck with that, now." She stepped into Nunn's space and wagged her finger in his face. "You guys took a long time processing the scene. Much longer than usual. We were out of town following up on leads when you released the crime scene late last night. We heard Ms. Sanchez's sister was permitted to move back in. Which is unheard of! Our lawyer requested we be given access before allowing her to do so, but someone higher up decided it was too much of a burden."

Officer Nunn glanced at the house for the fourth time. He was clearly out of his league. Sam was throwing hundred-mile-an-hour heat, while he was the little league kid relegated to the bench and asked to keep the scorebook. Detective Callas saved him from further unease and embarrassment when he came out the front door, did a quick search, located us, and marched over. Nunn was relieved. When Callas arrived at the squad car, he asked Nunn, "Whaddaya got?"

"Nothin' yet. I'd just started questioning them."

Callas studied his young partner. It didn't take a seasoned detective to see Nunn was shaken. "That's okay," Callas said to Nunn. "I'll take it from here."

Detective Nunn stole a quick glance at Sam before speeding off as if he'd heard his mom call him for dinner. We watched him scurry away. Callas looked at me and asked, "Why are you smiling?"

"It's good to know I'm not the only one Ms. Summers has that effect on."

He swung his attention to Sam. "What'd ya say to him?" he asked in a threatening tone as if Sam was his number one suspect in his new case.

"I didn't like his attitude," Sam said. "I don't care much for yours either."

"Too bad," Callas said. "I just walked in on the second murder in the same house in less than a week. And I don't give a shit what you think or how ya feel."

They went silent, each refusing to break eye contact. I jumped in. "Detective Callas, we understand." Sam glared at me. I ignored her and said, "We want to discover who did this because we're fairly certain it wasn't Trey Williams."

Callas responded with a derisive grunt.

Sam straightened to her full height and peered down at Callas, who stood five-nine in elevator shoes. "You have this wrong," Sam said. "Our client didn't kill Anita Sanchez. I'm even more certain, he didn't kill her sister."

"How'd you know it was her sister?" Callas asked, growing suspicious.

As if she was a tenured college professor lecturing an incoming freshman, Sam said, "First of all, it's her house. She is the most logical person to be inside. Second, although I couldn't see her face, she was wearing the same shoes as the woman in the photo hanging in the hallway, pictured with Anita Sanchez."

Callas didn't hesitate to hide his skepticism.

"Check it out," Sam said. "Second picture on the left. They were identical twins. Mirror twins, actually. Rare but obvious when you look at the picture more closely. You'll probably find one was right-handed, the other left, their fingerprints nearly identical.

"Third," Sam said, "you called out to her when we arrived, which makes me believe you expected her to be here. You probably called an hour or two ago to announce we were on our way."

"Two, actually," Callas said, retaining his surly attitude.

"There you go," Sam said. "Last, despite your attempt to discreetly tell Detective Nunn-nuts who the victim was, I read your lips and saw everything you said to him. By the way, we didn't insist on coming here, no matter what you said."

Callas went quiet a moment, then said, "What makes you sure your *boy* didn't do it?"

Uh-oh, no, you di'int. I felt Sam's righteous indignation spring to life.

"First off, Trey Williams is hardly a boy. You should consider eliminating that word from your vocabulary when speaking of a grown man, especially one of African-American descent."

"Don't lecture me, honey," Callas said, raising his voice.

Sam stepped into Callas' personal space. "Listen, De...tec...tive, you need to retake the sensitivity course. Get your attitude out of the 19th century."

"Excuse me all to hell," Callas said, "if I'm not the most PC guy in the world right now, but the fact remains, your guy killed Anita Sanchez. And I'll find a way to make sure he takes the fall for this one, too."

"Good luck with that. When are you going to release the rest of the police report to us? You're not going to spring them on us at the last minute, I hope, Ayópi."

"What did you call me?"

When Sam didn't answer, Callas moved in closer. The two were nose-to-nose. It reminded me of a dispute at home plate. If Sam had been wearing a baseball cap, she'd have spun it around and worn it backward.

"You'll get the rest of it when we're ready to give it to you," Callas said. "Maybe we'll wait 'til after we've processed this crime scene and give 'em to you at the same time to save us both time and effort. I'm sure you'll have to investigate this one, too."

"Try not to take as long processing this one. Besides, after what I saw, I don't think it will be hard to prove you're swimming in the wrong stream. You should step out of the water and reexamine what you think you have."

Sam grabbed my arm and pulled me toward my car.

"Hey, I'm not done with you two yet," Callas yelled to our backs.

Over her shoulder, Sam said, "And, Ayópi, if you have any more questions, talk to my lawyer. John Anthony Thomas. Use your twentieth-century phone book."

"If I catch you interfering with my investigation," Callas said, "I'll see your license is pulled. Do you hear me?"

Everyone on the Southside had heard him, so I'm pretty sure Sam had too, but I still asked, "Did you hear what he said?"

She knew by my tone I was yanking her chain and kept marching forward. I looked over my shoulder to see if Callas was chasing after us. Sam increased the pressure on my elbow. I had trouble keeping up with her long, angry strides. "We should do this more often," I said. "This is great exercise. I can feel my heart rate going up. And what does 'ayópi' mean?"

"Asshole. Reminds me of Rainey."

"Ayópi means asshole?"

"What?" Sam asked perplexed. "No, of course not. Ayópi means boy in Greek."

"Greek? You think Callas is Greek? It doesn't sound Greek to me."

"It was common for persons of Greek ancestry to shorten their names because few people here could pronounce, much less spell them. Like when your grandfather's Polish name was changed from Evashevski to Evans at Ellis Island. Callas is probably a shortened version of something like Kalogiannis or Kalogeropolous."

"But he didn't understand what you called him. I find it's best when you insult someone, you call them a name they understand."

"So, I should only call you names a five-year-old understands?"

Why do I do this to myself? "What's it to you, poopy head?"

She smiled and pulled out her cell phone. I opened the car door and watched Sam wait for the call to go through. "Hi, it's me." She listened. "I know. Let me ask you something. Does Trey own a gun? Or ever shot a gun?" … "Good. Now, do you happen to know if Anita moved the items on Trey's shelves when she dusted, or did she just dust around them like your current cleaning service?" Sam listened once more to a lengthy explanation. "Have the Merry Maids been out to your place since we were there?"… "Great. Tell them not to come until we've had a chance to get there first. I need to check something."

When she hung up, I waited to hear what she'd unearthed. She said, "You'll see."

FIFTEEN

Sam refused to answer the vast majority of my questions, saying she needed to "check something out" first. The one question she did answer, "Did you actually read Callas' lips?"

"I did, but I could also hear him."

"With everything going on, and half of the people talking, you heard him?"

"I have selective hearing."

"Selective hearing? That reminds me. A guy's girlfriend says to him, 'It's been so long since we've done anything romantic, it hurts!' He told his buddy, 'She broke up with me because she said, 'It's so long it hurts.' ' "

"I can tune out extraneous noise, like that bad joke, and home in on the person I want to hear. Even if they're whispering."

"Uh-huh."

"You've heard of how the other senses of a blind person become heightened as a form of compensation?" She didn't wait for me to answer. "While I was in high school and college, I taught myself to adjust my senses for any given situation. I'd walk around my house and dorm room with a sleeping mask on, forcing myself to use my other senses. For example, when we walked into the flat, I smelled gunpowder in the air. The murder must have taken place within the last hour for it to be that prevalent. From the strength of the odor, I'd say, the person fired at least two shots. No one will report having heard them because the shooter used one of the homemade pillows to muffle the sound. Most likely, the one missing from the chair in the living room. The chair next to it had a decorative, homemade pillow. It stands to reason the first chair should have had one, as well."

"Huh?"

"Poly-fill pellets were on the floor inside the entryway to the living room. They're used for filler to make inexpensive throw pillows." She snapped her fingers and pointed out the windshield. "Keep your eyes on the road."

I'd been snatching quick glances at her as she explained what she saw and deduced from the new crime scene. When I turned back to watch the road, she mentioned we'd have a few minutes to spare because two other detectives were at the Williamses' home questioning Trey. John Anthony Thomas, Shannon had explained to Sam, was on his way to their house. Sam calculated we had close to two hours to kill.

We went to Kopp's Frozen Custard Stand and bought double cheeseburgers and fries. We took our food and sat in my car so people milling around, eating at the stand-up tables, wouldn't overhear us.

"Can you leap tall buildings in a single bound?" I asked.

"You'd be surprised what I can do."

Trust me, I wouldn't. Over the years, I'd come to know most of Sam's secrets, including her ability to detect smells, like the gunpowder, or hear conversations others felt were out of earshot.

She asked, "How much richer did you come home from our little trip?"

I did a quick calculation. "Guess."

She added everything in her head. "While I was around you, you pulled in $80,000 from EZ and the guys. You tipped Squeaky and Pepper ten, and the dealer two. Plus, the thousand to each of them to get you a seat at the table. Your new clothes cost you $3,500. Mine cost $4,000. It'd have cost more, but I used the same shoes two nights in a row."

"How gauche."

"You cheapskate," she said with a twinkle in her eye. "The cab rides, ...and you lost $1,000 at roulette. What were you thinking? Roulette. Drifting out of your lane, again?' Sam grunted a laugh at her little joke, then went on, "The last night, after my golf lesson, you won another $40,000, but you were forced to report it because it was a sanctioned casino event, minus taxes and tips and the two meals.... $85,560, give or take a few dollars."

"You forgot the golf club rentals, $85,360. Not bad for a few night's work. But the best thing about the trip was seeing the expressions on those guys' faces when they saw the prize-winning fish swim away."

"Who're you calling a fish?" she asked with a disgusted, grossed-out expression. "They were lechers."

"Most of them have been given anything they want since someone saw them shoot a large orange ball through a slightly larger metal hoop. They're twenty-something millionaires who seldom have to buy their drinks or food, and who have women throwing themselves at them every time they go out for the night. It's why I suggested we use the tactic we did. I knew they'd never figure out we were interviewing them as suspects."

Sam got lost in the memory. She shivered.

"I guess they never saw anything like Samantha Summers. I promise you they went out and found someone else, but it was you they pictured in bed with them."

I didn't receive the smile I thought I would with my perceived compliment.

"I seem to have that effect on people." Sam waited a few seconds, before she added, "I did find what Sonny said intriguing, though."

I raised my shoulders and hands, indicating I'd no idea what she meant.

"The child support. The whole 'it don' amount to much.' I researched it online. With the money Trey makes each year, he'd owe anywhere from five to six-hundred-thousand dollars a year in child support."

"Holy shit! How does that not amount to much?" After my initial shock, I said, "Speaking of Sonny, something was off in the way he talked to you about the murder. His answer appeared too practiced."

"What do you mean?"

"It was as if he suspected he'd be asked about Trey or Anita or a 'Where were you?' type of question. But I'm not sure why."

"Okay. We'll examine it some more." Sam glanced at her phone to see what time it was. "Let's go."

I played the gentleman. I let Sam throw away the trash while I found the restroom. We climbed back into my car and headed north to Mequon. Once again,

Shannon was waiting for us at the door when we arrived.

We took our usual places in the den, but this time John Anthony Thomas filled in for Dr. Foucher. Sam walked over to the shelf, where Trey's Citizenship of the Year Trophies were displayed and picked up the one that'd been moved to the front. Sam smiled and replaced it where it'd been resting.

"What can you tell us?" Attorney Thomas asked once Sam sat next to me.

"I can tell you how to save a lawyer from drowning," I said.

"I've heard this," John Anthony Thomas said, shaking his head in disgust.

I could see Trey, however, was interested in hearing the answer. I said, "Take your foot off his head."

Trey laughed. Shannon and Atty. Thomas were aghast I'd be telling jokes at a time like that.

"Ms. Summers, please," John Anthony Thomas said as if pleading for his life. I thought he was about to insist she take control of her pet or put me outside where he thought I belonged.

Instead, Sam asked Trey, "Tell us what the police said or asked when they questioned you earlier."

Trey looked at Shannon and Thomas. "They wanted to know where I was between 9:00 and 10:30 this morning. I told them I was here. Unfortunately, Shannon was at the grocery store shopping. So I guess I don't have an alibi."

"When I left at 7:45, Trey was sleeping. He was still in his pajamas when I got back just before noon."

"I was *still* in my pajamas when they showed up. They asked me if I knew Juanita Sanchez. I told them I'd met her once, last summer when we had a barbecue. Anita brought her as her guest. Anita told me they were mirror twins. Never heard of that before. Anyway, they asked me if I owned a gun. Which I don't. Then they asked me if they could swab my hands."

Trey passed it off to John Anthony Thomas, who said he'd objected because he hadn't had a chance to speak with Trey yet but relented when Trey said he had nothing to hide.

Trey added in a confident voice, there wasn't anything to be found. He'd only fired a gun once in his life, near the end of last season when the team had a gun safety lesson. "I remembered how powerful it felt squeezing the trigger. It scared the hell out of me. I can see why so many people cling to their guns. But it wasn't for me." He added, whenever he went out for the evening and didn't feel safe, he hired a bodyguard.

Shannon broke in. "You sound as if you've discovered something. What is it?"

Sam pointed to the trophy case. "The trophy that killed Anita was already at her house the night she was murdered. The flower stand in her hallway held a minute layer of dust except for a small section where your fourth Citizen of the Year trophy rested after taking it from here." Sam walked over and picked up the trophy. "You see the sharp edges?" Sam gestured to the base of the trophy and the small pointed edges sticking out a millimeter from the corner. "This is distinctive. I've not seen another trophy with this type of base."

"The stand was twelve feet away from where we were," I said in amazement.

"Your point?" Sam asked, dismissing my comment.

Shannon ignored our little banter and focused on the place where the trophies rested. "You said the trophy has been missing since around New Year's Eve, and Anita hasn't been back since she left in October. We changed the locks. She couldn't have gotten in unless..." She gave Trey a fierce glare.

"What? You still don't believe me. Do you?" Trey said, both hurt and defiant.

"How do you explain the test?" Shannon asked Trey. She repeated her question to Sam, "How do *you* explain the test?"

"We haven't figured that out yet. Let's take care of the bigger problem first, then we'll work on it." Sam gave Shannon a sympathetic, reassuring smile.

Shannon nodded warily. Trey glared at Shannon malignantly for the first time since we'd known them. Sam went on to explain her theory to bring the two of them back to what she'd discovered. "The trophy, this one," Sam hefted it in the air, "was moved at your party on New Year's Eve. It was moved because one of your guests – here I'm speculating – someone over 6'1", noticed the other trophy had been removed, and took the one from behind it, placing it where the first one had been on display."

She stopped to make sure we were following her explanation. Satisfied, she said, "A layer of dust was under this one, which wouldn't be there if the trophy had been moved at the same time as the one which was stolen. Stolen by Anita, by the way. If Shannon is correct in what she told me on the phone, and she witnessed Anita move everything on the shelf when she dusted, you'll see the area underneath the two remaining trophies are dust-free."

Trey lifted one of the other trophies. He swiped his hand over the shelf, where the trophy rested and held up his hand to show us it was clean.

"How'd you know?" he asked, astonished.

"I noted the place on the flower stand at Juanita's house and determined it's where the statue had rested. The most logical explanation was the dust I'd seen the first time was from the second one being moved. I knew when we moved it, we'd find dust underneath."

"That's great," Thomas said, "but how do we prove it?"

"We don't have to. I'm sure the police took pictures. Besides, it doesn't prove anything. They'll reason, Trey saw it and used it to kill her. They may even say it was another thing which made him angry."

"I don't get it? Why do you think this is significant?" Thomas asked.

"It goes to this being a crime of passion, not premeditated. If someone removed it from here *after* Anita had moved out, it'd make it easier for the cops to pin this on Trey. Now anybody who entered the house had access to it."

John Anthony Thomas said, "But it doesn't prove Trey didn't."

"True, but..."

"But what?"

Sam avoided looking in my direction. "Let's say, for right now, I'm convinced and leave it at that." She didn't want to tell him, or Trey and Shannon, her belief was based in large part on the word of a flake.

"Why take the trophy in the first place?" Trey asked. "That makes no sense."

"Are you missing any other items?"

Shannon and Trey shared a quick, uncertain glance before Shannon said, "I'm not sure. We didn't think of looking."

"I would, if I were you," Sam said before moving on to another point. "There is one other thing I noticed while we were at Juanita's house this morning. A faint impression of somebody's footprint lay inside the door. It was a shoe from its midpoint to the toe, but it was there since the first murder. Someone, probably Anita's murderer, tried to wipe his feet on the mat. He didn't get it all."

An uncomprehending John Anthony Thomas asked, "A partial shoe print? How does that help?"

"Because it came from a size 12 or 13 shoe, Trey wears a 15." Trey and Shannon looked down at Trey's feet, wondering how Sam knew.

"But it could have been there any time before the murder, couldn't it?"

"Not likely. We know Anita was a clean freak. Few people take the time to lift items on a shelf they can't see when dusting. She was killed on the only day it snowed in the last three weeks. Nineteen days to be exact. It's been too cold to snow. That afternoon it got into the teens. We received a dusting of snow before dropping to sub-zero temps again."

"That's hardly enough to convince a jury, Ms. Summers."

Sam didn't get a chance to respond. We heard a knock on the door, and Shannon hurried to answer it.

Detective Callas marched into the den a few seconds later. "Treymon Williams, you are under arrest for the murder of Juanita Sanchez. Stand up and turn around." Callas gave Sam a condescending smile as he stepped toward Trey. A stunned Trey did as commanded.

As Callas secured the cuffs, John Anthony Thomas said, "Don't say a word. I'll be right behind you. Do. Not. Say. One. Word. Do you understand?"

A catatonic Trey didn't respond.

John Anthony Thomas asked Detective Callas, "Based on what evidence may I ask?"

"You may. We found his fingerprints at the crime scene...again. You'll need to leave the premises so we can search the house."

SIXTEEN

Early the next morning, we met with Attorney Thomas and picked up a copy of the preliminary forensic report on the death of Anita's twin sister, Juanita. She was shot twice with a 9mm handgun.

The first shot hit her in the chest, penetrating her heart's left ventricle. The second was to the center of her forehead. Both shots were fired through a throw pillow as Sam had deduced. Trey's fingerprints were discovered on a spent shell casing, which rolled into a crevice in the floor near the fake fireplace. The other casing hadn't been found. Neither had the gun.

The other report Sam received told the story of Anita being bludgeoned by Trey's Citizenship of the Year trophy. A single blow led to her death. The lone prints were Trey's and Anita's.

"This doesn't seem too favorable," I said to Sam when I'd finished reading the report.

"You think?" Sam said with a little more than a hint of cynicism. "The statue can easily be explained, but the fingerprints on the shell casing is going to prove more challenging."

"How can the statue be easily explained? First off, they're his. Second, his..."

Sam held up her hand. "His fingerprints are on it because it *was* his. Her fingerprints are on it because she stole it and kept it at her house."

"The shell casing?" I asked.

"The shell casing is another matter. I have some ideas, but I want to talk with Trey first," she said. "I certainly don't like these." She flipped a stack of eight-by-ten-inch photos.

Sam's body language hinted there was something else. Something even more incriminating. I waited for her to tell me.

Sam grimaced. "They released the 9-1-1 call."

When she paused, I asked, "And?"

"When the operator picked up, the only thing Anita said was, 'Trey Williams.' "

We were not allowed to see Trey that afternoon, but were given an appointment first thing the next morning. Attorney John Anthony Thomas joined us as we waited in a ten-by-fifteen-foot room. Trey was brought in with ankle bracelets and handcuffs shackled together by another length of chain. An officer placed him in the chair across from the three of us and re-handcuffed him to the table.

Trey gave an upward head nod to Sam, then me. "Hi, how're you doing?" He tried to give off an air of confidence, but the façade was crumbling. He had a sadness, which showed how much shit he knew he was in, and it kept getting deeper and deeper.

"I want to ask you some questions," Sam said. "I need you to answer me honestly this time."

Trey showed a flash of irritation. "I have been," he said and sulked.

"We'll see. Right now, there's a great deal of evidence incriminating you, especially the 9-1-1 call. Plus, the police believe you're the one person with a clear-cut motive to do both of these."

Trey's head sagged, he stared at his shackles, wagged his head and said, "I didn't do this. Any of this. How can this be happening?"

In a sharp voice used by parents to make a child own up to what they'd done, Sam asked, "Is the baby yours?"

Trey lifted his head. "No. It must be the lab. They screwed up, or the guy must 've been paid off." The anger was back in his tone. If he was lying, I was going to ask him to give me lessons on how to sound so sincere while doing so.

Sam stared at him. He returned it. She said, "A black SUV was seen outside Anita's sister's house the night she was murdered. You have a black SUV."

"There's gotta be hundreds of black SUVs in the city. Half the players have black SUVs."

"That by itself is easy to deflect. But with the paternity test, the 9-1-1 call, the statue and the shell casing with your fingerprints on it, the woman upstairs hearing Anita call out your name and with us not being able to establish an alibi for you, it doesn't appear too promising."

John Anthony Thomas said, "That's all circumstantial."

Sam shut him down with a stern glance. Earlier, she'd instructed him to not speak at any time while she asked Trey questions. He shifted in his seat. I felt his pain. I'd been there…way too many times.

Sam turned back to Trey. "Even though it's all circumstantial, a jury might add it up and come to the conclusion you did this."

"What reason do the police think I have for killing her sister?"

"Tell me about the phone call?"

"What phone call?"

"The one you received from Juanita early the morning she was killed. The one the cops pulled off your 'recent calls' log from your phone."

Trey's eyes went wide. "It's not what you think."

"What do I think?"

Trey stayed silent for a minute. His eyes glazed over before he said, "She told me she had pictures of Anita and me together. She kept calling me 'darling you' for some reason. I thought she was making stuff up to blackmail me. I told her she was crazy. I didn't kill her sister, so she could do whatever she wanted with her so-called proof. I'm telling you, she was nuts. I hung up. That's it."

"Why didn't you say anything to us earlier?"

"I mentioned it to Mr. Thomas, but I didn't want to speak about it in front of Shannon. She's upset enough as it is."

Sam looked at John Anthony Thomas. He gave her a nod of confirmation.

"You don't know what pictures she was talking about?"

"Not a clue. I was sure she was bluffing. How could she have pictures if I already knew I didn't do this? I thought she was trying to...I don't know."

I watched Trey struggle with the idea, Anita and her sister saw him as their personal ATM.

She took a stack of five photos out of the file and slid them across the table. "Do you think these are the pictures?" At first, Trey didn't comprehend what Sam had asked. She spread them out, allowing Trey to examine each one. Sam had requested John Anthony Thomas refrain from mentioning they existed so I could gauge Trey's reaction when she showed them to him.

Trey scanned the photos before scrutinizing each one. "But... How?... It's not..." Trey said. When he finished, he addressed Sam. "Someone must have photoshopped me into these."

The five photos were taken from a camera positioned above. They showed Anita on her back, having sex with Trey. Although the pictures didn't show Trey's full face, the part visible was the back of his head and much of his profile. A tattoo on his back – "Shannon" – stretched across his shoulder blades.

"Uh-uh. We checked. Our expert said the photo has not been retouched in any way. You lied to us. You slept with Anita."

Trey shot out of his seat and slammed his palms on the table. He leaned as far across as he could and thrust his face toward Sam. "I didn't sleep with her. If you don't believe me, I want someone else to investigate this."

His actions and rage brought a guard rushing into the room. Sam said to the officer. "It's okay. He's okay." She said to Trey. "Aren't you." It wasn't a question but a direction.

He regained his composure, stood as straight as his restraints allowed, and in a calm voice, said, "Everything's cool," and sat.

Once the guard left, Sam glanced in my direction, asking a silent question. I nodded. She looked back at Trey. "We'll figure this out.

Unfortunately, you are stuck here. There's no way they're going to let you out on bail again."

Trey's head slumped to his chest. "This will kill Shannon."

SEVENTEEN

We spent the rest of the day trying to verify Trey and Shannon's alibis for the night Anita was murdered. I checked out Trey's, and Sam worked on Shannon's. Sam gained access to some of the mall stores with video surveillance of people entering and leaving their establishments. Shannon, or at least a woman who appeared to be Shannon, could be seen wandering, trance-like through the hall. The distance plus the lack of video clarity proved inconclusive.

I'd no such luck. I found few cameras on Lake Shore Road, which ran along the Lake Michigan coastline Trey had taken to Port Washington. It was mainly country homes most of the way from Mequon until I neared Port Washington. I took South Wisconsin Street into town. There were no cameras in the parking lot where he'd parked while reflecting on the paternity results. I drove so slowly up and down Lake Shore Road, I backed up traffic and had people leaning on their horns out of frustration. When they eventually passed me, their reactions ranged from slight head shakes to people rolling down their windows to scream at me. I took my cue from the Madagascar penguins, I just smiled and waved.

When we'd finished, Sam and I met at her office in the heart of the Third Ward. I talked with Adrianna Truwell, Sam's Administrative Assistant, while Sam accessed her mail, office email, and scanned her phone messages. When she finished, we drove to Mequon to speak with Shannon. Sam showed her the set of pictures. She examined them for so long that Sam tried to regain her attention by asking with as much compassion as I've ever heard from her, "Do you still believe Trey?"

Shannon didn't answer. She stared at the eight-by-ten-inch glossies. Sam placed her hand over the pictures to break Shannon's trance. "That's our bedroom," Shannon said as she continued to stare at the spot where Sam had laid her hand as if it were made of glass. With overwhelming disbelief, she said, "She's wearing my diamond necklace."

"After seeing these pictures, do you still believe Trey didn't sleep with Anita?" Sam asked in a near whisper. Shannon eyed Sam but remained silent. "Shannon, I have to tell you there's so much evidence piling up against Trey, you should prepare yourself for the worst. Is there anyone who can come and stay with you? Trey's mom, perhaps? Or someplace you can go? I don't think it's healthy to be here by yourself."

Shannon shook her head. "Trey told his mom he didn't want her here. He didn't want her to see him like that. He said it'd kill him. She reluctantly agreed as long as we called her every day to tell her what was going on." She went silent as her eyes drifted to the pictures once more.

"How about your sister?" Sam's asked, her voice cracking. I'd never seen Sam so close to tears before.

Shannon stared unseeing as if Sam's question hadn't registered. I tried to think of something to say, but I was so caught up in watching Shannon and Sam's raw emotions, for one of the few times in my life, I was speechless. Shannon's world had turned into a runaway train, and it was becoming more apparent to her by the second, she had no power to stop it. Sam was distraught seeing someone she cared for so much, suffering such despair and hopelessness.

After a long minute, Shannon said, "That's not him. That can't be him. Not Trey." With each subsequent pronouncement, she gave her head a more violent shake.

When Sam objected, Shannon gave her a fierce scowl. "It. Is. Not. Trey!" She placed her hands on top of the pictures, flung them back across the desk, and said, "You two should leave."

Without waiting for us to move, Shannon stood and stormed out of the room.

EIGHTEEN

Maria Alvarez – Woman Who Lives Above Anita's Flat

As we pulled out of the subdivision, I continued to sneak glances at Sam to see if I could discern what she was thinking. I'd hate to play poker with her. She gave away nothing. After a minute, I broke into her thoughts. "Where are we?"

"In Mequon. Don't you have GPS?" Sam asked with a bit of an edge.

I gave off a fake laugh and slapped my hand against my thigh. "That's so funny," I said. I made a showing of getting myself back under control, before, in a much more serious voice, I asked, "With the case?" When Sam didn't respond, I added, "I sense you're beginning to think there's too much evidence stacked against Trey."

Sam released a deep, long-held sigh. "Way too much. Most of it's circumstantial, but it doesn't look good."

To get her to refocus, I asked, "What's next on our to-do list?"

Sam showed a renewed determination in her voice and manner. "I want another look at the crime scene. We have to go to the gun club. We also have to set up interviews with the other people on Trey and Shannon's list. The sooner, the better. You're going to take one more crack at finding Trey on camera the evening of Anita's murder. I don't care if you have to pull over and ask every business owner on Lake Shore Road. We also have to see who else on Trey and

Shannon's list has, or had, access to a black SUV. Then I want to interview the neighbor who saw the car, and the woman who lives above Anita's sister who heard the argument. We also have to talk to the lab tech who did the DNA paternity test. While we're out there, it might be helpful to speak with Trey's mom to see if there's anybody she can think of who Trey and Shannon didn't. Someone who might have it in for Trey...or something, which may have happened years before. And I want to get ahold of the 9-1-1 tape to hear it for myself."

I stared at her as we drove on I-43 toward downtown Milwaukee. "Keep your eyes on the road. I don't want to regret bringing you along on this investigation, and if I'm maimed or dead, I might."

I focused on the road and said, "What do you want to do the next day?"

Happy to release the tension, Sam burst out laughing. With a slight chuckle, she said, "We could go to the beach. This time of year, we'd have it to ourselves."

"I'll bring the sunscreen. You bring the hot chocolate."

Sam pulled out her phone and dialed a number by heart. She held up her index finger, telling me to wait. "Hello, may I speak with Detective Callas?" After a pause, she said, "Samantha Summers." She was put on hold and said to me: "There's a few... Hello, Detective Callas. This is Samantha Summers. Attorney John Anthony Thomas asked me to view the crime scene once more, seeing as we didn't get a decent chance to do so the first time."

She smiled at what Callas told her, before saying, "That'd be great. We'll see him there." Whatever Callas said next brought on an even wider smile. "Thanks." She said to me, "He says he's too busy to deal with us right now, but he's sending Detective Nunn-nuts to let us in."

"Why the huge smile?"

"When he told me he couldn't be there, he said, 'This *boy* has too many things on his plate.' "

"So he found out what 'ayópi' means?"

"He didn't sound too pleased with me. His schedule was an excuse not to be near either one of us. Which is fine. I won't have to put up with his condescending, Rainey attitude."

We drove in silence to the Southside and pulled up to the curb outside Juanita Sanchez's flat and waited for Detective Nunn. He was either instructed to take his time or reluctant to be subjected to Ms. Summers again because it took him over an hour to arrive.

Sam didn't say a word when he showed. He avoided eye contact, led us up the stairs, opened the door, and stepped aside. We entered Juanita's place. Nunn followed a couple steps behind, noting everything Sam took in. She methodically checked every square inch of the three-bedroom flat, paying particular attention to the different locations where they'd found the bodies. She squatted down in the front room and studied a spot on the hardwood floor. Detective Nunn tried to determine what Sam found so intriguing. Instead of elucidation, it ended with him shaking his head and throwing his hands in the air in frustration.

After two hours of toe-tapping by Detective Nunn, Sam told him she'd finished. "Can you inform Callas we might want to come back here again?"

Nunn's shoulders slumped, knowing he was the one who'd have to come back to observe Sam going through her paces. He nodded when Sam continued to stare at him, waiting for an answer.

We climbed into my car and pulled away from the curb. "Go around the block," Sam said, "and come back here."

Being a good boy, I did as instructed. When we circled the block. Reaching the corner, Sam told me to wait until Detective Nunn drove away. We stopped and watched. He appeared to be writing something in a notebook before starting his unmarked squad car and took off.

Sam said, "Pull up to the house again."

"You need more time in there?"

"No. I saw everything I needed to within the first ten minutes."

"But, we were there two hours."

"Yeah?"

"Mind telling me why?"

Sam shrugged.

"You were jerking him around."

Sam shrugged once more.

"Let me guess. Payback for keeping us waiting."

"Pretty much. I was waiting until the woman above Juanita's flat returned. I wanted to interview her while we're here. I didn't hear anything coming from above when we arrived, so I took my sweet ass time until I heard her come home."

"How can you tell it's her and not her husband or her kids?"

"It's not kids. Their footsteps are different."

I didn't bother to hide my skepticism.

"Ever hear of the pitter-patter of little feet," Sam said. "Even teenagers have a different walk. They weren't heavy enough to be a man's. It's her. As long as we had to wait, so did Nunn-nuts."

"That's a little petty, don't you think?"

"Your point?" Sam didn't wait for my answer. She threw open the car door and walked up the front steps we'd descended a few minutes earlier. She rang the bell to the upstairs flat and waited. Less than a minute later, a Latino woman pulled back the sheers and peaked out.

Sam gave her a friendly wave and spoke through the glass. "Hola, senora. Me llama Samantha Summers. ¿Le importa si le hacemos algunas preguntas?" Sam flashed her state private investigator's badge. Before the woman could get a decent look, Sam put it back in her pocket. I knew what she was trying to convey, so I put on my best cop expression, the one implying I was bored and impatient. I knew enough Spanish to understand Sam had asked the woman if she minded if we asked her a few questions.

Upon seeing Sam's badge, the woman's face registered momentary panic, but relaxed when Sam assured her we were not with the INS. The woman introduced herself as Maria Alvarez.

They continued to speak in Spanish. Sam asked, "What can you tell me about the argument?"

"Which one?" Maria asked.

"The one the night Anita was murdered." Before Maria could answer, Sam asked, "There were others?"

"Yes, many."

"Between Anita and a man?"

"No, her sister."

"Her sister?"

"Yes."

"Could you tell what they were arguing about?"

"No."

It was still cold outside, so Maria motioned us in and led us upstairs, where we sat around her kitchen table. Sam gave a cursory examination of the flat. Maria offered us coffee. She poured three cups, adding milk and sugar. Sam glanced at her phone, a slight smile played across her lips. Maria launched into her story. She was in her dining room, cleaning up after dinner when she heard people talking downstairs. She thought the sisters were going to go at it again, but then realized it was a man's voice. She explained the walls and floors were thin, most everything could be heard, especially if people were talking in a raised voice. Maria said the conversation started off calmly, but because she spoke little English, it made no sense. At first, she tuned it out but, as the voices rose, she paid more attention.

Sam asked, "Did you recognize the man's voice?"

"No, I never heard it before."

"Do you think you'd recognize it if you heard it again?"

Maria shrugged. "I am not sure."

Sam pulled out her phone and opened her voice memo app. She held out the phone after pushing the play button. Trey's angry voice came out of the speaker.

Maria listened and gave a tentative shake of her head. "I am not sure. It is close. Maybe."

NINETEEN

Theresa Garza – Witness From Across the Street

"How pissed will John Anthony Thomas be when he finds you taped Trey's interview?"

Sam shrugged. "Who cares? I'm looking for answers, not absolution."

By the time we reached the bottom of the stairs at the house of our next interviewee, it'd dawned on me. "You planned this all along, didn't you? You knew he'd react that way when you showed him the pictures and accused him of sleeping with Anita."

"I suspected. I wanted him angry, so I'd have something for Maria to compare it with."

I gawked at her in amazement. I'd a whole new appreciation for Sam's skills. I smiled and asked in a conspiratorial voice, "What do you have planned for this interview?"

Sam scrunched up her face. "I'm going to ask her to verify what she thought she saw."

"That's it?"

Sam noted my disappointment. "What? Not every interview needs to have sleight of hand. I want to establish the when and the who, that's all."

"Sounds like fun," I said, the sarcasm hanging heavy in the air.

Sam rang the bell. A mature, Hispanic lady opened the inner door, greeting us through the screen. I wondered if the storm window, which should have been there, had been lost years ago, or if the slumlord didn't want to take the time to install it for the cold winter months. The woman studied us for a long moment before asking in Spanglish, "What you want?"

"Do you mind if we ask you a few follow-up questions of the night of the first murder across the street?" Once more, Sam pulled out her badge and flashed it at the woman.

She put it back in her pocket, but the woman said, "See it again?"

Sam slid her eyes in my direction. I thought the interview might be over before it began. She removed her badge and presented it to the woman. "We represent Treymon Williams' lawyer. We're trying to establish whether what the police wrote in their report is accurate."

The woman's demeanor changed. She reached out, unhooked the latch from the door, opened it, and motioned for us to come inside. She showed us to her living room and gestured for us to sit on the couch. "I get you something?"

"No, but thank you so much. That's kind of you. I'm Samantha Summers. This is my partner, Chancy Evans."

"I am Theresa Garza."

"May I ask you something, Ms. Garza?"

"Certainly."

"When we first arrived here, and, I'm assuming you thought we were the police, you were standoffish." Theresa didn't understand, so Sam said, "You didn't appear happy they were here again."

"Si, yes. The policeman was a culo."

I looked to Sam for the translation.

"She thinks he's an ass."

"Si. Ass. Not the burro."

The three of us smiled.

"Theresa, what can you tell us about that night?"

"I no see or hear much. I sit on my sofa." She pointed at the couch where the two of us sat. "I hear cars fast down avenida. I look to see if I can recognize them. It problemo. It mas every day. When they drive on, I look over the calle...um, street and see a muy big...caro..."

"Expensive?" Sam asked.

"Si, expensive...automobile park in front of el casa." She pointed across the street to Juanita's house.

"What color was it?"

"Negro."

"Black?"

"Si."

"Are you sure?"

"Si, muy."

"Did you see who was driving it?"

Theresa shook her head. "No, it dark. Noche. The streetlight, not good. All I know is the man not from aqui."

"You mean the neighborhood?"

"Si. He have diferente walk. No Hispanic. No white."

"You think the man was black? African-American?"

"Si." Theresa bobbed her head the way people do when they're not 100% sure.

"Could you see his face?"

Theresa shook her head and repeated, "It was noche."

"Could you tell if he was old or young?"

"No joven. But no viejo."

"Neither young nor old?"

"Si."

"Could you tell how tall he was?"

"He alto." She held up her hand above her head to indicate he was much taller than she. "How mucho, I no tell. He was presentimiento. But alto."

"He was hunched over?" Sam hunched her back to make sure Theresa knew what she was saying.

"Si. Un poco."

"A little hunched over?"

Theresa nodded.

"Do you remember what he was wearing? Coat? Hat? Scarf?"

"He have long coat. Dark. El cuello up."

"The collar was up?"

"Si. It hid face."

"Anything else?"

"A hat. Like India Jones. Dark like coat."

"Indiana Jones?" Sam asked.

"Si, him."

"Was he wearing it back on his head or pulled down?"

Theresa didn't understand. Sam pantomimed like she was placing a hat on her head. First, she placed it so it was perched on the back of her head. Pretended to take it off, then set it low across her forehead.

"Si. Ese." Theresa said, seeing Sam place it forward on her head.

"Could you tell if he was wearing gloves?"

Theresa gave some thought to Sam's question, before she said, "Si, but not hasta que he on porch."

"Until he was on the porch?"

"Si, yes."

Sam asked, "Why then?"

"The light on." She pointed at the ceiling, indicating the porch light.

"Did he ring the bell or knock on the door?" Sam pantomimed to make sure Theresa understood what she was asking.

"He knock on door."

"Is there anything else you remember? Something you didn't tell the police?"

"Si," Theresa said. "He use his left hand to knock on door?"

TWENTY

"Do you think it's significant?" I asked Sam as we drove to the Third Ward.

"What? Using his left hand to knock on the door? Possibly."

The way Sam had answered, I knew she'd found something else more significant. "And?"

"And nothing." Sam turned her head and stared out the passenger side window as we made our way along 16th Street and across the viaduct. I glanced over to my left and saw the Potawatomi Resort and Casino. We may have purchased Manhattan for a song, but the Native Americans were making it back a million-fold with their casinos spread across America.

"I've had some great times there," I said to break Sam's reverie.

Her head moved ever so slightly. Her focus shifted from something she alone could see, to decipher what I was blabbering about. She caught a glimpse of the resort.

"Isn't that where you played poker with Trey and Dr. Foucher?"

"How'd you know?"

Sam ignored my question. "Being late, or early in the morning, why didn't you stay there instead of coming home? I hear it's nice."

"I wanted to, but I didn't have a...reservation." I drummed my hands on the steering wheel in the ba-dump-bump rhythm to punctuate my joke.

With a quick shake of her head, Sam returned to staring out her window again. "You're really disgusting sometimes."

"You think that's bad. I know this Native-American dude. One day he walked past a pawnshop and noticed a bronze rat displayed in the window. He went in and asked how much it cost.

" 'Three dollars,' said the owner. 'But a thousand for the story behind it.'

"My friend declined the story but bought the bronze rat. As he walked along the street, he noticed rodents were coming out from their hiding places, following him, he walked faster. Soon thousands of rats were chasing him. He ran to Lake Michigan and threw the bronze rat as far as he could into the water. To his surprise, all the rats leapt in after it and drowned. Seeing this, my buddy rushed back to the pawnshop.

" 'Do you want to hear the story, now?' the owner asked my friend.

" 'No, but do you have any bronze white men?' "

Sam didn't turn, but I heard a grunt of laughter. Still focused on whatever only she could see, she said, "We're going about this all wrong. This all began with the paternity suit. If we determine who's behind it and how they did it – that's assuming Trey is telling the truth about not sleeping with Anita – we'll be able to solve who's also behind her death."

"Which means what?"

"We start by going to the lab to interview the tech who did the test results."

Hartford, CT – CDC Testing Center

That's how we ended up in Hartford, Connecticut, two days later, at the CDC testing center. We obtained a notarized copy of a letter from Trey and his lawyer, giving us permission to talk to the company as to their procedures regarding the test he'd submitted and the results. The real trick would be to get the company to release the name of the technician who performed the test or the clerk who processed the results.

When I asked Sam what she planned on doing if they refused to give her the information she wanted, she gave me a mischievous grin, wiggled her eyebrows, and said, "I've got another ace up my sleeve," then laughed. It was my turn to do an eye roll.

When we arrived at the facility, we were led to a waiting room to meet with the lab's general manager. We were shown into her office – a white, sterile room with her framed Ph.D. hanging on the wall. No personal items were on display anywhere. The room felt cold and off-putting, much like CDC's manager.

"Hello, I'm Naomi Buddy. Please have a seat." Ms. Buddy motioned to the two white, plastic chairs opposite her steel-framed desk. She was a stout woman, under five-feet tall, in her mid-fifties. Her dark hair with streaks of gray was pulled back in a tight bun. She wore readers with a librarian's eyeglass chain around her neck. She had a strength about her that reminded me of a huge feline cat, with long fingernails to match. My hands reflexively covered my groin. I decided to let Sam ask the questions. Ms. Buddy leaned back in her black, high-backed office chair, waiting for us to speak.

160

Sam slid forward and gave her the letter from Trey and John Anthony Thomas. "We were hoping to talk to you about this."

Ms. Buddy read the letter and studied the notary seal before placing the refolded letter on her desk. She leaned back in her chair and scrutinized Sam.

"Mr. Williams and his attorney have given us permission to investigate the test results your company ran. Can you explain to us the procedure you use?"

Ms. Buddy stared at me but spoke to Sam. "Mr. Evans is not on the request sheet. I'm afraid he will have to leave the room."

"Your procedures aren't covered by the non-disclosure agreement, just the results," Sam said.

Ms. Buddy swept her attention back to Sam, locking eyes. Despite my better instincts, I broke in. "Let me see if I can help here. If you do this the way everyone else does, it goes like…"

"I assure you we're *not* everyone else. We are one of the most respected clinics in the States. In the world, I dare say."

I held my hands up in surrender. "What I meant, either you or one of your satellite clinics, collect a sample from the mother and father. These can either be something like saliva from a buccal swab or blood."

Ms. Buddy gave me a hard glare – I suspected I was winning her over.

"The clinic or you," I said, "require two forms of picture ID as well as each party's social security number. What we'd greatly appreciate is to see Ms. Sanchez's ID."

She went wide-eyed as if I asked her to take off her clothes, step up onto her desk and do a handstand. She glared at me, then addressed Sam. "That, I can only show you." She picked up the letter and waved it.

"I promise I won't peek." I crossed my heart and held up two fingers. Unless she had exceptional peripheral vision, she missed my gesture. I'm not sure she hadn't tuned me out altogether.

"How accurate are your test results?" Sam asked, although she already knew the answer.

"They're 100% accurate." Ms. Buddy's response was tinged with an edge of defensiveness. She couldn't believe Sam suggested it was anything but perfect.

"Even if someone tampers with the results?" Sam asked.

"Excuse me?" Ms. Buddy sat upright in her chair. "Are you suggesting we'd falsify results?"

It was my turn to speak. "Anyone can be bought. We all have our price."

She spun on me, pinning me to my seat with a glare my grade school nuns would have found admirable. Out of habit (sorry), I shrank back in my chair. I should have stayed with my first instinct and kept my mouth shut.

She thrust her arm toward the door. "I want you two to leave."

I stood. Sam grabbed my arm. I sat. Talk about being between a rock and a hard place.

"Ms. Buddy, we're sure you're above reproach, but there's a substantial amount of money involved here. Although I'm sure you pay your techs well, I doubt it's in the six-figure range. What we'd like to do is talk to the tech who performed the test."

Ms. Buddy leaned forward, placed her hands on the desk, stood (although it was hard to tell), and in a stern voice said, "What you're proposing is impossible. Each case is assigned a number. The techs have no idea who the samples belong to. It could be theirs for all they know. The chain is anonymous. I don't even know."

"Someone must. How else can you send the results back to the people who've requested the test."

That gave Ms. Buddy pause, much of her righteous indignation gone.

"Is it possible for the person who controls the file to either mix them up or someone was able to pay them off to falsify the results?"

"We've never..." Ms. Buddy said, then went mute. She was silent for a long time. "I suppose for enough money, anything is possible."

Sam knew from a preliminary investigation, CDC had a clerk who unintentionally switched files, leading to a major lawsuit against CDC. They settled the case out of court for tens of thousands of dollars. What saved them from total catastrophe was, they'd caught the mistake and brought it to the attention of the parties involved.

Sam pushed a little more. "Can we interview the person who handled Trey's file?"

Buddy gave us a defiant shake of her head.

"It'd save us a great deal of time."

"I'm sorry, but I'm going to have to insist you acquire a court order for something like that."

Not receiving what we wanted most, Sam changed tactics. "How much damage to your company would it do when people find out you might have screwed up another test, or worse, one of your employees is under suspicion of falsifying the results?"

Ms. Buddy's eyes grew wide. Sam's implied threat sent paroxysms of fear through her. "You wouldn't!"

Sam's eyebrows raised a millimeter.

Ms. Buddy's face went crimson. She grabbed Trey's letter and motioned for us to follow her. She marched ahead of us. "This didn't happen. If I hear otherwise, I'll deny it to the bitter end."

We trailed her into another sterile room, stacked with huge filing cabinets from wall to wall. "Cailey, this is Ms. Summers. Please answer her questions." She flipped the notary paper up and down to convey we possessed the legal right to be doing what she'd asked. She spun on her heels and started to walk out of the room. I felt a tug on my coat sleeve. When I turned, she said, "This is where you get off. You'll have to leave."

"And just when I thought we'd achieved a breakthrough moment."

I told Sam I'd meet her in the waiting room. Fifteen minutes later, Sam came out and headed straight for the door. It took me a few seconds to gather my coat and scarf and rush after her.

"What gives?" I asked when I closed to within ten feet.

"Anita and Trey's I.D.s matched. Cailey denied even knowing who Trey is. Ice-skating is the one sport she claims she ever watches – and it's only every four years during the Winter Olympics. I wish you were in there. It'd be nice to have your impression whether she was telling the truth. She was totally relaxed as if she didn't have anything to hide. I have her full name, though. We'll run a check on her finances to see if she's made a substantial deposit lately. But if she's smart, she'd wire it directly to an offshore account."

TWENTY-ONE

Storrs, CT – Adelphia Williams – Trey's Mother

We drove from the clinic to Storrs, where Trey's mother lived. Sam called John Anthony Thomas to explain he should have the paternity test rerun. When she hung up, I asked Sam what she hoped to gain by talking to Trey's mom.

"I'm just throwing shit against the wall to see if anything sticks."

"It seems as if you've thought this through."

"Think of this along the same line as the time I agreed to live with you. I'm desperate."

"Sounds like my love life."

"Quit whining and do something about it."

"Sure. As soon as we get back."

"What? You found a deaf, dumb, and blind person?"

"Yes, but she's built like a brick shithouse."

Sam's eye-roll was so dramatic her irises disappeared into the back of her head.

"Seriously, what are you going to ask her?"

"I'm exploring his background. Moms can sometimes shed light on events their children can't."

We found Adelphia Williams' two-story, redbrick home in the gentrified section of Storrs off the UConn campus. Adelphia greeted us with warmth and ushered us into her parlor. We sat around a wrought iron table on comfortable wrought iron chairs where she had coffee and cookies waiting for us.

"I have milk if you'd prefer it instead of coffee."

Adelphia looked more like Trey's older sister than his mother. She was a touch under six-feet tall with light brown skin and shoulder-length hair streaked blond. She either worked out religiously or was blessed with a metabolism that kept her figure youthful.

"We're sorry to intrude at a time like this," Sam said. "We know this is hard for you."

Adelphia's head drooped. She slowly raised it and said, "I appreciate that. I know every mother says this about her child, but Trey couldn't...wouldn't do any of those things. Since he met Shannon, he's matured. He loves her with all his heart. She's been good for him. This is one enormous lie. I wish I could be there, but..."

"May we ask you some personal questions? We don't mean to pry, but my experience shows, you often find answers in the most banal of questions." Sam's voice was soft and soothing, setting Trey's mom at ease. Adelphia shifted in her chair, expecting the worst.

Sam asked, "Is there anybody you know who might want to harm Trey in some way?"

"Like who?"

"Somebody from his past. A rival of some sort? Someone who resented Trey's success?"

Adelphia slowly shook her head. "Trey was teased a lot as a kid. When he became good at basketball, it all changed. There were rivals from other teams, but it was always a healthy rivalry. One of mutual respect. Not jealousy. I can't think of anyone."

"How did Trey and his father get along? Could he be trying to get back into the picture somehow?"

Adelphia withdrew into herself. Her eyes glazed over, and she became catatonic.

"Ms. Williams? Ms. Williams, are you okay?"

She woke from her trance and stared at us, wide-eyed as if she was surprised to see two strangers in her home. She turned away, frightened, unsettled. She wrapped her arms around her as she stared off into the distance.

Sam asked in a gentle coaxing manner. "What can you tell us about Trey's father? We promise it'll go no further than this unless it is necessary to help free Trey."

Adelphia shifted once more, and stared at her hands, encircling her coffee cup. She spoke in a halting whisper. "You have to understand, I've only told my therapist what I'm about to tell you. Trey doesn't even know, but... I try not to think about it. I'd just turned fifteen. To make ends meet, my mother – my father had died in an accident at the factory where he worked – my mother took in boarders. A young man, an eighteen-year-old, named Walter Davis, rented one of the rooms. I thought he was kind of cute. We flirted a little, harmless teenage stuff. One night he came home from his second shift job, drunk. My momma and I were already in bed, sleeping. He came into my room and raped me." Adelphia's voice caught, a tear leaked from her eye. "I couldn't do anything. He caught me by surprise. He held one hand over my mouth and a switchblade to my throat with the other, threatening to kill me if I screamed. When he was done with me, he choked me until I passed out.

When I came to, I was so frightened, I didn't move for hours until I heard mama rummaging around the kitchen. When she saw the bruises on my face and neck, she asked me who did it. I looked toward Davis' bedroom but stopped because I couldn't bring myself to speak his name. But she knew. 'Davis,' was all she said. I closed my eyes and cried. She grabbed a carving knife, went to his room and killed him where he slept. She plunged the knife into his chest, then calmly called the police."

Sam and I sat stark still, stunned.

"As I said, Trey doesn't know. No one knows. My mother went to jail, and they placed me in a home for wayward girls. Trey was born there. I've been in therapy ever since."

"Where was this? I mean, where did you live at the time?"

"We lived in Flint." … "Michigan," she added to make sure we knew where Flint was located.

"When I was eighteen, I got a job at one of the factories, raising Trey by myself. My mother died in prison. I never told Trey the truth. He thinks his father and I were in love. I told him his daddy was killed in the First Gulf War. He believes it's why I've been seeing a psychiatrist for the past twenty-plus years."

She looked so forlorn, I said, "We're so sorry. We didn't mean to dredge up bad memories."

At first, I didn't think she heard me. In a guttural voice, she said, "It was the worst experience of my life. What he did to my family and me was horrible." She reflected on her experience so many years ago, before adding, "Trey was the only good thing that came from it." Adelphia paused once more.

"Trey was recruited by every major university in the South, East, and Midwest. We were so close, he told me he wanted me to move to wherever he went to college. I didn't want to live in the South, and I wanted to get away from there. When the final decision, which he made on his own, was UConn, I couldn't have been happier."

"You had no input?" Sam asked.

"We discussed the different schools. Trey knew my feelings about the South, but the decision was his. I wanted him to be happy, not to do it for me."

"Do you think he sensed you wanted to leave Michigan and the Midwest?"

"Probably. He knew I was unhappy there, I'm sure it influenced his decision."

"You never married?" I asked.

"No. Trey was my sole priority, besides, after what happened...."

When Adelphia didn't continue, I asked, "But you stayed here when he moved to Milwaukee?"

"Yes, this is my home. Plus, you know the NBL. He could be traded or move when he becomes a free agent. I didn't want to have to pack up everything every time he did. He's a grown man. I did my job." She moved her attention away from me, and stared hard at Sam. "Now I expect you to do yours. He'd never do something like this. Find out who did."

It sounded as if she was dismissing us, but Sam had one more subject she wanted to discuss. "I want to ask about Dr. Foucher. There are rumors..."

"Yes, I'm aware of them. Sometimes the sports agents are worse than little old ladies. I never got over what happened. The last thing I wanted in my life was a man. I still don't. The thought is repulsive, even after all those years of therapy. Yes, Dr. Foucher has been a close friend. His concern and care for Trey is something I truly appreciate."

"You had no say in the decision to take him on as his agent?"

Adelphia became a bit indignant. "No, it's another one of those baseless rumors. I did take to Dr. Foucher right off the bat – at least in the business sense."

We thanked her for her hospitality and left. As we walked out the door, Adelphia said, "Trey's my whole world. Please fix this."

"We'll do our best," Sam said and started to walk away. I gave her a slight nudge and motioned to Adelphia. She stepped back inside and hugged Trey's mom for a long, long time. When she moved away, she gave Adelphia her warmest smile. We made our way to the rental car and drove back to the airport. While we waited for our flight to depart, Sam called the Muskies' offices to set up interviews with Carroll and Rosario. We were told Carroll could meet with us after we landed in Milwaukee, but Rosario wasn't available for a few days because he was in the middle of new negotiations with the team's sponsors.

TWENTY-TWO

Joe Carroll – Muskies' Head Coach

On the plane, we discussed what we'd unearthed. From the list given to us by Shannon and Trey, we determined we could discount EZ and Ahmad, but still needed to take a closer look at Sonny Stokes. We were also getting a different picture of Dr. Foucher, much to the chagrin of one Samantha Summers. I, too, was seeing him in a whole different light than the public perception fueled by rumors. Although he was a screw up as everyone else's agent, he went out of his way to take great care of Trey. Sam hated to admit it, but there appeared to be little motive for him to be behind the paternity suit laid on Trey by the deceased Ms. Sanchez number one.

That left six people on the Williamses' list – three if Dr. Foucher was correct. The three everyone agreed on were: Tim Howard, the team's special events coordinator, Miles Phillips, the team's trainer, and Andres Rosario, the team's CFO. Also on the list were: the aforementioned Sonny Stokes, head coach, Joe Carroll, and team owner, Ronald Landrace.

We drove from the airport straight to St. Francis and the Muskies' training facility. Coach Carroll said he could meet with us at 2:00 that afternoon. We pulled into a parking spot adjacent to the facility. We noticed seven cars in the lot, including a black Cadillac Escalade, a black Ford Escape SUV, and a black Lincoln MKX. Four other cars – a Honda Civic, a Chevy Cruz, a Nissan Stanza, a Jeep Cherokee, and the Muskies' team van – were parked there. It meant, either, everyone took the bus to practice, or most of the players and coaches had left for the day. We walked into the lobby, where a male secretary greeted us. He escorted us into Carroll's office, a medium-sized room with a desk, two chairs, and a loveseat. Coach Carroll was talking on the phone.

Numerous awards rested on the shelf behind Carroll, along with a picture of his wife and kids. His jerseys from his days at NC-State and when he played in the old ABL hung on the wall above the couch. Off to his right was a window overlooking the practice court, a floor below. As he talked, he motioned for us to sit in the chairs in front of his desk. Over the years, I have become accustomed to the males and a few of the females we encounter sizing up Sam, but the guys in the NBL took it to a level never seen by mortal man. Coach Carroll watched her longingly as she took the chair closest to the window.

Carroll laughed at something said on the other end of the line before apologizing that he needed to cut their conversation short. With the way he eyed Sam, I'm sure it had more to do with Carroll's eagerness to get to know her than being polite. After he hung up, he reached across the desk to shake hands with Sam and me. When I introduced myself, the coach continued to stare at Sam. I was back to being the invisible sidekick.

"Are you ready?" Carroll asked.

"Ready?" Sam answered, confused.

"For the sauna."

"Sauna. What sauna?"

"Sorry, I thought Trey's attorney had passed that on to you. I have a busy schedule. We're preparing for the Chicago Minotaurs. We finished practice a couple of hours ago. This is the only time in my day I have to use the sauna. The players are gone, and, in an hour, I have to leave for a speaking engagement. I told Trey's lawyer, and he said it'd be fine."

He stood and walked out of the room. He was two inches taller than Sam and had put on sixty pounds since his playing days in the ABL. Sam and I walked behind him, sharing questioning glances. I gave her a did-you-have-any-idea look. To which she responded with an it's-all-news-to-me shrug. She gave me a twist of her head, which I took to mean, if-you-can-handle-it, so-can-I. Sam gestured for me to notice his gait and his stooped shoulders. He possessed a slight limp, which made him appear like he was pimping. It fell into the category Theresa Garza had described.

We reached the bottom of the stairs and rounded the corner. Sam ran headfirst into Sonny Stokes. It took a second to register with Sonny, who Sam was because she was wearing tennis shoes, jeans, a white blouse, a sports coat, and little makeup. When it dawned on him, he said, "You lookin' for me, sweet thang?"

Sam motioned toward Coach Carroll. "I came to talk to your coach."

Sonny's eyes narrowed. He swung his attention to Carroll then back to Sam. His abacus was missing half its beads, so he had difficulty adding up what was happening.

Carroll asked, "Do you two know each other?"

"We met in Vegas during All-Star Weekend," Sam said.

Carroll asked Sonny, "Did you meet her partner...ah, shit! What's your name again?"

"Chancy Evans."

Sonny studied me. He knew he knew me, but the name didn't ring a bell. "I thought you were in the business?"

I shrugged as a way of saying I'd no idea of what he was talking about.

"They're private investigators looking into Trey's situation," Coach Carroll said.

Sonny's face darkened when the realization hit home. It was all an act in Vegas. I don't know if I've ever seen any human so pissed off in my life, and I caused so much trouble growing up, my mother thought of selling me to the gypsies. He swung his full attention to Sam and stared malevolently. Sonny's hands clenched into fists. I knew if Coach Carroll and I hadn't been there, he'd have tried to beat the shit out of Sam for making such a fool of him.

Noting his loathing, Sam slid her jacket aside. Sonny shifted his attention to the gun, resting in Sam's shoulder holster. The two of them locked eyes. To break the spell, I said, "My friend set the marksmanship record for trainees when she attended the police academy in Madison. She can shoot the testicles off a flea from fifty yards." I added, "From what we've heard, you offer a much larger target."

Sonny glanced at me to see if I was joking. I gave him a subtle shake of my head to let him know I was dead serious. He took a step back and motioned for us to pass. Sam moved around Sonny, pivoting so she could keep him in her sights. Sonny watched for a few seconds before heading upstairs.

As he rode out of sight, we heard him say, "Fuckin' bitch."

Carroll asked, "What was that about?"

When Sam didn't answer, I said, "Sonny hit on Sam in Vegas. He didn't know we were working for Trey."

My explanation mollified Carroll. "I'm a little surprised he's still here," he said. "Usually, by now, everyone's gone. Our guys and my staff leave here every day like we're holding a fire drill, except no one comes back inside when it's over." He chuckled at his little joke. "Ms. Summers, there's a room over there with a woman's bathroom. Change in there."

"Change what?" Sam asked, taken aback.

"Your clothes, of course. Unless you want yours steam cleaned." Coach Carroll laughed once more. "Don't worry. We have extra-large towels. I'll have Harold, our equipment guy, bring you one." He said to me. "Come with me. There're towels in the coaches' locker room." He stopped, pointed to an entryway, and more to Sam than me, said, "The sauna's in there. Just let yourself in. I have the steam set for 110 degrees. Cleans out the pores. We'll be in for half an hour. Grab some water from the cooler before you come in."

Five minutes later, Carroll and I were sitting in the sauna. The steam and heat were so thick I thought I might barf. He climbed to the uppermost bench and plopped down with his legs spread, exposing his nether region for much of the Milwaukee area to see. I hoped for Sam's sake the steam might soon envelop the room, saving her from the same sight to which I was exposed.

No such luck.

Less than a minute later, Sam strolled into the room with a towel the size of Texas wrapped around her only to have the first sight she witnessed be Coach Carroll's splayed legs. Her response was not what I'd expected. She burst out laughing after unsuccessfully trying to stifle it. She spun as if searching for a place to sit while getting herself under control. Not finding any seating on her side of the sauna, she walked over to the bench cornering where Coach Carroll sat.

"Why don't you sit over here?" he suggested as he patted the place next to him. "It'll make it easier for us to talk."

"Thanks, but no. I want to be able to see your face."

"Just move real close and turn your head."

Sam ignored his offer and moved to the top bench – all the better to not see you, my dear. At least not your nether region.

Coach Carroll removed his towel. "Hope you don't mind. This is much better for your skin. Every part of your body exposed. You should try it."

"No thanks. I'm a little shy." Carroll ignored my comment and turned in hope to Ms. Summers.

"Sorry, I only let my girlfriend see me naked."

"Ah," Carroll uttered, catching on. I could see him running various scenarios through his mind. The one I think he settled on was the fantasy where James Bond turns Pussy Galore from the dark side. He smiled. To be honest, it was more of a leer. "What is it you wanted to ask me?"

"Why don't you guys run more? You walk the ball up the floor when you have these young, athletic studs."

He didn't appreciate my comments or criticism of his coaching philosophy. "I thought this was about Trey?"

Sam said, "It is. Chancy's just being himself, the worst…and the only advice he's ever followed. How's your relationship with Trey?"

"Not the best, I suppose."

"Why's that?"

"Look, Sam. May I call you Sam?"

"You just did."

He ignored Sam's censure. "I'm old school. I believe in defense and being tough. Trey treats the defensive end like a place he has to hang out until we get the ball back."

"So do EZ and Sonny," I said.

Carroll glared at me with revulsion. "Not all the time. EZ will foul someone hard once in a while, and he'll take the ball to the basket, like Sonny. If Trey thinks someone's going to foul him, he pulls up for the jumper. He'd prefer to stand out by the three-point line and let it fly."

"He's shooting over forty percent from there. It's like shooting sixty percent from the two-point area."

"Your point?" Carroll asked, in a curt, fuck-off kind of way.

"You guys believe a guy shooting fifty percent for the game is great, yet he's shooting the equivalent of sixty."

"Yes, but it doesn't get anyone from the other team in foul trouble, does it?"

Sam jumped in. "I'd love to listen to this all day, but Coach has someplace he needs to be." The two of us shut up. Sam went on, "We hear you went to Landrace and asked him to trade Trey." I think Sam threw up in her mouth when she mentioned Landrace's name.

"It was after a tough loss to New York. After the game, I wanted to trade everybody, including my coaching staff. Hell, I wanted to trade me. As much as I don't like Trey's super-soft nature, your buddy, Chauncy…"

"Chancy," I corrected him. He ignored me.

"Didn't touch on the thing which makes Mr. Oh So Pretty oh so valuable. His ability to make the three opens up the court for Sonny and EZ. Besides, he shoots over forty percent from out there."

I gave myself a fist bump, followed by open hand explosions.

"You don't want him gone?" Sam asked.

"Not unless I can get LeBron James for him." Carroll waited a beat. "You sure you don't want to sit next to me? I don't bite unless you want me to."

"Sorry, I haven't had my rabies shots yet. Besides, I thought you were married?"

"I am, but it's an open relationship."

"Your wife's okay with you sleeping around?"

"Sure, why not? It's what we agreed to before we were married. I knew I couldn't be satisfied with just one woman, it was one of the conditions I insisted on before jumping the broom." Carroll slid a few feet along the bench to move closer to Sam. "So, what do ya say?"

"I say if you move an inch closer, you'll be able to guard a harem. Men are such pigs. All you guys think about is sex and sports."

"Don't forget food," I said.

Sam slid farther away from Carroll. "I still prefer women. Nothing's changed since I first set foot in this place, especially after seeing you in the flesh."

"So, you're still open to the possibility."

"What? Are you freakin' deaf? How'd you come to that conclusion?"

"Because you said you 'prefer' women, which means you still might be open to being with a man."

"Wishful thinking on your part. Let me amend that. It's closer to delusional. Besides, I thought you needed to be somewhere?"

"I can show up late."

"Is that your Escalade in the parking lot?" Sam asked.

Sam's change of subjects didn't faze him. "Pretty sweet, don't you think?" he said. "I can take you for a ride if you'd like."

"That's tempting, but I don't want to have you miss a day of cleaning out your pores."

"We could go someplace and clean out another part of my body." Carroll glanced at his groin, then back at Sam as if she found his exposed reproductive organ irresistible.

Sam gave him a crooked little smile. "Sorry, I left my magnifying glass at home." As an afterthought, she asked, "Isn't your wife a bit disappointed? Who could you possibly satisfy with that?"

"The only person who matters – me. Besides, I have other talents." Carroll stuck out his tongue and touched it to the tip of his nose. I could tell Sam was impressed, but not enough to take him up on his offer.

"Ugh! Chauncy, please get me out of here."

"Chancy," I said sullenly.

"Since we've been on this case, I have a whole new respect for my lack of respect for men." When she reached the door, she said to Carroll. "Two more questions. Did you go with the team to the gun safety lesson at the end of last season?"

"We all went. The whole staff and a couple of guys from the front office."

"Do you own a gun?"

"You wanna see it?"

She glanced at his crotch. "No thanks, I've been disappointed enough for one day. What kind is it?"

"It's a 9mm Browning."

TWENTY-THREE

Twenty minutes later, after showering and dressing, we met in the lobby and headed to the parking lot. Sam and I bantered about the sauna experience as we climbed into my car. While we were inside, we had a light dusting of snow. I noticed somebody had been kind enough to clean off my windshield. I also noticed the Ford Escape, the Lincoln MKX, and the Muskies' team van were now absent.

Having driven in Wisconsin since I was sixteen, I didn't consider the powder to be much of a problem. When we exited the facility and turned south to head back to I-794, the car slid a bit on the fine layer of powder.

"A little out of practice, Ace." I didn't know if Sam was pissed because of the lechery she'd been exposed to for most of this case or whether she was sticking it to yours truly, as was her norm.

I turned right again onto Howard Avenue, the car slid and shuddered once more. "Are you sure you don't want me to drive?" she asked. "Seeing Coach Carroll naked has thrown you." She took a dramatic pause before adding, "Or excited you."

"Not as much as hoping you were going to take him up on his offer to take off your towel."

"In your dreams, Big Boy."

We entered the on-ramp to I-794 heading north toward downtown and the Hoan Bridge, rising a hundred and twenty feet above where the Milwaukee River empties into Lake Michigan. A few years back, a section of the bridge had collapsed. Fortunately, no one was on that segment when it fell into the river below. I cruised around the forty-five mile an hour speed limit for the first stretch of the interstate by-pass. In anticipation of increasing my speed to the fifty-five mile per hour limit ahead, I accelerated as we approached the curve.

Once more, my car slid, but this time the front left side of the car dropped to the pavement, and I saw my front tire continue down the road. The rear of my car slid over into the other lane of traffic toward the concrete barrier, which prevented vehicles from sailing off the bridge and into the water over a hundred feet below. Fortunately for us, most of the afternoon traffic was heading away from downtown. *Unfortunately*, one of the few cars traveling in the same direction as us, was in the next lane. The driver was unable to stop and collided with the back left side of my car, sending us spinning in circles. The eight airbags deployed, throwing us back against our seats and the headrests.

"Are you okay?" I asked Sam once the car came to a stop.

"Yeah. How about you?"

"I'm fine. What the hell...? How did that happen?"

"Your nose is bleeding," Sam said as she handed me some napkins.

I raised my hand to my face and came away with a hand full of blood. I grabbed the napkins and held them tight, pinching the sides of my nose to staunch the flow. I felt it ooze down my throat. The metallic taste brought back memories of lying on my back on the UW football practice field with our All-American linebacker standing over me.

I peered out my window and watched my left front tire roll along the side of the road. It wavered and tipped over. I jumped out and ran back to the woman driving the other car. She was shaken and scared. I rapped on the window. She cautiously turned her head to me, wide-eyed. The sight of blood running down my face onto my chin shocked her even more. Her eyes grew as wide as SETI Satellite dishes, and her mouth dropped open. I motioned for her to roll down the window. When, with a shaking hand, she did, I asked, "Are you okay?"

She said in a squeaky voice, "What happened?"

"My left front tire came off somehow."

She eyed the front of her car and slumped. "I just bought this yesterday."

"Don't worry. I have insurance. I'll make sure it's as good as new." As the words left my mouth, steam rose out of her radiator into the cold afternoon air.

Sam called 9-1-1 and reported the accident. Within minutes, I heard the State Patrol cars headed our way. The woman and I exchanged insurance information and talked to the two officers. I explained to the state trooper that the tire had just came off.

He wagged his head in disbelief. "I've heard this model has a problem with the lug nuts coming loose. But all five at once?" He made a notation in his logbook. "We've called a tow truck. It should be here soon. You're lucky. If this'd happened while you were on the bridge, you could've died."

TWENTY-FOUR

My car was towed to a repair shop in the Third Ward. Sam and I called for a cab and returned to General Mitchell International Airport to rent a car. I wanted to lease the Cadillac CTS, but Sam convinced me to go with the Nissan Altima because it handles better in Milwaukee's unpredictable winter weather.

We discussed what had transpired over the last forty-eight hours as we drove back to our loft. We once more walked the five flights, and I opened the door. Sam scooted past me and headed for the computer. On the way home, she'd received a text from Adrianna. Sam contacted her earlier to delve into the financial resources of Cailey MacDonald, the young lady who'd handled Trey's paternity test. Sam downloaded the attachment and read Adrianna's report. I walked up behind her, reading over her shoulder.

"Do you mind?" Sam chastised.

"Not at all. What does it say?"

That got me a look reminiscent of the one my mother gave to the sex reassignment surgeon when he refused her request to turn me into the little girl she wanted. I found myself relegated to the couch until she finished analyzing it. I watched Sam grow more disappointed the longer she delved into the report. When Sam finished, she looked at me.

"Let me guess," I said. "There's no apparent link between Ms. MacDonald and the possibility she'd a hand in falsifying Trey's report." Sam looked sideways at me and made a circular gesture with her hand for me to continue. "I take it her finances, and her standard of living hasn't changed dramatically over the past year. No new expensive purchases. No new car or new furniture or a grand wardrobe makeover. No cruise, no trip overseas, or to Disney World, or a Caribbean vay-cay. Etc. etc. etc."

"You could tell all that by watching me read her report?"

"Like a book."

Sam let go a huge sigh. "I guess we'll have to wait until we see the new paternity test results, which should be here any day. It appears more and more likely, the baby is Trey's."

"So, he was lying about sleeping with her?"

"There *are* those pictures. Despite Shannon's insistence to the contrary, Trey may have cheated on her. Whether he killed Anita because of it, I'm not sure. I'm leaning that way. The only reason I'm not going all in, to use a phrase you can relate to, is your unshaken belief he believes himself to be innocent."

Sam waited for an implied answer. "What?" I asked puzzled.

"Are you sure?"

"That he's innocent or believes he's innocent?" Sam's eyes sparked. I chuckled. "Both. I still believe Trey is telling the truth when he says he's not the father, and he didn't kill Anita or Juanita. He's been too consistent with his tone and body language. Nobody's that good. At least no one I've ever met or known."

Sam's wasn't completely sold on my theory. "I guess so. But something doesn't add up. Let's face it, perhaps he's a sociopath. It'd explain a lot."

"It doesn't fit," I said. "His tiny bursts of anger, the care he has for Shannon, his drive to be the best three-point shooter, the fact he has a healthy sex life, all of which says he's not. I agree with Shannon, he didn't do any of this." My statement came out with more conviction than I felt.

Sam caught it. "You don't sound as if you're entirely convinced with what you said." I shrugged. The silence grew for a few minutes before Sam asked, "What happened today?"

"With the interview or the car wreck?"

"Yes."

"I think Carroll told us the truth. Asking Landrace to trade Trey was out of frustration with the loss to New York, nothing more. Do I think he'd trade him if he could? Sure, but only if he was offered a sweetheart of a deal."

I noted Sam's skepticism.

"Maybe not a sweetheart of a deal, but I believe he sees him as an asset, much like Landrace. One more piece of meat he can use to sweeten any trade."

While Sam contemplated my hypothesis, I muttered more to myself than her, "I don't know if I've ever seen anyone as pissed as Sonny today. Except for my mom, of course." Sam gave me her best you-have-to-be-kidding-me expression. "Or Rainey," I added.

"He was not a happy camper," Sam said.

"Like one of those kids who finds out someone put a snake in his sleeping bag?"

Sam stared at her computer screen and didn't respond. To draw her attention, I said, "Or his hand stuck in warm water while he was sleeping. Or his anaconda super-glued to his leg. ... Or..."

Sam rotated her head a smidgeon and gave me an intimidating glare out of the corner of her eye. Okay, so my stunt worked. Maybe a little too well. Now that I had her full and undivided consideration, I said, "So much for Sonny being a 'pretty decent guy.' Foucher might have to reevaluate his opinion of him. I read his tone and body language more along the lines of an entitled brat who didn't get his way and who was super-pissed at being conned. But, what could be his motive? Do you set someone up for murder for an additional fourteen million dollars?" Sam raised her eyebrows. I concurred. "I guess so."

We went silent again for a couple of minutes contemplating everything that'd been said. I shrugged my shoulders and let out a huge sigh.

"What?" Sam asked.

"My car will never be the same."

"Buy another. With the money you won in Vegas, you can afford a new one, and you'd still have enough left over for a healthy down payment for a second one for me."

"Speaking of which – the accident, not Vegas – it wasn't, was it?" I asked.

"An accident? No. One or two, but not all five. Someone loosened those hoping we'd be critically injured. Or sent to the morgue."

"Do you think Sonny might have done it?"

"Yeah," Sam said without hesitation. She added, "But you also have to understand we were in the shower long enough Carroll could have been the person who loosened them. He's tall and has a strange gate. Plus, he does walk a little stooped over."

"Would he run out wearing nothing but a towel?" I asked.

"Why'd he have to wear nothing but a towel?" Sam had difficulty unraveling my logic.

"He certainly didn't come into the locker room while I was showering, to get dressed. I'd have heard him."

"You didn't notice the wardrobe closet in his office?" Sam asked.

"Huh? He has a wardrobe closet in his office?"

"Mr. Observant. How do you win at poker?"

"Reading people's reactions is different than observing your surroundings."

"Sure it is." Sam's comment was so acerbic it gave me acid reflux. Seeing my reaction, Sam softened her tone. "I'm sure the closet held a change of clothes. He'd have something he could throw on – like sweats – run outside, loosen the lug nuts and get back before we finished showering and dressed."

"I suppose." I didn't buy Sam's theory, not because I thought what she was saying wasn't feasible, more because I read Carroll as someone who'd told us the truth. He was more interested in playing with Sam's body than breaking it. On the other hand, he'd like to see me shattered into a million pieces because I questioned his coaching philosophy.

Sam interrupted my thoughts. "You don't believe he'd do something like that." Her tone suggested she didn't agree with me.

"I'm not saying that," I said. "He was too focused on you. Besides, he admitted he wasn't particularly fond of Trey. As I said, I believe he sees Trey as an asset. Setting him up for this pretty much negates that."

"So all we have right now is Sonny. ... And Trey."

I bobbed my head in agreement. "I hate to admit it, but if I were forced to choose between the two, based on everything we know, I'd pick Trey."

TWENTY-FIVE

Miles Phillips – Muskies' Trainer

Kenny Miller called to tell us Miles Phillips was scheduled to attend a meeting of Milwaukee Wealth Builders on Thursday night. Some of Milwaukee's wealthier business people started MWB. Entrepreneurs needing capital brought their ideas and inventions to them in hopes of acquiring seed money for their projects.

I called MWB's offices and told them of an idea I believed could make millions. I explained I'd designed a new golf shoe that took the pressure off the forward knee on the downswing. They gave me an ID number and told me to be at the club at 7:00 p.m. I brought Sam as my design partner.

We arrived a few minutes ahead of schedule to survey the place. A long wooden table with five high-backed leather chairs was set up for the potential "investors." Five feet in front of them was another much smaller square table with a couple of chairs for the "presenters." Off to the side was a second room where the various entrepreneurs, all a bit on edge, gathered while waiting their turn. Sam and I, holding the diagrams we hastily put together of the "designs" for our revolutionary new shoe, parked our asses in the waiting room. It wasn't hard to spot Miles Phillips. He sat at the end of the second row near the refreshment table. He'd sit for a few seconds, pop up and pace. He'd march to the back of the room, pivot, then tramp back to his seat. I expected a doctor might walk through the door any minute to tell him it was quintuplets, one of each kind.

Based on the way the rest of the men in the NBL had reacted to her physical charms, I suggested it'd work best if Sam played the ingénue once more to strike up a conversation with Phillips. In no uncertain terms, she told me she'd rather hang by her thumbs over a roaring bonfire. She was still having nightmares concerning Vegas and insisted on acquiring the information the old-fashioned way, by approaching Phillips and engaging him in conversation.

No matter how hard she tried to seduce him with her verbal skills, he continually brushed her off. After her third failed attempt, Sam gave up and slumped in her chair. "I guess I don't have that effect on *everybody,* after all. Any ideas?"

"Aside from you playing the harlot once again?" When Sam's eyes narrowed, I quickly added, "I do. Sit tight. I'll be back in a minute."

I went to the refreshment table and grabbed a cup of coffee. I waited for Phillips to sit, counted to twelve then made my way up the aisle. My timing was perfect. As I arrived at the spot a step behind where he sat, he stood, turned, and hit the cup I was carrying, spilling my coffee on me.

"Oh shit, I'm sorry," he said. "Are you alright?"

I pretended to be scalded by the coffee, although I'd placed a couple of ice cubes in my cup. "Ouch, ouch, ouch." I pulled my shirt away from my chest. "Now what am I going to do, I can't go in there like this. My shirt is ruined."

"I'm sorry. ... Here, take my jacket. If you button it, maybe they won't be able to see the stain," as if the light brown spot, covering the entire front of my shirt, wouldn't look so bad if I wore a sports coat. I put the jacket on. It was too small – my arms stuck out past the cuffs – and too big at the same time – I'd have to go on a three-month diet of spaghetti and ice cream before it came close to fitting me.

Phillips said, "Maybe if we dab some cold water on it right away, it'll come out."

I handed back his coat, and we moved to the restroom where he grabbed a handful of towels and, using his left hand, dabbed at the stain.

"That's okay, I can take it from here," I said. He watched while I tried to remove the coffee from my Cucinelli dress shirt. It gave me the chance to strike up a conversation. "What brings you here? I mean, I know why you're here. What's your invention?"

He hesitated as if I might be a corporate spy, but seeing my dilemma, he decided it was okay to tell me. "I have this new orthotic insole that will revolutionize sports. The design helps prevent people from tearing their Achilles."

"Is that a huge problem?" I asked as I rewet the paper towel and gave another swipe at my shirt. "I mean, is it a common injury?"

"With the increase in the runners and the explosion sports we have these days, it's becoming more and more so, especially among women who wear high heels all day long, then exercise. My idea is going to change the world." He made it sound like the orthotics were a cure for cancer and heart disease in one.

"Wow. Sounds exciting." I stuck out my hand. "I'm Beau Brummel."

Phillips once more hesitated before accepting my hand. "I'm Miles."

"So...Miles? Are you having trouble finding financing, too? I've got this great idea for a golf shoe that takes most of the stress off the knee. The shoe pivots as you turn forward. I betcha Tiger'd love to have had something like that."

Phillips wasn't impressed and muttered, "I bet." He appraised my shirt. "That's much better. I should go in case they call my name."

"Hey, no problemo. Good luck. Let me know how it goes. If they turn you down, I just might know someone else who'd be interested."

He brightened. "Really?"

"For sure," I said as if securing him a start-up loan was a foregone conclusion.

When I walked out, Sam caught sight of me. She raised her eyebrows, sat up straighter, and searched my face for the answer she'd hoped to see. Phillips must have been called to make his presentation because he was nowhere in sight. When she saw me scan the waiting area, she confirmed my suspicion. "He's in there." She gestured toward the other room. She asked, "How'd it go?"

"It went well. He thinks I can find him his funding if he strikes out."

"Let's hope his presentation is a huge swing and a miss."

Five minutes later, Phillips returned to the room. It didn't take an expert in body language to see the committee had rejected his idea. He walked straight to me. "Would your guy listen to my presentation?"

"For sure. When we're done here, let's go someplace and talk."

"Great. That'd be great."

After Sam and I made our presentation to the committee, we gathered our diagrams and headed to the waiting room to gather Miles Phillips, as well. He suggested we go to Applebee's. He grabbed his long, dark trench coat, and his Indiana Jones fedora. He pulled it down low over his face, flipped up the collar, and made his way to the parking lot. We followed him to the restaurant. Sam needlessly pointed out he drove a black Ford Escape SUV. We huddled in a booth, and the waitress took our drink order. Before she could turn to fill our request, an eager Phillips asked, "What'd the committee think about your idea?"

I gave him a shoulder shrug and a head tilt, implying we'd bombed out.

"Me too. Can you believe those guys? I've got something that's going to revolutionize sports, and they tell me it's not worth their time."

Sam scrutinized Phillips for a few minutes, then said, "I've seen you someplace before."

"I doubt it." Phillips dismissed Sam's statement while keeping his focus on me. "You said you know somebody who might be interested in backing something like this?"

Sam persisted. "No, I know I know you." She snapped her fingers as if she remembered where. "On TV. I've seen you on TV. I'm sure of it. But where?"

"No, I'm pretty sure you're mistaken," Phillips said without much conviction.

"Sports. Some sort of sporting event. Football? No. Basketball! You're one of those people who have courtside seats at the Muskies' games. You're always sitting next to the team and the head coach. Whatshisname?"

Phillips offered Sam a weak smile. "Carroll."

"No, that's not it. It's a guy's name."

Phillips subtly shook his head. "His first name is Joe. His *last* name is Carroll." He said to me. "Can you introduce me to this guy you know?"

Sam didn't let me answer. "How do you afford such amazing seats? Those tickets have to cost you a small fortune."

"They're free." Once again, Phillips had eyes only for me while he answered Sam. They were filled with immense hope and deep longing, the same way I'd looked at Shannon that first night.

"How'd you pull that off? Are you a good friend of the owner, whatshisname? Lecher?"

"It's Landrace, and no, I'm not."

"You must know someone to get such great seats?"

"It's one seat."

"Oh." Sam sounded like she'd just found out her date with Charlize Theron had been canceled. "So, you can't take us sometime?"

I could see Phillips' determination to keep it a secret, as to who he was, vanish. "Listen, lady, I work for the Muskies."

"How wonderful. What do you do? Are you somebody famous?"

It was as if Sam had kicked over an opened can of paint, everything came spilling out. "I'm the trainer." He returned his attention to me. "Can you set something up with this guy? I'm sure he'd love my idea. I've got graphs and charts and studies. The whole nine yards."

"Shouldn't it be the whole ninety-four feet?" Sam asked.

"Huh?" Phillips said to Sam, "It's an expression."

"It doesn't fit if you're in basketball. Nine yards. The courts ninety-four feet."

"Okay then, the whole ninety-four feet. Can we move past that?" Then to me, "What do you say?"

I opened my mouth, but Sam asked, "If you work with all those rich athletes, why don't you ask *them* for the money?"

"They wouldn't know a great deal if it bit them on their asses."

"So, you've tried?"

What little determination remained in Phillips, melted faster than snow at the equator. "Yeah, I tried. I went to one of the guys, but he turned me down like those jerks tonight."

"I bet that pissed you off."

"No, not really," he said, but it was as hollow as a politician's campaign promise.

"Oh, come on now. Those guys are rich. They've probably got so much money they throw away on drugs and women, surely they could've spared a few dollars for a guy they work with."

"That's what I thought, too. But no." Phillips' face had gone crimson. "He told me it was done in Australia, and failed. But it's not the same. Sure, it's where the idea came from, but I've improved on it. I even paid an independent company to run some tests. It works. Did he listen? No! Him and the asshole agent of his."

"You sound pissed."

"I was at first, but not anymore. Besides, the guy got his."

"What do you mean by that?"

"Nothing."

"It doesn't sound like nothing." Sam had sunk her teeth in so far, she was determined to hang on until she extracted every last bit of information she could.

"Listen, I'm telling you it's nothing. The guy's going to be spending so much money crawling out from under something else he's into, he's not much use to me now."

"Treymon. You're talking about Treymon Williams. Wow. Can you believe that shit?" Sam got up from sitting next to me and moved to the other side, where she forced Phillips to slide further along the bench seat. "Did he do it? I hear he knocked her up then offed her. Her sister, too. He must be some kinda bad man." Sam added some awe to her voice as if being a murderer added to Trey's allure.

Phillips moved as far away from Sam as he could, plastering himself against the wall. He shot me a glance, questioning what kind of people I hung around with. I gave him a what-can-I-say raise of my eyebrows. He stared wide-eyed at Sam, who'd moved in for the kill.

Phillips tried to become one with the wall. "Listen, lady, I just work with the guy. I don't know anything about his personal life. And I don't want to. To be honest, most of the guys are jerks. You know what NBL stands for? Nothing But Losers."

"Yet, you wanted him to finance your project."

"Why not? It's not like I asked him to be the godfather to one of my kids. Besides, it'd made him millions more. A win-win for both of us."

"Do you think he did it? I mean, killed those two women?"

"Sure, why not. If you're in this league long enough, you realize anything is possible. Even murder."

"You don't like Treymon much. Do you?"

"Not any more or less than the rest of those guys."

Sam slid a little closer. "Do you own a gun?"

Phillips turned sideways, his back flat against the wall. He raised one knee, placing it on the bench seat to prevent Sam from moving closer. "I have three of them. I believe strongly in the Second Amendment. I also own a couple of rifles. What does that have to do with anything?"

Sam's eyes grew large as if he'd told her he was an astronaut who'd walked on the moon. I thought Phillips might climb across the table and run out of the restaurant, but Sam had leaned so far into him he'd need a crowbar to pry himself free.

"Calm down, lady. It's no big deal. Most of the guys in the NBL have guns. It's the nature of the business. All those crazy fans and stalkers. Relax, already."

Undeterred, Sam said, "I'd love to see yours. Is one of them a 9mm handgun? I love those."

"Nobody sees my guns. I don't even show them to my wife."

"You're married?" Sam couldn't contain her disbelief that this reprobate had found somebody who'd agreed to marry him. She slid three feet away.

"Yeah. She's home doing what all women should be doing," he said pointedly to Sam. "She's taking care of my house. Which reminds me, I hope she did a better job of shoveling the drive this time."

Now *I* was dumbfounded. "You make her shovel the driveway?"

"Sure, what else has she got to do? Last time she didn't get the edges straight, so I made her do it over again. Hopefully, she learned her lesson."

I understood why he hid his guns from his wife.

Sam gawked at him in disbelief. She dropped all pretenses. "Where were you the night Trey's housekeeper was killed?"

"Huh? What? Who are you people?"

"I'm a private investigator. I'm looking into who could have done this and set Trey up."

"A woman P.I.? Really?"

"Yeah, and I carry a gun." Sam pulled aside her jacket to show Phillips her Sig-Sauer P229. Sam had finally stumbled onto something that made him excited to talk to her.

He moved away from the wall and inched closer to Sam. "Can I see it?" he asked as he reached for it.

Sam slapped his hand away. "Reach for it one more time, and you won't be able to tape ankles for a year." He smiled. Sam caught his reaction and returned it with one of utter disgust. "Where were you that night?"

"I was probably at home with my wife. Why? You don't think I had anything to do with it?"

"We hear you threatened to get even with Trey for not sponsoring your project."

The realization of the situation hit home. Phillips stared at me. "You don't know an investor, do you? It was a ploy to bring me here to discuss Trey. You knew who I was all along." He said to Sam, "Get out of my way. I want to leave, right now."

"Why, so you can go home to make sure the driveway's shoveled properly?"

"Among other things." He remained resolute, waiting for Sam to move.

"One final question. Did you go with the team to the gun safety lesson?"

Phillips remained silent. Sam refused to budge until he answered. He wisely decided to not challenge a pissed-off woman with a gun. "I was one of the people responsible for setting the whole thing up. Why?"

Sam didn't say anything and slid out of the booth. He slithered along the bench, keeping his focus on the spot where Sam carries her gun. As soon as he could stand, he grabbed his coat and hat off the rack and stormed out of the restaurant.

Sam watched with interest. "Look," she motioned to Phillips, hurrying away.

"What?" I asked when I didn't understand what it was she wanted me to notice.

"Look at the way he walks."

I noticed something different.

"It's neither white nor Hispanic," she said to enlighten me. "He's also hunched over a bit."

She was right. He owned a strange walk, one stride longer than the other, closer to an angry strut than a hard walk.

Once he disappeared from sight, I asked, "What do you think?"

"He's right. The NBL stands for Nothing But Losers." She let it sink in and asked, "What was your take?"

"He's a credible suspect."

"I agree." She smiled before adding, "A good thing you didn't tell him the committee liked your golf shoe idea or you may have been next on his list."

TWENTY-SIX

Andres Rosario – Muskies' CFO

The Muskies left the next day for the first game of a back-to-backer, or as Milwaukee's Southsiders say, a D-N-B, a dare-n-back. Sam felt it was a perfect opportunity to speak to one of the last two people on Trey and Shannon's list. Sam called first thing Friday morning to set up a time to talk to Andres Rosario. She explained we represented Trey and were interviewing character witnesses in case it went to trial.

When we arrived, we were asked to sit and wait because Rosario had someone he'd be finished meeting with momentarily. Five minutes later, his door opened, and a man in his early forties took a couple of steps backward out of the office. He pivoted when he saw Sam and appraised her from head to toe. He was dressed in a thick winter coat and rolled his newsboy hat in his hands. After giving me a cursory glance, he turned back to Rosario standing in the doorway and offered him an abbreviated nod. He walked past us and regarded Sam once more, offering her a slight bow before heading for the door.

Rosario apologized. "Sorry to keep you waiting. Come in, come in." He left the door open and returned to his desk, where his lunch was spread out. He'd laid a few sheets of paper toweling on top of it to protect from any spills or drips.

I was surprised at the size of his office. I thought an NBL team's CFO would have a large, ornate workspace. The room was fifteen-by-fifteen feet. The desk was gouged and scratched and was missing the glass top, which should have covered the surface. One filing cabinet, a cloak rack, and two modest cloth chairs filled the rest of the office. I'd seen better furniture at school rummage sales.

A photo of him with his family of five rested on his desk. The space possessed one saving grace: it was a corner office with windows overlooking 4th Street and a section of the employee parking lot.

He grabbed his sandwich and took a bite before he sat. In mid-chew, he waved at us to sit across from him. He chomped on his food and swallowed. "Sorry, this is the only time I have to eat. My day is crammed full of meetings and deals. I'm going to be stuck here all day. I hope you don't mind."

"Thanks for seeing us," Sam said. She motioned toward the doorway. "Who was that?"

"Who?"

Sam gestured toward the door once more.

"Oh, him. Nobody really. A guy I knew from my old neighborhood. Wanted to know if I could find him a job with the team."

"And?" Sam asked.

"I told him I'd see what I could do." He took another bite of his sandwich and grabbed a handful of chips. "Why do you ask?" He popped the chips into his mouth.

"Nothing really. Just the way he looked at me. Like we knew one another."

"Sam," I said, "you get that from every guy, even the blind ones."

That received one more head shake from Sam. She focused on Rosario and said, "We appreciate even a little of your time." Sam was acting so sweet I thought Rosario might forego his dessert.

"What can I do for you?" he asked as he stuffed another handful of chips into his mouth.

"We're part of the team investigating the Treymon Williams situation." Sam made it sound as if Trey had been caught J-walking instead of being accused of two counts of murder.

"Sad," Rosario said with a shake of his head before taking another huge bite of his sandwich.

"Can you shed some light on where the negotiations were on his new contract before this went down?"

"I'm sorry, what? I was told you were here to see if I could act as a character witness for Trey."

"We are, but part of it is assessing your relationship with him. His lawyer doesn't want any surprises when you're cross-examined."

Rosario bought Sam's explanation. "There's not much to tell. Foucher and I had a couple of conversations, but nothing concrete. It was more of a feeling-out process."

"Can we ask whether you were going to meet Foucher's demands?"

"They were hardly what I'd consider demands. Besides, every detail is brought to the attention of Mr. Landrace before it's approved. I'm just the middleman."

"We heard you receive a bonus if you keep the team's cap under the league threshold."

He hesitated and took another bite. "It's modest, but I do get a bonus. Mr. Landrace, despite what you might have heard, can be quite generous."

"A half-mil bonus is more than 'quite generous.'"

"I'm not sure where you got that figure, but I assure you that's grossly overstated. Not even close."

"Either way, you must look forward to the bonus no matter how small it is?"

"Of course, but what does that have to do with Trey's situation?"

"We're under the impression the organization was being pressured by your sponsors to make sure the team extended Trey. His new contract was sure to put the Muskies over the cap. There goes your bonus."

Rosario shifted his attention between Sam and me, settling finally on Sam. "What are you saying? I framed Trey so I could keep making a bonus? That's quite an accusation. It's just money. I've been in this business long enough to understand it's cyclical. Sure, what Trey asked for was a cap buster, but there are other ways to cut salaries. Plus, Trey wasn't going to be with us forever. One day he'd be gone, and we'd be back under."

"In the meantime, it's a blow to you financially."

He shrugged to convey it mattered little to him.

"Do you own a gun?" Sam asked.

The non sequitur threw him. When he recovered, he said, "No, they scare me. I don't want them anywhere near my kids."

"Did you go with the team to the gun safety lesson last year?"

"I was there, but I couldn't bring myself to handle one of the guns. I sat and observed. That's all."

"You didn't pick one up or hold one?" I asked. "Why even go?"

He glanced at Sam then back to me. "I was asked to go to represent the front office. A team-building exercise for the organization. When I arrived, Miles Phillips was so excited about his new gun, he showed it to me. He reminded me of the kid who wants to show his buddy the Playboy magazine he'd found in his dad's drawer. It was a little creepy. He thrust it at me. Before I knew it, I was holding it. As I said, it scared me. I immediately handed it back to him. I didn't shoot it. He assured me the safety was on, but I couldn't be sure."

"Have you ever fired a gun in your life?" I asked.

"When I was a kid, a long time ago. It was so powerful it practically knocked me over. Right then, I knew…" He didn't finish his thought, drifting off to a place neither Sam nor I could follow.

"Do you remember where you were when Anita Sanchez was killed?"

He hesitated once more before saying, "My wife and I were at the all-school concert at University School. My daughter was a solo artist. My sons were part of the school's ensemble orchestra."

"One more thing before we go, then you can return to your lunch. What kind of car do you drive?"

"A Ford Fiesta. Why?"

"Just curious. Thanks for your time. Oh, does your wife have a car?"

"She drives a Chevy van. With the school functions and kids activities, she puts thousands of miles on it every year."

"Thanks, again," Sam said.

We went across the street to Turner Hall, where we ordered their famous Friday fish fry. Over lunch, we talked about our latest interview.

"Give," Sam said once the waiter left to get our drinks.

"Something's off," I said as I tried to figure out what was bothering me about our Rosario interview.

Sam gestured with her hand to continue.

"I suspect he lied about the bonus, at least the amount. He made it sound as if it was much lower than what Trey and Shannon told us. Despite his insistence, it didn't mean much to him, it did."

"It costs over $20,000 a year per kid to send your children to University School. He has three of them." As a follow-up question, she asked, "Do you believe he could have done it?"

"I'm sure you'll check his alibi, but, despite his protestation about guns and his attempt to convince us they scare him, I got the opposite impression. Something in his eyes told me he enjoyed the feeling of power that came with handling the gun Phillips showed him."

"I'll check with the school. With the number of rich kids who go there, their security must be exceptionally tight."

We were sitting near one of the windows overlooking 4th Street. Sam sat up straighter when she caught sight of something outside. "What do you think he's doing there?"

I spun in my seat to see whom she was talking about and caught a glimpse of Sonny Stokes in his Lincoln MKX, leaving the parking lot.

TWENTY-SEVEN

University School – Brett Warner – Head of Security

Saturday was "alibi checking" day.

We drove to Fairy Chasm Road, the location of University School of Milwaukee. The high school was slated for several athletic contests: in the afternoon, they hosted the finals of a four-team hockey tournament, then two high school basketball games that night.

Sam had learned the name of the head of security, Brett Warner. She called him earlier that morning to see if he might have a moment to talk.

We were greeted at the entrance by one of his security people. After we identified ourselves and showed him ID, we were told to follow the hallway to the end, take a right, and we'd find Warner's door on the right-hand side.

We knocked and heard a deep male voice say, "Come in. It's open."

Warner was an inch or two shorter than me, with wavy, dishwater-blond hair and a bit of a paunch. When we introduced ourselves, Warner asked, "You're private investigators? That's something I've thought I might like to do when I'm done here in a couple of years. You make a decent living?"

I laughed.

Sam glared at me then answered Warner's question. "It pays the bills."

Other than her clothing, car, business expenses, and most of her food, well, some of her food, I tried to remember what bills Sam paid, came up blank, but refrained from making any comment.

"That's what I thought. This job ain't so bad. They pay us well. The lone drawback is havin' to put up with the attitude of wealthy, entitled teenagers. But like I said, they pay us well. But, enough of the small talk. What can I do for you?"

"We're checking up on various people and their alibis. Not that we believe this person did anything, you understand. We're just crossing all our T's, dotting all our I's." Sam made it sound as if she was confiding a national secret to Warner. He leaned in as if they were colleagues sharing top-level information. Sam asked, "Do you keep a log of people who attend the different events here?"

"Nah. We don't do nothing like that. Most of the people who send their kids here are minor celebrities in the community. They expect to be recognized. Askin' them who they are, don't go over too good."

"We were told you held an all-school concert on the 10th of February."

Warner looked over his shoulder at a large calendar hanging on the wall. "That's right," he said.

"Can you tell us who was on duty? We want to see if a certain someone was here."

He studied the calendar for a moment. "Len Mathews and Charles Taylor worked that night."

"Will either of them be here today?"

"Charles is scheduled to come in at 5:00 this afternoon for the basketball games."

"Oh." It was clear Sam was disappointed we'd have to wait that long.

"We do have video," Warner said.

"Does it show the audience?"

Warner seemed confused. "That's the only thing it shows. We don't care 'bout the performance. That's for the drama and music departments. We're interested in seein' what happens, if anythin', in the seats. In case somethin' goes down."

Sam slid forward in her chair. "Can we see it?"

"Sure. Give me a minute." Warner opened a large filing cabinet door and pulled out a drawer. He played his fingers along a row of DVD cases, stopping when he came to the one from that night. He extracted it and slid it into a DVD tray built into his desk. The screen on the wall sprung to life. Within seconds the video was playing. "Who're we looking for?"

"Andres Rosario."

Warner grabbed the remote from his desk and fast-forwarded through the video. "Stop," Sam said. "There. Is that him?"

The timestamp read 18:42. Rosario was walking down the aisle, with a stocky, dark-haired woman. They grabbed seats halfway down the auditorium and a third of the way across the row.

"Can you speed it up to see if he stays for the whole performance?"

"Sure." Warner hit the fast-forward button, we saw everyone move or walk in jerky, double-time. Rosario and his wife watched the entire performance and never left, not even to go to the bathroom. During the twenty-minute intermission break, they remained in their seats. The video moved on and showed the Rosarios, like everyone else, giving the performers a standing ovation when the concert ended at 20:54.

"Thank you. You've been a great help." Sam reached out to shake his hand when the video ended.

"No problem. Anytime." He gripped Sam's hand, holding onto it longer than conventionally acceptable. He gave her his best, warmest, yet nervous, smile. He attempted to say something but babbled incoherently until Sam extracted her hand from his.

"It was nice meeting you," he said once his tongue became unglued.

We made our way to Lake Shore Road and turned north toward Port Washington to see if we could spot any cameras pointed at the road. Sam noticed a few places she thought were prospects, but at the first two – the Red Bull plant in Grafton, and Lake Wind Elks Farm – we found the cameras positioned to cover the employee parking lots and not the road.

We decided not to stop at Flying S Ranch or the Jehovah's Witnesses Church. (Sam didn't want to get stuck having to listen to someone preaching to her about her lifestyle.) The WE Energies Power Plant had cameras, but, like the first two places, they were focused on their parking lot.

The sixth place, About Nature Construction Company, used digital video, but to save space on the hard drive, it recorded a frame of video every five seconds. We explained to the manager what we were trying to find, and he allowed us access to their collection.

We reviewed the video from the night in question for over an hour and caught a few frames of dark SUVs passing by the company. None of the stills of the cars speeding past were of much use. The one frame of video that looked encouraging didn't show the driver of the vehicle, or the license plate. Nonetheless, we copied the image onto a thumb drive, thanked the manager, and continued our search.

We stopped at four more places: Lakeland Title Services, Vines to Cellars, Bernie's Fine Market, and a bicycle store called Zuzu's Pedals. The last had a digital video camera, but the resolution was of such poor quality most of the passing cars were indistinguishable from one another.

On our drive back, I said, "That felt like a waste, like me going to bars, picking up women waste."

"We have that one frame of video, and it was from the right timeframe, we have to hope we can clean it up. I'll give it to Christy Nichols, the woman I use for my photo and video work, to see if she can get something off it."

"Do you have any operatives who aren't female?"

"No, why would I? Women are much more trustworthy and reliable."

"And?"

"They' don't hit on me as much as you guys." She must have thought back to Warner and how tongue-tied he'd become just touching Sam's hand because she added, "Or try to."

"That's what I thought. Anyway, we're kind of back to square one, as far as Trey's alibi goes."

"Our best hope is if the paternity test comes back negative," Sam said. "Although it won't prove much other than he was telling Shannon the truth. The prosecutor will say, at the time of the murder, he was under the impression the kid was his. It doesn't change his motive."

"I've been giving this much thought, as I'm sure you have, if Trey *is* telling the truth, and he didn't sleep with Anita, how could the baby be his?"

"I'm not sure. What worries me more are the pictures. Christy assures me they haven't been photoshopped."

"When you put it all together," I said, "the case is exceptionally compelling against Trey. He had motive and opportunity. His fingerprints on the statue – I know you've already explained it – and his fingerprints on the shell casing, which is much harder to explain. He has a black SUV. The pictures, tattoo, blackmail phone call, and worst of all, the 9-1-1 call."

"Are you sure you're reading him correctly?"

I shrugged. "I hate to admit it, but I'm beginning to have serious doubts."

TWENTY-EIGHT

Tim Howard – Muskies' Game Day Operations

We had to wait until Monday to interview Tim Howard, the Muskies' game-day operations guy. Sam and I posed as representatives of Tri-Awards Statues and Souvenirs, a company specializing in bobblehead dolls. Howard suggested we meet at the Muskies' warehouse to discuss returning the 10,000 Treymon Williams' figures the team no longer planned to give away.

"What happened to Gene Morales?" Howard asked after we'd introduced ourselves as Alexandra Davis and Derek Andrassy. I was Alex and Sam was Derek. Just kidding. We called the offices of TAS&S earlier and asked to speak with the Muskies' representative, sending him on a wild goose chase – or, in this case – a wild Muskie chase to FIB-land.

"Gene has picked up a larger territory," I said. "You'll be working with Der…Alex, I mean, from now on." Howard considered Sam. She gave him her best neutral expression.

When we'd set up the meeting, we were unsure of how to handle it. I loved seeing Sam play the harlot seductress in Vegas and recommended she go that route. She didn't agree. At least I don't believe she agreed. She never responded verbally to my suggestion. She did give me a two-handed, one-fingered salute along with a penetrating glare, making me shrink to the size of a Hobbit. I guess we'll play it by ear.

He stepped away from Sam toward me. In a conspiratorial whisper, he asked, "She's the new rep?" I sensed his ill ease dealing with a woman.

Sam picked up on it too and pounced. She took a menacing stride toward Howard and thrust her hand forward to shake. When they clasped hands, Sam forced the base of his first and last fingers to slide over the other bones in his hand, clenching it tight. He jumped as if Sam had hit him with a cattle prod. He took a huge step back, shaking his hand. He fell over one of the boxes labeled with "our" company name and a second label proclaiming they held Trey's bobbleheads. He popped back up, acting as if it never happened.

Sam took another intimidating stride toward him. He glanced in my direction, pleading with me to step between him and Sam, aka Alex, to rescue him. When I made no effort to intervene, he backed up two more steps and nearly stumbled a second time.

"No offense, Derek or Alex, but I was comfortable with Gene."

"That's pretty selfish on your part to expect him to give up a sweet promotion to make *you* feel more comfortable." Alex, aka Sam, said.

"I guess so," Howard said without any feeling. It was apparent Howard felt slighted that Morales wouldn't pass up his promotion for him.

With a bit more force, Sam said, "We were told you want to discuss returning the Trey Williams' bobblehead dolls."

"Huh? What? Oh, the bub...bubble...I mean bobble things. We were hoping we might, somehow, be able to return them." After trying to hold Sam's unwavering stare, Howard gave up and scanned the warehouse planning his escape route.

Sam gave him her best, you're-shit-out-of-luck expression. "I'm sorry," she took another step toward him, backing him into some shelving where old merchandise was stored, "but what use would we have for them?"

Howard leaned away from Sam despite little room for him to move. His voice cracked as he said, "Perhaps we could receive a credit, even a partial one." He glanced my way once more. It reminded me of the way victims in movies react when they realize they are about to be tortured, then murdered.

With a tone lacking any hint of sincerity, Sam said, "I'll see what I can do, but maybe you can hold onto them 'til then? Who knows, perhaps Treymon is innocent, then you could use them after all."

Howard regained a slight bit of composure with the turn of subject. "Not likely."

Sam cocked her head sideways and regarded him with overwhelming skepticism. "Why do you say that?"

Howard glanced in my direction but said, "From what I hear, lady, they've got him pretty much dead to rights."

"That's too bad. A young guy like that."

"Yeah, a real shame," Howard said without enthusiasm.

Sam took offense. "You don't sound like you feel the same way." She reached out and poked him in the chest.

He tried to speak but couldn't. He cleared his throat. "When you work with these guys long enough, you see their true natures."

Sam took a half-step back, allowing Howard to relax. In a calm but questioning voice, she said, "He seems like a nice guy. Taking time to sign autographs. He appears especially good with the kids."

A repulsed Howard snarled. "He should've been an actor. It's all show. He hates kids. Can't stand 'em. It takes him a couple of hours to calm down after he has to deal with 'em."

"Really?" Sam sounded as if she didn't buy any of Howard's b.s.

He caught her tone. "I could tell you stories."

"I'd like to hear them." She narrowed her eyes and pinned him with her best, you're-in-deep-shit stare.

Howard looked at me once more. Despite his wishful thinking, I hadn't moved an inch to save him from the tall, blonde menace pinning him against the shelves. He glanced at Sam, then me, then back at Sam. It reminded me of someone sitting at Wimbledon's center court watching the mixed tennis finals. Every time his eyes found me, they pleaded. Every time they saw Sam, they held a new level of terror. They'd reached Defcon One.

"I take it you don't like him much," Sam said.

"Not really. He was trying to get me fired."

A look of incredulity crossed Sam's face. It was also in her tone, "Why?"

Howard searched the warehouse and for an answer that might not set Sam off. "I'm not sure. I was called into the GM's office and told Trey wanted me gone."

"And he didn't say why? That doesn't seem right." Or feasible.

"Who knows with those guys? Probably wanted the organization to hire one of his relatives or something. Most of the guys in the league are prima donnas. You don't hang their uniform up the way they want, they get all pissy. Bunch of little girls." Howard realized what he'd said. He turned to Sam to see if she'd taken offense. Sam's eyes spit fire. He changed directions in an attempt to placate her. "Despite you guys doing an outstanding job with the bobbleheads, if one of those assholes thinks it doesn't look exactly like him, he wants to sue."

As if his compliment had soothed the raging beast, Sam decided to let him off the hook. She spoke in a breezy tone. "You sound like you have a pretty decent handle on things around here."

Howard relaxed. "I've been here since day one. If they'd ever put me in charge, I'd straighten this organization out. Make it even more profitable."

"You think you'd be any good at it?" Sam made it sound as if they were on a first date, getting to know one another.

"Not good. I'd be great."

Sam offered him a reassuring smile. "I guess I can see that." She let her tone grow increasingly agitated. "Trey trying to have you fired must've made you angry. I know I'd 've been upset if I was in your shoes. Taking away a person's livelihood should be a crime punishable by death." By the time Sam had finished, her voice had reached heavy-metal proportions while pinning Howard against one of the shelves with an intimidating glare.

Howard swallowed hard. Beads of perspiration broke out on his forehead and ran down his face. "Sure, it pissed me off," he said, as he tried to regain his composure.

"I bet you're glad he's outta the picture."

"I guess so. It certainly doesn't bother me none."

"I don't blame you. If I were you, I'd be glad he's out of my hair." Sam stepped back and glanced around the room. Her whole demeanor changed in an instant. Her face lit up, her tenor cheerful once more. "There must be tons of valuable stuff here. A collector's wet dream. I'd think you'd better be armed or, at least, have a gun handy if someone broke in here."

Howard stared at Sam like she were the craziest woman he'd ever encountered – scary one minute, happy-go-lucky the next. "I have one handy," he said.

"Really?" Sam was back to being skeptical. Her eyes moved rapidly back and forth, giving off a demented, frenzied appearance. "Ever since I was a little girl, guns have fascinated me. Can I see it?" It came out more of an order than a request.

Howard turned his attention to me and gave a slight shake of his head. I'm sure he pictured Sam unloading all ten rounds in him before leaving. When Sam caught the head shake, she took another forceful, threatening step in his direction.

"Oh, all right," he said. He walked over to his desk, took out a key, and unlocked the upper, right-hand drawer. He opened it and extracted a 9mm Glock. He checked to make sure the safety was engaged, discharged the clip and the chambered bullet before handing it to Sam.

Sam weighed it in her hand. She broke it down, then put it back together within seconds, and aimed it at the window over Howard's left shoulder. He blanched and took a huge step sideways to get out of her line of fire.

She flipped it over, nodded approvingly, spun it, and gave it back to him, butt first. "Do you know how to handle it?"

He swallowed so hard I thought his Adam's apple might have to be retrieved from his bowel movement the next day. "We had a gun safety class last year. I received the top score for accuracy." He spoke with increasing confidence. I suspected he'd moved past Sam intimidating him.

It took a second to remember Sam's alias. "Der...I mean, Alex, we need to move on to our next appointment."

Sam stepped into Howard and tapped him on the chest one more time to show me she still had control of the situation. "Sorry, Jim, but I'll get back to you regarding the bobbleheads."

"It's Tim," he said, more than mildly disappointed she didn't remember his name.

"Tim, then," as if calling him by the incorrect name was no biggie. "I'll talk to the office, see what I can do."

She walked past Howard and turned around. "It might help if you could bring them back to our warehouse yourself. We could even talk guns while you're there. Do you have a personal vehicle large enough to carry them all?"

"The SUV sitting outside the door is mine." He reconsidered the volume of boxes and added, "But I'll probably have to use the team cargo-van. Anyone can sign it out when they need something bigger."

"Give me a call," Sam said, back to being Susie Sweetheart. As she turned to leave, Howard's body trembled in one an exaggerated piss shiver.

A lone vehicle was parked outside the door. It was the same Ford Edge we'd seen in the Muskies' parking lot the day someone loosened my lug nuts.

TWENTY-NINE

Mequon – Shannon Williams and Dr. Foucher – Trey's Agent

We received some bad news on our way back to our loft. Sam's phone rang. By her replies, I could tell whatever she'd heard wasn't making her day all seashells and balloons.

When the call ended, I asked, "What's up?"

"That was Rose Marie, Attorney John Anthony Thomas' secretary," Sam added to make sure I remembered who Rose Marie was. When I nodded, she said, "The paternity results are in, the baby *is* Trey's. No doubt whatsoever. He's the daddy."

"Shannon must be devastated." I pictured her sitting in their five-bedroom house in Mequon by herself, having to deal with the news. "What do you think she'll do?"

"I don't know. She was sure Trey wouldn't do anything like this, yet…"

"That sucks." I didn't know what else to say.

"Thanks," Sam said. She took hold of my hand.

"For what?"

"For not making some smart-ass remark."

"Hey! I'm as sensitive as the next guy."

"After everything I've been exposed to by your gender, that's not saying much."

"Well, when you put it that way."

She smiled a sad smile, and we remained silent, holding hands as I wound my way through the Third Ward. Five minutes later, Sam said, "That may not be the worst part." I couldn't imagine anything, at least in Shannon's world, being much worse. I waited for Sam to enlighten me. "There was blood on Anita's sweater that wasn't hers. It's Trey's." Sam went silent once more. I took a quick peek and saw the consternation on her face, but before I could say anything, she added, "Keep your eyes on the road. You've already demolished enough cars for one week."

Sam called Shannon to ask her how she felt. Sam gave me a whirligig sign with her finger, which either meant, she wanted me to speed up, turn around, or sit on her finger and twirl. When I thought back over the past few weeks and how disgusted she'd found the male species, I suspected it was the latter. She didn't use her middle finger, so I found it a positive sign. She saved me from having to guess any further when she put her hand over the phone and mouthed, "Turn around. Mequon."

I drove around the block, headed to the I-43 expressway, and went north. We entered the subdivision and pulled into the circular drive. We parked behind a purple/green SUV. "Foucher's here," I said. When I glanced Sam's way, she didn't appear as upset by that development as I thought she'd be.

We rang the bell. I watched through the etched glass as Foucher lumbered down the Williamses' hallway toward the door. "Thanks for coming," Foucher said as he stepped aside, allowing us to enter. "She's distraught. She could use a woman to talk to right now. Her sister's on the way, but won't be here for another hour or so."

"Where's Shannon?" Sam asked. He pointed to the back of the house and the kitchen. Sam headed in that direction. Foucher and I followed. Sam stopped abruptly and, without turning around, held up her hand. "For right now, it should be a woman thing. You two make yourself scarce."

Such finality infused her tone, Foucher and I froze. We didn't move until Sam had disappeared into the kitchen. The two of us shared admonished looks and headed for Trey's study. I took my place on the loveseat. Dr. Foucher sat in his usual chair. Neither uttered a word as we strained to hear the conversation in the kitchen. All we caught were indistinguishable words mixed with sobs.

I broke the silence. "That's a unique paint job on your car. Where'd you have it done?"

"There's a place on the Southside of Chicago specializing in pimping rides."

When he didn't say anything else, I asked, "Is it expensive? It seems like it'd be expensive."

He waved off my question. "Not really." He looked toward the kitchen. He felt uncomfortable not being able to hear what Sam was saying to Shannon.

"How long have you owned it?"

"What? You mean the SUV? I buy a new one every year. I picked it up at the end of summer." He glanced back toward the kitchen once more.

"You appear particularly close to Trey. More so than your other clients."

"You never forget your first."

"But to the detriment of your other clients?"

He shrugged as if it didn't matter.

"We talked to Trey's mom when we were checking on the way the clinic handled Trey's case," I said.

"She mentioned it to me."

"Did she tell you we asked about you? The rumors you two were involved?"

That garnered his full attention. His eyes narrowed, his face flushed red with anger. "That shit was started by other agents. We didn't hook up. I couldn't... She's been through too much in her life. Carries a lot of baggage. Besides, I grew to know Trey. I didn't want anything to come between us. It'd be like, like...like sleeping with my sister."

"You're fond of him, aren't you?"

"He's like a son." He waited before he added, "Don't you have something better to do than sit here and ask me questions about Trey's mama?"

"Not at the moment," I said with a smile.

"Wouldn't your time be better spent trying to see who set him up?"

"Don't look at me. I'm just along for the ride. Come to think of it, that's a bad analogy. Or is it a metaphor. Because I'm the one who's driving. Besides, Sam's the one you need to be lecturing."

"It's neither. It's an idiom." He swung his attention back to the conversation taking place in the kitchen. He leaned toward the doorway in hopes of better hearing what the women were saying to each other.

"How's she doing?" I asked to draw his attention while motioning to the back of the house where the ladies were ensconced.

"Not well. She took the news hard. Trey's blood on Anita's clothes was a bigger blow than the paternity test. I suspect deep down she knew the baby was Trey's, especially after seeing the pictures of Trey with Anita in their bedroom."

His statement triggered a thought. I asked, "Who took the pictures? When we showed them to Trey, he was genuinely taken aback. At first, I thought it was because they'd surfaced, but the more I thought about it, the more I realized he was stunned there were any in the first place."

Foucher searched my face as if the answer could be found there. "I don't know. I didn't ask him. Do you believe he didn't know about them?"

I cast my memory back to the moment when we confronted him with the pictures. "I'm sure of it. He didn't know. He showed no guilt on his face or in his body language. His reaction was one of disbelief as if it were some bad, cruel, sick joke."

Foucher sat up a little straighter. "But they swear it wasn't photoshopped. It must be him."

From the entryway to the room, we heard, "Can I see them again?" It was Shannon.

"They're in the car," Sam said. "Chancy, please go get them? I threw them in the backseat when we switched cars."

I retrieved them and handed the manila envelope containing the prints to Sam. Shannon – her face puffy, her eyes red and swollen – sat behind Trey's desk. Sam took out the pictures and spread them out in front of Shannon. She dabbed at her eyes, studied the picture then raised her head. "That's not him."

Sam didn't attempt to hide her skepticism, but Shannon shut her down. "No, I'm not delusional. The tattoo. Here." She pointed at the second photo on the desk, the one with the clearest picture of Trey's tattoo. "You see this?" She tapped her finger on the tail end of the tattoo that stretched across Trey's back from one shoulder blade to the other, which "Shannon."

Foucher and I moved to get a better look at what she'd shown Sam. The three of us looked at the place she'd laid her finger. Sam shrugged, "What?"

"See the O?"

"What about it?"

"There're no dots. They're not there." Shannon opened Trey's middle drawer and extracted a magnifying glass. She let it hover over the photo, magnifying the "O" in the tattoo. "There should be two small decorative dots in the center. When Trey had his done, he made sure to point it out to me. He said he'd asked the artist to put it there to emphasize I was the 'only one' in his life."

We leaned in and found no dots.

"That's not Trey," Shannon said. "I knew it." Shannon scraped the photos together into a pile, scooped them up, and slid them back into the manila envelope. She handed it back to Sam. Shannon said, "Find out who this is, you'll find out who's behind this."

THIRTY

On our way back to downtown, Sam dialed Attorney Thomas' office. "Hi, Rose Marie. This is Samantha Summers. Is Attorney Thomas available for a minute? Thanks." She held her hand over the phone. "We need to talk to Trey."

I could hear Rose Marie's voice come through Sam's speaker. "That'd be great. Thanks. We're on our way."

When we entered John Anthony Thomas' office, Rose Marie greeted us holding two cups of coffee from Starbucks and showed us directly into Thomas' office. He walked around his desk. It took less time for Usain Bolt to run 100-meters.

To save time, he perched his left butt cheek on the front edge of his desk and asked, "How can I help you two?"

"We want to see Trey again. We believe the pictures are fake. Not so much fake as it's not Trey in the photos but a doppelganger."

I said to Sam, "I thought that was something that showed the weather?"

Thomas took the bait. "No, that's Doppler radar."

"I thought Doppler was a horse?"

"No, that's a dobber."

"Isn't that something they use in bingo games?"

"That's a dabber."

"Oh, I thought that was the name for somebody who dresses sharp."

"Huh? No, that's dapper."

When Sam saw how exasperated Attorney Thomas had become, she said, "Chancy, stop it. Quit screwing around. We have more important things to do."

I focused on Thomas. "A doctor comes to a kiosk selling brains. The doctor sees a sign: doctors' brains available for $8.00 a pound. Nurses' brains are going for $12.00 a pound, while truck drivers' brains are $45.00 a pound, lawyers' brains are $90.00 a pound."

"I've heard this."

"Really? You sure?" When he didn't answer, I said, "The doctor asks, how come doctors' brains are so cheap, yet a lawyers' brains are so expensive? The man says..."

Thomas, in a bored, singsong voice, spoke over me and said, "Do you know how many lawyers it takes to make a pound of brains?"

"Oh, you *have* heard it?"

He gave me a condescending smile before shifting his focus to Sam and Sam alone. "Let me call to see when I can get *you* in."

Sam caught the slight. "I need Chancy to be there, too."

Thomas involuntarily glanced my way and shook his head in disgust. When he spoke into his intercom, he said, "Rose Marie, please call the county jail to see when Ms. Summers..."

"And Mr. Evans," I said.

"And Master Evans, can get in to see Trey again? Thanks."

Thomas addressed Sam. "How's everything else going?"

I started to answer, but he held up his hand. "With the investigation?" I could see why he was considered one of the top trial lawyers in the Midwest. It took him only a couple of times being around me to know the best way to phrase his questions.

"We've made some headway. Not as much as we'd like, but we've narrowed the potential suspect list to a handful of people. We believe we have a plausible explanation for the fingerprints on the statue and now the pictures. I'm still working on how Trey's blood was transferred to Anita's sweater."

"How many possible suspects do you have?"

"We've ruled out some people because they either have strong alibis or they are highly unlikely. We have three individuals who don't have an alibi – Sonny Stokes, Miles Phillips, and Tim Howard and a few others who might have motive, including Ronald Landrace and Joe Carroll."

"Joe Carroll, really?"

"Yes. Immediately after interviewing him and Landrace, someone tampered with Chancy's car. We were almost killed. Although a case can be made for Sonny because he was there at the same time."

Thomas gasped. "Oh, my goodness!"

Sam explained in detail our interviews with Landrace and Coach Carroll and our run-in with Sonny at the training facility, before describing the accident. During her story, Thomas watched her with undisguised concern. When he turned in my direction, his expression changed, it registered regret, knowing I'd been spared.

When Sam finished, he said, "It sounds like you've rattled somebody's cage. I don't like it much that whoever this is, made an attempt on your life," he shot me a furtive glance making sure I knew he was referring to Sam and Sam alone, "but it's a sign you're on the right trail."

The intercom buzzed, he pressed a button. "Yes, Rose Marie?"

"They said they can come to see Trey at four this afternoon."

"That'd be great," Sam said. "Please set it up. Thank you." She added, "I need to hear the 9-1-1 tape. Can you call Callas and have it sent over here?"

"Sure, I'll do it right away." He stood up from the desk and shook Sam's hand. "Let me know how it goes." He gave me a hesitant nod, and we left.

THIRTY-ONE

Trey came into the interview room dressed in an orange jumpsuit. A chain led between his cuffed hands and his shackled ankles. Despite it, he smiled. The guard led him to the table where he sat across from us. They'd searched us before we entered the room, instructing us not to reach across the table or touch the inmate. A camera in the upper corner of the chamber observed to make sure we followed their instructions.

"Hey, you two. What's up?" Trey asked as if we'd bumped into one another on the street.

Sam said, "Hi, Trey. How're they treating you?"

"As well as can be expected, I guess." His eyes held a sadness I hadn't seen before.

"We just came from seeing Shannon and Dr. Foucher..."

Trey interrupted her. "How's she doing? She's only been here a few times since..." He stopped. I could tell he was thinking back to the pictures we'd shown him the last time.

"That's one of the reasons we wanted to talk to you." Sam removed the pictures from the envelope and spread them out in front of Trey. Sam pointed at the photos, "Do you notice anything?"

Trey studied the pictures. I could tell his attention was drawn to seeing Anita naked. Sam's right. We're pigs. He slowly shook his head. "No, not...wait a minute. The tattoo."

"What about it?" Sam asked.

"It's not right. Mine has a couple of dots in the O. I don't see any here."

"Dots? Why are there dots in the O of your tattoo?"

"I asked him to do it, the tattoo guy I mean, because I wanted to show Shannon she was the only person in my life. The dots signify she's the 'only one.' "

His explanation seemed a tad off. It was the first time I'd been able to "read" him since we'd met. I touched Sam on the arm. She motioned for me to go ahead. "What aren't you telling us?"

"Whaddaya mean?"

"It's not the whole story, is it?"

He shifted in his seat. His head drooped. After a few seconds, he raised it again. "The guy kinda screwed up. I didn't want anything there, inside the O, I mean. But he got carried away." He pointed to the lettering. "It's some kind of Old English script. He put two decorative lines in the center. I didn't know it until I looked at the tat in the mirror. I made up the story to explain it to Shannon. I thought, what could it hurt? Plus, it sounded good. I figured it was pretty cool. I knew she'd like that, so it's what I told her. If I'd thought of it when I went in, I'd have done it." He slid his eyes back and forth between Sam and me. "Please don't tell her."

"We won't," Sam assured him. "Do you recognize the guy in the picture?"

"Uh-uh. It does look like me, but I knew it couldn't be because I was never with her."

Sam acknowledged she believed him. "We have a few more items we want you to help clarify. First, the blood on Anita's sweater…"

Trey's head dropped once more. Before Sam could finish her question, he said, "I don't know how it got there. It makes no sense unless someone planted it. That's the only thing I can think of. The police are saying it's the reason I had the bandage on my left hand, even though I told them what happened at practice."

"This is what we're going to do," Sam said, "You have to trust me. I want you to close your eyes." When he did, she said in a calm, soothing voice, "Relax. Take some deep breaths."

Trey's body became lax.

"Return to any time while Anita still worked for you when you may have injured yourself." He began to shake his head, but Sam stopped him. "Don't move. Stay still. Think. Let your mind drift back. Don't respond to what I'm going to ask you. Did you cut your hand or arm while you were around your home?"

Trey didn't move, but I could see his eyes darting back and forth under his eyelids. They froze and shot open. "I'd been shooting hoops on the basketball court at home. I went in for a dunk, came down awkwardly, and tripped. I stumbled and hit my head on a table near the end of the court." He tried to point to a spot above his right eyebrow. "Right here. It was sliced open. Shannon wanted me to get stitches, but I said I didn't want the tabloids getting' hold of something like that.

"Shannon held my shirt against the cut, and Anita ran to get some towels. When she returned, the two worked together to try to stop the bleeding, but weren't having much luck. Anita went to get another towel and some ice. When she came back, she took the first towel from me, then handed the second one and the ice to Shannon. Between the cold and the pressure, it eventually stopped. Shannon put a couple of butterfly bandages on it while Anita held the skin together.

"You can still see the scar." He tried to lift his hand once more to his forehead, but the cuffs and chains didn't allow him to raise them much past the tip of his nose. He gave up and leaned forward to let us examine it.

"What did Anita do with the towel?"

Trey shrugged. "I'm not sure. I remember her taking it from me, but that's it. I do remember both of them with blood all over their hands, though."

"Can you describe the sweater she wore?"

He leaned back and gave Sam a side-eye glance for asking the dumbest question she'd ever asked him. "What guy'd remember that? Hell, I don't even remember Shannon's wedding dress." He brightened. "I bet you Shannon would remember, though. She can tell you what she wore the first time we met. Hell, she can tell you what *I* wore the first time we met. She says she can remember what clothes she wore on every important day of her life. It's freaky, but she swears by it."

"That's great. I'll call her when we're done here and ask. Okay, when you guys were at the gun safety class, what did they teach you?"

Trey guessed at the answer Sam was searching for, "Gun safety?"

"No, no, not that. Let's do this again. Close your eyes, return to that time, starting from the beginning. See everything in your mind. Now tell me what you did from the moment you stepped out of your car until the time you left the range."

Trey relaxed once more, and, as before, his eyes moved rapidly behind his eyelids. He spoke as if narrating one of his games. "I saw Miles Phillips in the parking lot. We gave each other a head bob. His assistant, Brad Selig, came over and shook my hand. He asked me, 'Are you ready for this?' I told him no because guns scare me. He slapped me on the back, and we went through the entrance to the main room where most of the rest of the guys and the coaching staff were standing around, talking. Andres Rosario was there. Phillips walked over to him to show him a gun. Miles was pretty excited, so I assumed it must've been new.

"The instructor, his name was Jeff...somethin'. For the next hour, he instructed us on the proper way to handle a gun. Where the safety can be found, but not all guns have them. He demonstrated the proper way to hold and fire them.

"He ushered us into the shooting range where we took turns shooting at targets. We wore ear and eye protection. We each took five turns. Phillips jumped in to take extra turns. Someone kept score. I remember hearing Tim Howard got the highest, which pissed off Phillips. He claimed it was because he was unfamiliar with his new gun."

"How'd you do?" Sam asked.

Trey kept his eyes closed and laughed. "I don't know if I hit the target. I know I got one of the worst scores. Me and Rosario."

"Rosario? He took a turn shooting?"

"I think so. I'm not sure. I don't remember. What I do remember was watching my teammates. Most of them had brought their own guns. They kept waving them around as if they were filled with water instead of bullets. It scared the crap out of me. I'm amazed someone didn't get shot." Trey laughed.

"How many bullets did each clip hold?"

"I think it was ten."

"When you fired all ten shots, what did you do?"

"I'm not sure what you're askin'."

"When you emptied a clip, did you give the gun to someone else to reload, or did you do it yourself?"

"We did it ourselves. It was part of the class. We engaged the safety, discharged the empty clip, checked the chamber, pulled the slide all the way out, then reloaded the clip. We were instructed to leave it out until it was our time to shoot again, and we were in position in the booth. Then we reinserted the clip with the barrel pointed at the ground. Finally, we chambered a round and began shooting."

"Did you use the same gun the entire time?"

"Yeah. Those who didn't bring a gun were assigned one and told to hang on to it until we left."

"Did you reload the gun after the last time you shot?"

Trey needed to think about what she'd asked. "No, I don't believe so. The guy said to leave it empty after we checked to make sure no more bullets were chambered in the gun."

"Do you remember what shooting station you were at?"

"It was number four," Trey said, "like my uniform number."

"Good. Who else used that station?"

"I don't remember. Guys were moving around a lot."

"That's okay," Sam said. "We'll figure this out. Next, can you possibly give any explanation why Anita said your name when she called 9-1-1?"

Trey's eyes became vacant. "I've been trying to figure that out since we were told, but..." He continued to shake his head and shrugged.

"Last thing, did Sonny know Anita or her sister?"

"Yeah. He hit on the two of them at the barbecue we held last summer."

THIRTY-TWO

Jeff Tomlin – Owner of Cream City Shooter's Supply

I hadn't seen Sam that excited since she'd led the Badgers to the Big 10 volleyball championship. The events of the day proved encouraging. She believed the momentum, like in an athletic contest, had shifted in our favor, and, now that it had, she was eager to follow up on what we'd learned and find answers to explain away the rest of the evidence against Trey.

Our first stop was Cream City Shooter's Supply near West Allis. The owner, Jeff Tomlin, stepped out from behind the counter to greet us. Once he got close enough, Sam flipped open her state private investigator's license. After examining it, Mr. Tomlin smiled. "We have deals for law enforcement officers."

"I'll consider it," Sam said as she scanned the sales office. "Nice place."

"Thanks, we bought this less than a year ago. We're still remodeling it."

Sam was disheartened by Tomlin's revelation. "Exactly when did you purchase it?"

"End of April."

"Did you own it when the Milwaukee Muskies held their gun safety class here?"

"I set it up. It was the beginning of May – before we opened to the public. I was trying to promote some business. I thought this might help us with some much-needed publicity."

"Did it?"

"Nah, not really. The Journal-Sentinel NBL beat reporter came out and did a piece, but we didn't pick up much business." He shrugged. "What made you ask that?"

"You may have heard about Trey Williams."

"Yeah. Nice guy. I worked with him the most. The rest of the players were pretty handy with guns. At least they thought they were. It scared the shit out of me. Sorry. Pardon my language." His apology was aimed at Sam. She waved it off. Satisfied he hadn't offended her, Tomlin went on. "For the most part, they were nonchalant with the way they handled their guns. I thought the only publicity I was going to get was from one player shooting another. When I'd tell someone to be more careful, they blew me off. I swear I won't ever do that again."

"How was Trey?"

"I could tell it wasn't Trey's thing. He gave a lot of respect to the gun and followed my instructions to a T, but he was relieved when he handed it back at the end of the night."

"Do you have a record of which gun he used?"

"Sure, I keep a log. Want me to get it for you?"

"That'd be great."

We followed Tomlin back to his office, where he grabbed his logbook and flipped toward the front, ran his finger down the page, and told us it was one of their 9mm. Rugers.

"Who else did you sign guns out to?"

"Let me see. The players were Joe Thompson and Mark Peters. Then Andres Rosario and assistant coaches Jerry Timmerman and Mike McMasters."

"Are you sure? I mean about Rosario?"

"Yeah." He spun the book and pointed to Rosario's name.

"Did you see him fire it during the event?"

"Come to think of it, I didn't. He stayed in the corner most of the night. He could've, I suppose, but I couldn't swear to it in court." He paused before adding, "I don't believe he did because his gun was still loaded when he turned it in at the end of the night."

Sam asked, "Do you know what station each guy used?"

"Nah. I told everyone to keep to the same station, but it was like herding cats. Trey was the one guy I remember staying where he started. He was at station number four."

"Who else used that station?"

He shrugged. "Two, three other guys at least. As I said, they kept moving from one to the other like they were at a cocktail party. I appealed to their head coach, but he was one of the worst." He snapped his fingers, "Tim Howard and Miles Phillips didn't move either. They were at station three, right next to Trey. They were locked in a contest to see who was the better shot. I recall both of them did well."

"Can we see the range?"

"Sure."

"And bring the gun Trey used?" I nudged Sam. She added, "Please."

"No problem. Follow me." He stepped back to the counter and extracted three pairs of earmuffs and goggles. He handed one to Sam and me, then put on the third set, letting the ear protectors hang around his neck. He unlocked the cabinet below the counter and extracted a 9mm Ruger. He double-checked the serial number and relocked the cabinet.

Tomlin held the door for us. We walked into a forty-by-ten foot room. Eight booths, each five feet wide with a small tray-like table, were positioned at the front of each area. One shooter occupied the rifle range and a second a handgun bay. Beyond the row of booths stretched a second section forty-feet wide and close to two-hundred-fifty-yards long. I could make out the targets set at various distances anywhere from ten to two-hundred-plus yards.

"I thought there'd be more people here this time of day," Sam said.

"We get most of our business on weekends," Tomlin said. He went on to describe the range. "This first section is for rifles, although it can be used for handguns. We can set the targets back to two-hundred-forty-yards. This section over here," he walked us to the far side of the range, "is strictly for handguns." He moved to station number four and motioned for us to take a look. There wasn't much to see.

"Would you mind if I took a few shots?" Sam asked.

"Be my guest," Tomlin said.

Sam pulled her Sig-Sauer P229 handgun, pointed it at the ground, released the safety, jacketed a round, took her stance, and pulled the trigger four times in rapid succession. She reset the safety, released the clip, ejected the shell in the gun, caught it in mid-flight, slid it back into the clip, reseated it, and replaced it in her shoulder holster.

Tomlin hit a button, and the target – set at forty yards – came rushing toward us. It swung to a stop. Tomlin bobbed his head as a way of saying, *not bad.* He turned to Sam, but she was busy studying the floor to see where the spent cartridges had landed. Three were in front of the table in the target section. The fourth was at her feet.

"That was pretty decent," Tomlin said. "Three dead center. You missed the last one."

Sam reached out and pulled the target off the clip. She pointed at the bulls-eye, where one of the holes was slightly larger than the other two. "I hit this spot twice. It's not perfectly round. It's more oval." Sam made her statement without a hint of pride or gloating. She smiled at Tomlin. "Now it's your turn."

Tomlin's mouth dropped open. His focus switched from the target to Sam with unrestrained admiration. He examined the target more closely and, in a reverential tone, said, "Wow!"

To give off an air of confidence, he hiked his shoulders, took two long strides into the booth, hung a new target, then pushed the button to move it to the forty-yard range. He fired off four rapid shots and retrieved the target. When he gaged his marksmanship, his shoulders drooped. "I did hit the center three times, but missed a little high on one." With each word, I sensed his ego dropping like an express elevator.

"Still, that's respectable shooting, especially with a gun you're unfamiliar with," Sam said as a means of encouragement. Her full attention wasn't on Tomlin, however. Instead, she searched the floor, once more, to see where the cartridges had landed. One rested near Tomlin's foot, two on the edge of the range, while the last one had bounced behind him two feet. Sam bent over and picked them up and slid them into her pants pocket.

"Who cleans up the mess?" Sam asked.

"The shooter. They're told they must police their station before they leave." He pointed to the back of the room. "There's a push-broom against the back wall. If they don't, we charge them an extra fee on their credit card we keep on file."

"Did you make the players police their own brass?"

He shook his head. "Are you kidding? I was happy to have everyone leave here without someone being shot. We told them to leave them on the ground, we'd clean up later."

"Did you see anyone pick up any casings?"

Tomlin gave it some thought before saying, "One or two guys in the beginning, but after a while, everyone left them wherever they landed, including Trey."

"Do you remember who those 'one or two guys' were?"

Tomlin hesitated then shook his head. "Sorry, no."

"You don't remember who else used station number four?"

"When I noticed how careless everyone was acting, I focused more on keeping everybody safe. I could almost read the next day's headlines – Muskie Player Killed at Cream City Shooter's Supply."

I said, "You know there's no such thing as bad publicity."

Tomlin disregarded my reply. "That's not the reputation I wanted to start my business with – an unsafe gun range." He paused before adding, "It's bad enough there were no working cameras in the place. We've had some since then to make sure we know who's accountable for what if anything bad happens."

"There were no cameras in place?" I asked.

Tomlin explained the last owner had placed dummy ones around the building. The lone camera that did work, pointed at the gun display case. The new cameras were scheduled for installation the day after the class. He said, "We scheduled the Muskies' gun safety class before we knew the cameras didn't work. I'm kicking myself for not checking before I bought the place. I just assumed. What idiot runs a shooting range yet doesn't have working cameras?"

Sam acknowledged she understood. She extracted one of her business cards from the small card-case she kept in her back pocket, and gave Tomlin a sincere smile as she handed him the card. "If you think of anything that might help us, such as, who else used station number four, or anything unusual, please give me a call."

He looked at it and reminded Sam of the deal for law enforcement officials.

When we were back outside, I said, "The lack of patrons and having to admit there were no working cameras made him uneasy. I think he was hoping to make a better impression on you."

Sam shrugged off my comment.

I asked, "Why'd you pocket the casings from Tomlin's gun?"

"You'll see."

THIRTY-THREE

Dana

It was after 8:00 p.m., and we still hadn't eaten dinner. We drove to the Third Ward and the Milwaukee Ale House on Water Street. We grabbed two stools at the bar and ordered specialty beers. Sam ordered an appetizer of Drunken Chicken, then asked me, "Do you want an appetizer, too."

"Nah, I'm good. I'm watching my figure."

"Me, too." She returned her attention to the bartender. "And a Bavarian Pretzel."

"I said I didn't want anything."

"I heard you. That's for me."

The bartender smiled. "Will that be all?"

"For now, but leave the menus."

After the bartender left, I said, "Please."

Sam gave me a what-does-it-matter shrug as she perused the menu.

I asked, "Did you ever wonder who'd taken the pictures? At Trey's, that is."

"Yes and no. And you're just asking that now? I thought it was evident."

"Evident?"

"Yes. That's the one part that didn't make sense and lent credibility to Trey saying it wasn't him. Who'd allow themselves to be photographed cheating on their wife."

"Couldn't there have been some sort of automatic camera setup beforehand?"

"Yes, but the camera moved ever so slightly. The pictures weren't all taken from the exact same angle."

I hadn't noticed the difference in any of the photos, but, then again, I was more focused on what the pictured showed. Satisfied with her explanation, I asked, "When are you going to tell me about the shell casing?"

"Not tonight. I'm still digesting everything we've learned today. Plus, I want to study the evidence some more. Relax. Enjoy your beer. I'm buying. Well, technically, Shannon and Trey are buying. But enjoy."

We sipped our beers while making small talk, discussing the past NFL season and how the Packers had finished.

"It's a shame Rodgers got hurt. They could have gone all the way," I said.

"Spoken like a former quarterback. You guys think the universe revolves around you." Sam got a playful smile on her lips and a mischievous twinkle in her eye. "I hear, as scout team QB, you spent more time on your back than a hooker on nickel night."

"Spoken like someone who knows something about spending time on her back."

"Jealous?"

I gave her question some thought before bobbing my head in agreement.

The bartender set Sam's appetizers down on the bar. I reached to take part of her pretzel. She slapped my hand. "Get your own. I thought you were watching your figure." She smiled. "Just kidding. Help yourself." As I pulled it apart, she hastened to add, "But not too much." She made a show of pulling back her jacket just enough to remind me she was carrying while giving me her best sinister smile.

When the bartender returned to see if we wanted anything else, we ordered dinner.

I said to Sam, "It's been a terrific day."

"No, but it's been a good one. What'd make this a terrific day is getting laid."

I gave her statement a quick thought. "I guess you're right."

Ten minutes later, the bartender placed a massive amount of food in front of Sam and told her to leave room for dessert.

"I always do," she said. He laughed, thinking Sam was being a smartass and walked to the end of the bar to refill an attractive brunette's drink. The brunette saw me looking her way. She smiled. I smiled.

"Pass the salt," Sam said, interrupting our flirting. She added, "Please," when I didn't move.

She finished her meal before I was halfway through mine and motioned for the bartender. When he was five feet away, Sam asked, "Can you make me a sundae?"

He glanced at the empty plates and chuckled. "Sure. What kind?"

"Hot fudge with caramel?"

"Coming right up." His shoulders rose and fell as he chortled the whole trip back to the kitchen.

I caught another glimpse of the woman. We shared another smile. "You should go introduce yourself," Sam said.

"Huh?" I asked, not because I didn't understand what Sam had told me, but because I thought she was so engrossed in her food, she hadn't noticed.

"She's nice-looking, *and* she's interested in you. Go talk to her."

I slid off the barstool and made my way to the woman. As I approached, she swung around. "Aren't you going to bring your friend, too?"

It stopped me dead in my tracks. I looked back at Sam, leaning on the bar with her forearms, reconnoitering the kitchen, trying to ascertain where the hell her sundae might be. "She's a little preoccupied right now," I said. "Besides, she's not much into men, so…"

"That's alright. She doesn't have to share you. She just has to be willing to share me."

I swallowed hard. I glanced once more in Sam's direction. Without catching her attention, Sam slid off the barstool and headed toward the two of us. She reached out her hand. "Hi, I'm Sam. This here is Chancy."

"Hi, I'm Dana." Holding Sam's hand raised Dana's excitement level.

"It's a pleasure, Dana. So you know upfront, *I* don't share."

There must be some unknown language between women because Dana knew what Sam implied. Choose, Sam or me. The disappointment was evident in Dana's face. Despite Sam leaning her head subtly in my direction, willing Dana to choose me, and me desperately wanting her to, I also knew if I was in her shoes, which of the two of us I'd pick. I was right. Dana offered me a sad little smile and turned to Sam.

With a slight shrug of her eyebrows, Sam whispered, "Sorry," before adding, "Give me a hundred."

I extracted a hundred from my wallet and handed it to her. She placed it on the bar. When the bartender came to collect on our bill, Sam pointed at it. "Keep the change. And the dessert." She smiled at Dana and held out her hand. The bartender swept the hundred off the bar and offered me a knowing smile, thinking I was the luckiest man in Milwaukee. Little did he know how wrong, but also how right he was.

THIRTY-FOUR

I awoke to the sounds of the women saying their goodbyes and smiled. It had been a great night. One I'd remember for centuries. The door closed, and Sam stuck her head in my room.

"It sounded like you had a good night…finally."

"It was. How 'bout you?"

"It was all right. I've had better. I sensed she was disappointed she couldn't have us together, but I could tell by the look on her face she was more than satisfied the way it turned out. After all, she did have both of us, and that's what she wanted, just not the way she wanted it."

I placed my hands behind my head. "The drought is over."

Sam laughed. "I could hear you guys. What was it two, three times?"

I blushed. "Three. Twice after she left your room then once more this morning before she left."

"I hope you used protection."

"Yes, mom." I pointed to the wastepaper basket next to my bed.

Sam screwed up her face in disgust. "God, that's gross." Her face lit up. "Get dressed. I figured it out."

Despite being a little before six, I heard Sam on the phone making arrangements to meet with someone. I threw on some jeans and a sweater over a dress shirt and walked out to find Sam ready to go. She chastised me, "God, you're slow."

"I think that's what Dana liked."

"I'm sorry I encouraged her to jump into your bed," Sam said. "Now, I'm going to have to hear about it for the next century."

I pulled out of our garage. She told me to head to Shannon and Trey's, and still refused to share whatever revelation had come to her while she'd lingered in my doorway. When we arrived at the Williamses' home, she opened the passenger door before I could put it in park. She rushed to the front door and pressed the bell, eager to share with Shannon what she'd found. I caught up with her as the door opened. Shannon wore an expensive robe and, despite Sam having just awakened her, was still stunning.

She stepped aside. Sam walked past her and asked, "Where's your bedroom?"

"Upstairs, on the left. Why?" Sam ran up the stairs and headed for their bedroom. Shannon turned to me and asked a question with her eyes.

"Sorry. As usual, I'm clueless."

She scurried after Sam, calling out, "What's going on?"

Sam didn't bother to turn around. She held up one finger as a way of saying she'd tell us everything in a minute. Sam stepped into the doorway and stopped. "Which side is yours?"

"That side. The left." Shannon pointed to the side closest to the bathroom. "I sleep on the left side. Trey sleeps on the right."

Sam moved to Trey's side of the bed, saw what she hoped she would, then looked back at us triumphantly. "You said you use birth control."

"Yes. Trey doesn't want kids. You know that."

"What kind?"

Shannon took a step back and wrung her hands as if she were about to reveal some deep, dark family secret. She glanced at me before returning her attention to Sam. She dropped her head, half turned her back to me, and in a hushed tone said, "I use foam. I was on the pill, but I got debilitating headaches and suffered from mood swings. The doctor took me off them. We heard contraceptive foam wasn't the most reliable method, so Trey also insisted on wearing a condom. Just to be sure."

Sam grew excited at the news. "I'm going to pry a bit more. It's vital." Sam waited for Shannon to agree. She gave Sam a slight, hesitant nod.

"When you're done making love, what does Trey do with the condom?"

"That depends. Most of the time, he goes into the bathroom and cleans himself. But more and more lately, he just threw them into the wastebasket."

"Who emptied the wastebasket?"

"Anita. ... Oh, my God. Is that how...? Oh, my God."

"What? What?" I asked, not catching on.

Sam said, "Anita took the used condoms with Trey's sperm and had herself artificially inseminated."

"Holy shit, is that even possible?"

"Sure, why not. She could easily keep the condoms in a cooler of some kind. Say she was going out to do errands and take the sperm to a clinic. It'd be best if it were local. The clinic could test to see how active the sperm was and save it for when Anita was ovulating. It may not have taken on the first try, but over time she was bound to hit the jackpot. She and her partner had to find someone at a clinic they could bribe to help them with their scheme because of the ethical issues involved."

Shannon staggered to the bed, sat down heavily, covered her face with her hands, and cried. Sam moved next to her, wrapped her arms around Shannon, and pulled her into a warm embrace. Shannon cried for a few minutes before she tried to talk. It came out in gulps. "I...I...I stopped be...be...believing him...mim...mim. I...I thought he lie...lie...lied to me...ee...ee. I fee...feel bad. Oh, my God. He...he...he was tell...telling the truth the who...o...ole time."

Sam smoothed her hair, and in a soothing voice, similar to a mother comforting a daughter over her first broken heart, said, "It's alright. The main thing is we're moving closer to the truth. Now what we have to do is put the pieces together and uncover who's behind it."

Shannon stared into Sam's eyes. The look they shared was one of love. It was the same look I'd always hoped Sam would honor me with one day.

"Thank you, so much," Shannon said.

"It's not over yet. We still have some areas to investigate, but now we can move forward knowing Trey is innocent."

Shannon let her head drop and rest against Sam's chest. She hugged Sam and sobbed. Sam rocked back and forth while she continued to brush Shannon's hair. I realized I had tears in my eyes.

When Shannon recovered, Sam said, "I have a couple more questions to ask."

Shannon grew wary, thinking Sam was about to hit her with the "bad news" of the good news/bad news conundrum. "Yes?"

"Do you remember Trey cutting his eyebrow sometime last summer?"

Shannon eyed Sam, perplexed. "Yes, he stumbled and fell into a table. What about it?"

"Do you also remember what Anita wore that day?"

"What Anita was wearing? I don't understand."

"Trust me. This is crucial."

Shannon gave Sam a second questioning glance before closing her eyes tight, scanning her memory from over eight months earlier. She opened them. "Let's see, I wore black capris pants, a sleeveless ochre blouse, and black flats. Trey was in forest-green basketball shorts with red trim, and a white, reversible top with his number four on it, his name on the back, and Muskies on the front. He wore high-top red basketball shoes with red laces. Anita...she wore a pale yellow, short sleeve dress, and cream-colored shoes. The dress had a white, Peter Pan collar with white trim around the sleeves and hem of her dress. It had three decorative buttons running down the first five inches of the front. She wore a light sweater. It was the same color as her shoes. She also had on the necklace she wore all the time. It was a silver cross on a silver chain." When she finished, Shannon focused her attention on Sam. "Now, can you tell me why you wanted to know?"

"I want to double-check, but I believe you solved another piece of the puzzle. It sounds like the same sweater she wore on the day she was killed."

Shannon's hands flew to her mouth. "Oh, my God!"

"Do you know where Trey had his tattoo done?" Sam asked.

"Yes, it was Custom Tattoo-Milwaukee. It's somewhere on the Eastside. Farwell, I think."

"Last thing." Sam handed Shannon a sheet of paper. "These are some of the items the police found in a drawer at Juanita's place. Do you recognize anything?"

Shannon studied the list. Her eyes grew wider the longer she read it. Dumbfounded, she said, "The three watches: the Rolex, the TAG Heuer, the Movado Sapphire are Trey's. The blue sapphire ring and the opal ring sound like mine. There's also the diamond necklace from the picture." Shannon raised her head to look at Sam. "Did she take these?" Shannon asked.

Sam gave her shoulders a tiny shrug.

Shannon returned to studying the list. With hurt and disbelief, she said, "We trusted her. We treated her like family."

"I'm sorry." Sam reached out to hold Shannon. The women hugged a long time. When they separated, Shannon stepped over and hugged me, but not for half as long as she hugged Sam. That's okay. I'm not greedy. Besides, the long losing streak, which was my love life, was over.

THIRTY-FIVE

Custom Tattoo-Milwaukee

We drove to Custom Tattoo-Milwaukee. It was located on Farwell, south of North Avenue. When we entered the shop, a voice from the back room said, "I'll be right with you. I just opened. I'm still setting things up."

"No problem," Sam said in a half-shout.

A minute later, a burly guy in his mid-thirties, with a scraggly beard, thinning hair, tattoos covering every square inch of his body, and too many piercings to count, came through a curtain, separating the counter room, with its hundreds of pictures of tattoos on the walls, from the area where he meted out pain. He smiled as he wiped his hands on an ink-stained rag. "How can I help you?"

"Can we get his and hers tattoos?" I asked.

Sam offered me a disapproving squint. "I'd like mine to say, 'I'm with stupid,' " she said. "With a finger that moves, always pointing at him." She jerked her head in my direction.

The tattoo artist laughed. "Haven't figured out how to make them move yet, but you could make sure he's always to your left." He looked Sam up and down and seemed disappointed. "No visible tats. Too bad. You'd make a beautiful canvas."

"How about me?" I asked.

He studied me. "I'm good," he said, "but not that good," and laughed once more. "Seriously, I can do anything you like." He motioned to the walls. "See anything you want?"

Sam stepped forward and held out the picture of Trey's doppelganger's tattoo. She'd folded the picture, so Anita was no longer visible. He reached for it, but Sam pulled it back. "Look. No touch."

He gave her a whatever-lady smirk and bent forward to take a closer look. "That's easy. Nothing much to it."

"Do you recognize it?" Sam asked.

"Sorta. I did something similar for NBL star Trey Williams, but that one's not mine."

"What do you mean, it's not yours?"

"Simple. It isn't. Heck, I don't believe it's real ink. Probably henna." He leaned in a little closer. "Yep. Positive. Henna. Depending on when the picture was taken, it might have disappeared by now."

"What do you mean?" Sam asked.

"The best henna tattoos last less than a month, that's if you take care and not wash it."

"You didn't do this one?"

"No, lady. It's close, but not up to my standards."

"Have any idea who might have done this?"

"Not really. There're fewer than forty decent shops in the city. You can rule out Moving Shadow Ink, Jedi, Horseshoe, and Serenity Ink because their work is better than that." He pointed at the picture as if to prove his point. He added, "That still leaves you with over three-dozen places. Good luck."

"Thanks," Sam said. "You've been an enormous help. Would you be willing to testify this isn't Trey, based on the tattoo?"

"Sure. Why not?" When we turned to leave, he said, "Leave me your number." I thought Sam was about to be hit on once more. "If I ever develop a moving tattoo, I'll give you a call."

Sam smiled. "Thanks, but I'll just buy the T-shirt."

THIRTY-SIX

Police Head Quarters- Detective Callas

We stopped at the Milwaukee police headquarters to talk to Detective Callas. Sam still refused to divulge what she wanted to discuss with him. When I asked how she planned to find Trey's "twin," Sam said, "We find the tattoo parlor. Hopefully, it leads us to the guy."

"That simple?"

"That simple. Of course, it might mean days of running around, showing the photo. I'll make a list of how we'll split up the tattoo parlors to make our search more efficient."

I wasn't too thrilled, knowing I was going to do so much grunt work over the next few days. "How do we know they had it done in Milwaukee? If I were them, I'd go farther away. Chicago, or La Crosse, or the Fox Valley."

"I know. I'm hoping someone from around here will recognize the style. These guys are a tight group. Each artist has his own signature."

We entered police headquarters and asked the desk sergeant if we could see Detective Callas. He took our names and our reason for being there, then motioned for us to sit in the waiting room. A half-hour later, Detective Nunn came and found us. He appeared "Nunn" too pleased (sorry) to see Ms. Summers once more. We followed him along a fifteen-foot hallway and into an elevator that took us to the third floor. Nunn led us along a shorter corridor to an open area with a series of desks positioned, so they provided almost no privacy for the room full of detectives. A majority of the cops raised their heads when we passed and greeted Sam like a long-lost relative. She called all the guys and gals by name and said something complimentary or funny to each one and hugged a couple of the women.

We approached Callas' desk, and Sam grew serious. Callas gave us a cursory glance and returned to typing with two fingers on his computer. Sam stood next to his desk, patiently waiting for him to finish. He considered her but didn't speak. He shrugged as if to ask what's-up?

Sam reached into her pocket, extracted the shell casing she'd picked up from the floor at the shooting range, and handed it to Callas. He took it from her without saying a word, rolled it around in the palm of his hand, and tossed it in the air a few times before holding it between his thumb and first two fingers. He examined it more closely. "How sweet. You shouldn't have. How'd you know it was my birthday?" Several of the nearby detectives looked up when they heard his patronizing tone.

"Your mother let it slip when we were in bed together the other night."

Some of Callas' colleagues tried to stifle their laughter but failed. Afraid Callas might draw his gun and start shooting, I took a step back. Instead, he smiled. "You've got quite a mouth on you, lady."

"Yeah, I find it useful for forming words and sentences." More laughter from the desks surrounding Callas'.

He shot his fellow detectives chastising glares before addressing Sam. "What's this?"

"A shell casing from the gun Trey used the night the team held its gun safety course. They lent it to him for the class. He returned the gun at the end of the night. You'll find it matches the one you found at Juanita Sanchez's murder scene."

Detective Callas wouldn't last two minutes playing poker with my usual crowd. He wasn't too happy Sam had poked another hole in his case.

Sam extracted the pictures from the manila envelope, took the top photo – the one Shannon, Trey, and the tattoo artist had identified – and placed it on Callas' desk. "This isn't Trey."

Callas slid forward in his chair to take a closer look at the picture. He gave Sam a sideways glance, grunted a mirthless laugh, and flung the photo aside. "Yeah, right," he said.

Unperturbed, Sam said, "Trey's tattoo has two small dots in the center of the O. Right here." Sam leaned over and tapped the photo. "Next time you interview him, he can show you. Also, the guy who did Trey's is confident this tattoo is henna. You might want to check with someone to confirm it."

Callas stared at Sam. As much as he didn't want to look at the picture on his desk, he couldn't help it. I could see him running the various scenarios through his mind, trying, without success, to explain away what Sam had uncovered. He gave up. "It still doesn't mean he didn't kill Anita Sanchez," he said. "How do you explain his blood on her clothes? Or his fingerprints on the murder weapon? Someone planted those too, I suppose?"

Sam shrugged, but didn't offer the information she'd uncovered. "If you put your mind to it, you'll figure it out." Sam's implication left little doubt she possessed the answers, but wasn't about to share. I wondered why she was holding back.

Callas scrutinized Sam while he rocked back and forth in his chair as if he were sitting on his porch swing at sunset, trying to determine why the light was fading so fast. He leaned forward, picked up the picture and the shell casing, and gave them to Detective Nunn. "Get these checked out," he said.

When Nunn had gone, Sam asked, "Did Juanita's phone turn up anything?"

Callas stared at Sam. "How'd you know about the phone?"

"A faint outline of a phone was evident on the recently polished floor. I suspected it was from her phone when she fell."

"It was smashed," Callas said. "That's why it wasn't in the initial police report. We couldn't get a thing from it. It's useless."

I thought Sam might hit him with a comeback – "You mean like you," – but she held her tongue.

"Was it a Galaxy S4?" She asked him.

Callas grabbed a folder from the corner of his desk and flipped it open. He slid his finger down the page, "Yeah." He studied her, attempting to understand how she knew, but he was tired of coming up short-changed in the brains department. He flipped the folder closed, put it back in the same place as before, then gave it a slight nudge, so it was perfectly in line with the edge of his desk. He went back to his computer and dismissed us with, "I'm swamped. I'd like to say it was a pleasure, but…"

Sam was three-steps away before it dawned on me we were leaving. I'd been staring at Callas, trying to read what thoughts might be running through his head. It wasn't hard.

When we pulled out of the parking structure, I asked, "How come you didn't tell him about Trey's accident and the blood? Or your explanation for why his fingerprints were on the trophy?"

"He'd have dismissed it. Too hypothetical. Plus, it's Attorney Thomas' ace in the hole if this ever makes it to trial. But I'm growing more and more confident it won't go that far."

"I could tell Callas tried to act as if what you presented him didn't mean much," I said, "but it was evident he's starting to have his doubts."

Sam, more to herself than to me, said, "I screwed up. I shouldn't have antagonized him."

"It doesn't matter," I said. "He was pissed at you before today."

"That's what I mean. I should've been more empathetic when we first met. I've been there when I was a cop. Until you prove otherwise, you suspect everybody and their motives. I should've cut him some slack."

I said, "So you do screw up once in a while?" and laughed.

She didn't acknowledge my question. Instead, she muttered, "Callas has a smugness that reminds me of Rainey. She's dismissive and arrogant, and condescending, too. We haven't gotten along since forever. When I came out to my parents, Rainey acted so superior as if she'd won some implied contest."

"How'd your dad take it?"

"He waved it off as if it was another phase I was going through. He still hasn't accepted it." Sam became reflective. "My Dad adored his little tomboy, and I worshiped him. When he came home from work and on weekends, he'd play with me. Endlessly. Of course, Rainey resented it."

Sam had left something unsaid. I asked. "What?"

She deliberated, debating whether she wanted to share with me what had crossed her mind. After a few minutes, she said, "Rainey says I'm the spitting image of my father. Dark hair and eyes, olive complexion. He's tall like I am. Mentioned, it's the reason she can't stand to be around me, much less look at me."

"Huh? You don't look anything like your dad."

Sam refused to answer my unspoken question. Then it hit me. "Holy shit. Your dad's not your biological father."

I waited her out. We drove for another ten minutes before she said, "Rainey told me on my sixteenth birthday. Said my biological father dumped her when he went off to college. His name is Tony D'Aquisto." Sam paused. I thought she was through, but then added. "She says every time she looks at me, it reminds her of her 'one true love.' "

"My God. I'm so sorry, Sam. Does your dad know he's not your biological father?"

"Yeah."

"But he doesn't care. Right?"

Sam didn't answer right away. Seconds past before she said in a wistful voice, "He loves me more than Rainey ever could. It's another thing that pissed her off. How close my dad and I were."

I'd never heard her speak of her dad. Her mom, we'd spoken of many times. We often tried to outdo one another with our horror stories of being raised by our un-mothers – you know, unfeeling, unloving, uncaring. They never hesitated to tell us how disappointed they were in their children.

I thought about what she said, and the past tense, "*How close me and my dad* were." I interrupted her thoughts. "Are you and your dad still close?"

At first, I thought she didn't hear what I'd asked. I debated whether to ask it again, but then she said, "Not really. My dad came to all of my games. Rainey, on the other hand, needed to be dragged to them. She'd read a book or talk to one of the other mothers who were more interested in gossiping than watching their daughters play sports. But my dad..." She let it hang. I felt her great disappointment at the loss.

"What?" I asked.

Once more, Sam waited to answer. "It's been different." She paused, then added, "I miss the closeness. That's been tough on me." ... "There's a wall or something. He doesn't know how to handle it." ... "He still loves me. But we avoid the subject. We'll discuss everything and anything, but not that." She deliberated whether to voice her next thought. She turned slightly away from me and talked to the corner of my windshield. "It's why our relationship, mine and yours, means so much to me. It helps fill the blank space." She looked out the side window, embarrassed for voicing such a personal feeling.

After a minute, I asked, "And your mom, how did she react to that?"

She spun back and glared at me. In a sharp, angry tone, she said, "Weren't you listening. Again?"

"Sorry," I said, feeling chastised for being misunderstood.

Sam grew contrite. "I'm so, so sorry, Chancy. I don't know what comes over me when I think of her. She was never caring or loving. When I started to become a woman, it got worse. There's a huge part of her that's glad I'm a lesbian. As if it makes her somehow better than me."

"Is that why you haven't found Ms. Right?"

"What do you mean?" Sam asked, confused.

"All your conquests. Finding fault with every single one of them. Except for Shannon. But she's off-limits, so she's safe. Perhaps you're searching for someone like your mom, but one who loves you for who you are. As if it'd fix that relationship in your mind."

She went back to staring out the window. "Thanks, Dr. Phil," she said. "Just drive and keep your eyes on the road."

THIRTY-SEVEN

That night Sam did a web search for tattoo parlors in the Milwaukee Area. She put together a list of forty-two places, including Milwaukee Ink and the four – Moving Shadow Ink, Horseshoe, Jedi, and Serenity Ink – that the Custom Tattoo artist told us not to waste our time exploring. Sam split the remaining thirty-seven into two groups by location. She gave me the parlors on the north and west sides, while she took the south and east sides. Sam had Christy Nichols email us copies of the photo Sam had left with Detective Callas.

I'd no luck at the first eight places I stopped but received a glimmer of hope at Waukesha Tattoo Company. I showed the store's owner, Mollie Simmons, the pic of the fake tattoo.

She said, "Justin Case."

"Huh? Just in case what?"

"Justin Case," she said again as she tapped the picture with her ink-stained index finger.

"I'm sorry. What do you mean just in case? You don't want to tell me because you're afraid of being sued? Help me out."

She continued to tap the photo. "This is Justin Case's work."

"That's a guy's name? Really?"

"Seven Seas Tattoo Shoppe, Little Chute."

"The artist's name is Justin Case, and he runs a tattoo parlor in Little Chute?" I asked to be sure.

She peered at me as if I were the dumbest person to ever inhabit the planet, then walked away.

"Thanks," I said to her back.

She shook her head in super-slow motion as she disappeared into the adjoining room.

Despite Mollie Simmons' certainty, I decided to continue knocking on doors to see if anyone else could verify what she'd told me. I struck gold seven places later at Jedi Tattoo. Although it was one of the places I knew didn't do the job, I thought I'd stop to ask if they recognized the artist. Jose Martinez told me it appeared to be the work of Justin Case from Seven Seas, confirming what Ms. Simmons had shared with me earlier.

Little Chute –Justin Case – Tattoo Artist

I called Sam to inform her what I'd learned. We agreed to meet at the park-and-ride off Highway 41, so we could drive together to Little Chute and the Seven Seas Tattoo Shoppe. We stopped along the way, grabbed some sandwiches from Quiznos, and ate as we made our way to the Fox Valley Area.

As I drove, Sam continually glanced in the side-view mirror. She lowered the sun visor, adjusting it so she could see the cars trailing us.

"What's going on?" I asked.

"Did you notice an SUV following you when you stopped at the tattoo shops?"

"No. Why?"

"There's been an SUV behind us ever since we left Quiznos. A black Ford Escape. It's five or six cars back."

I stared into the rearview mirror and drifted out of my lane. Sam grabbed the steering wheel, righting us. "Jesus, just drive. I'll keep my eye on him."

Sam returned to watching the Escape in her vanity mirror. It sped up and flew past us, going twenty-miles-an-hour over the speed limit. The driver was hunched over the wheel, his head turned away from me, staring out the driver's side window. The SUV was moving so fast, and the driver rode much higher than us, it was impossible to tell who it might be. I'd leaned forward, trying to catch a glimpse of the driver, inadvertently blocking Sam's view. She reached across my chest and threw me back against my seat, but by that time, the SUV was ten feet ahead of us. Sam stole a glance at the license number, but it was caked with mud, much like the rest of the SUV. The only letters barely visible were the first and last, an M and an R. We watched the SUV until it sped from view.

"Was he following us?"

"Uh-huh." After a few seconds, she added, "Interesting."

"What? What's interesting?"

Sam ignored my question. When she gets deep into her thoughts, it'd be easier prying the secrets out of the Sphinx. She didn't say another word until we reached the Seven Seas Tattoo Shoppe. It was located in a two-story brick building on Main Street.

A guy, in his late twenties to early thirties, was hanging pictures of tattoos on his wall to the left of his counter. His face and arms covered in colorful ink. His hands so deeply stained it appeared as if they'd been tattooed. He looked up when the bell rang. He seemed baffled to see two strangers enter his shop.

"Hi, we're looking for the owner," Sam said.

"That's me. Justin Case. Everybody calls me JJ."

"JJ?" I asked. "Shouldn't it be JC?"

He gave me a blank stare as if what I'd asked made absolutely no sense.

When I gaped back at him, he turned to Sam. "I generally don't take walk-ins, but someone just canceled."

"That's great," Sam said. "Can you do something like this for me?" He walked over and stopped in front of Sam. He leaned back. His rear-end and hands rested on the edge of the wooden counter. She held the picture up to his face. He flinched. It wasn't much, but it was there. "I could probably do something similar, but not an exact match," he said. "Is this for your boyfriend here?"

Sam laughed. "No, it's for me."

JJ asked me, "You want one, too?"

"Yeah. We're in lust with the same woman."

Not sure if I was yanking his chain, he asked, "Are you serious?"

"As an ingrown toenail."

He grew more uncomfortable by the second. "I can set up an appointment for both of you next week."

"I thought you said you have an opening?" Sam said.

"Yeah, but something this intricate will take more time than I have right now." He made a show of looking at his watch. "I have a client in two hours. This will take twice that long." He spun his appointment book, so he could better read it, and said, "How does next Wednesday work for you?" He glanced warily at Sam.

Sam scrunched up her face. "I was hoping to have this done today. Tomorrow at the latest. So more than two hours, huh?"

He said, "It's pretty intricate."

"Is that how long it took to do this one?" Sam moved the picture within six inches of his face.

"No. ... What I mean...meant...is...is it's not mine."

"Even if it's done in henna?"

JJ slid away from Sam and stood in front of me.

"Listen, as you probably guessed," Sam said, "I don't want the freakin' tattoo. Neither does Ace. What I want is information."

"What *I* want is for you two to leave!"

"All we need is a name."

JJ glanced around the room to make sure no one had snuck in while we were talking. He shook his head vehemently. "You've got to go."

"Who're you afraid of?" I asked.

"No one. I just don't appreciate the way you guys came in here, that's all. Now, do I have to call the cops?"

"Go ahead. You may want to talk to Detective Callas. He'd be interested in hearing what you have to say."

He shook his head more violently. "I don't know anything."

I felt something plunge into my side, knocking the air out of me. I fell to the ground as the storefront window shattered. I heard a muffled crack. JJ's face exploded. His body toppled over in slow motion.

I heard Sam groan as I hit the floor.

THIRTY-EIGHT

"Sam? Sam?" I must have sounded like some pre-school brat calling for his mommy after a nightmare.

"Shut up and keep your head down," Sam said.

I looked around and saw I was behind the counter. I have a vague recollection of being dragged there, but I couldn't swear to it. I found Sam. She motioned for me to move into the back room. It was most fortunate I did because two more shots rang out and bullets opened quarter-sized holes in the wood where I'd been lying before embedding themselves in the wall. It was all the incentive I needed. I scrambled as fast as I could on all fours, scooted through the doorway into the back parlor, and wedged myself behind a metal cabinet.

I tried to see where Sam was, but couldn't find her. "Sam, where are you? Are you okay?"

"Would you shut the fuck up, Ace?"

She was fine.

I pulled my knees into my chest and sat in a fetal position for what felt like hours. I heard sirens in the distance growing louder until they stopped outside the tattoo parlor. I moved ever so slightly to extract myself from my hiding place, but Sam yelled, "Stay there. Do. Not. Move."

"Yes, ma'am." I swear she can see through walls.

The next voice I heard came through a megaphone. "This is the police. Come out with your hands up."

"Officer, my name is Samantha Summers. I'm in here with Chancy Evans. The owner of the tattoo parlor is dead. We were shot at by someone with a high-powered rifle. Can you make sure the area is clear before we step out into the line of fire?"

"Miss, please come out with your hands visible so we can see them."

"With all due respect, officer, someone tried to kill us. He or she fired ten rounds. Please double-check and clear the area."

The police officer didn't respond. We heard a second, then a third squad car pull up in front of the building. A fourth stopped behind the store. Then a fifth. The back door flew open. Four cops in Robocop gear came charging into the place.

"Don't shoot, don't shoot," I cried as my hands flew into the air.

"Jesus, Chancy, you sound like you've gone through reverse puberty. Officer, I'm in the next room on the floor, spread eagle next to the brick wall," Sam called out, her voice five octaves lower than mine.

Two cops pointed their guns at me while I cowered in my hidey-hole. Two more maneuvered their way into the adjoining room. I heard one of them yell, "Secure." Three or four other cops came rushing through the front door. Sam said, "Don't be so rough. We're the victims here."

One of the cops held his gun on me. The other ordered me to stand and turn around, which I promptly did. "Put your hands on your head." I raised my arms. An officer grabbed my right wrist and twisted it behind my back. I felt the pinch of handcuffs attached. He grasped my other arm and cuffed it behind my back, as well. They marched my ass into the other room where Sam lay on the ground with her hands cuffed behind her.

One of the cops held Sam's gun. He examined it to see if it'd been discharged. "When was the last time you fired this?" he asked Sam.

"Two days ago, at a firing range in Milwaukee. I discharged four bullets and haven't replaced them yet."

Two officers helped Sam to her feet. They moved us to a couch and told us to sit.

"Someone call the ME's office. JJ's dead." I glanced toward the voice and saw one of the cops squatting next to JJ. I involuntarily looked at the dead man. The back of his skull had been blown off, his brain matter plastered on the wall behind him. I threw up. Everyone scooted away from me as my Quiznos hot ham and turkey, foot-long sub, splattered the floor. I wretched once more, and barfed up the breakfast sandwich I'd grabbed when we left my place that morning.

"Gross," one of the cops said as if me upchucking was more disgusting than seeing someone they knew lying on the floor with the back of his head blown away. Cops!???

They shuffled us into two separate squad cars and took us to the Little Chute police station. After watching too many cop shows on TV, my first instinct was to keep my mouth shut until I got a chance to talk to my lawyer. But I knew as soon as they placed me in a chair in an interrogation room, I'd spill my guts. Sing like a canary. Spill the beans. Oh well, you get the picture. I'm not the toughest nut to crack. As I said, too many cop shows.

They put me in a room with no window or mirror. The lone way in...and out... was through a single door. They took the cuffs off and left. I'm not sure how much later – it felt like hours – a guy in a suit my age, (the guy not the suit) came in and sat across from me.

"I'm Detective Van der Meir. What's your name?"

"Aaron Chancellor Evans." I said it so fast it came out as one long word.

Detective Van der Meir suppressed a smile. "Mr. Evans, what can you tell me about what happened at JJ's place."

"Sam and I, she's the woman who..." He nodded to let me know he knew who Sam was. "Sam and I were tracking a lead on a case we...she was hired to do. The Treymon Williams murder case?" He nodded again. "In the course of our investigation we...actually it was more like Sam, discovered the tattoo in a picture showing Trey's look-a-like was a fake. Not the guy. Okay, the guy, too, but I meant the tattoo." The detective's eyes were laughing, even though his mouth was set. For the life of me, I couldn't understand what he found so amusing.

"Go on," he said when I stopped because I'd found his demeanor unsettling.

"Where was I?"

"You were telling me it was a fake."

"We asked around some tattoo parlors in Milwaukee and we – this time mainly me – were told it appeared to be JJ's work. We came here to question him to see if he'd tell us who the guy was who'd hired him to do the tattoo."

"Did he tell you?"

"He said he couldn't. That's when some asshole started shooting at us."

My eyes must have glazed over as I replayed seeing JJ fall in slow motion with most of his face gone. The next thing I became aware of was Detective Van der Meir calling my name. "Mr. Evans? Mr. Evans, are you okay? You're not going to barf again, are you?"

I gave my head a quick shake and swallowed the bile rising in my throat.

"Go on."

"The rest is a blur. I remember getting knocked over." I gave my statement some thought, and added, "That must have been Sam knocking me down, out of the way. She tackled me before the bullet smashed the window. How'd she do that?" I pondered my little mystery for a few seconds before I added, "Holy shit, I was standing right in front of JJ. She saved my life."

"Mr. Evans." I'd traveled back in time once more. Detective Van der Meir yanked me back to the present.

"Two more bullets hit the desk I was hiding behind, but once more, Sam sensed they were on their way and yelled at me to move before they pierced the wood. Wow!"

"Mr. Evans!" Detective Van der Meir's voice brought me back to the moment again.

"Sorry. I crawled into the back room and huddled in the corner behind a metal cabinet until you guys showed up."

"How many shots were fired?"

I shrugged my shoulders. "I don't know four, five, six. Everything's kind of a blur."

"Would you be surprised if I told you ten?"

"Ten. Holy shit. Ten. Really?"

He gave me an Elvis smile and said, "Sit here for a minute. Someone'll come in and take your statement. Can I get you anything? Coffee?"

"That'd be great. Can I have a Soy Mocha?"

He laughed. "Where do you think you are? Starbucks? You want coffee or not?"

"Sure. Do you have cream and sugar, at least?"

"That we've got." I guess he found me entertaining because I could hear him laughing as he closed the door behind him.

An hour later, I exited the room after giving my statement one more time. I came upon Sam sitting at Detective Van der Meir's desk as if they'd known one another for years. They did. Sam and he had worked together in Madison for a few months before he left to come to the Fox Valley region and his hometown. No wonder it went so smoothly, and they didn't subject me to waterboarding or the rack.

Someone had driven our rental to the station, and we settled in for the two-hour drive back to Milwaukee. I shook so badly, I had trouble pushing the button to start the ignition. I finally hit the button, but nothing happened. After my third attempt, Sam said, "Switch. I'll drive."

We switched seats. Sam looked my way as she made a show of stepping on the brake before pushing the start button. The car came to life. Sam gave her head a slight shake, and we took off for home. I got lost deep in thought but noticed Sam kept sneaking quick peeks at me as she drove. "What?" I asked.

"Nothing, Casper."

"Casper?"

"Like the friendly ghost. I wish I could get my sheets that white."

I gazed out my window. "Keep your eyes on the road."

THIRTY-NINE

Halfway back to Milwaukee, I said, "Thanks, by the way." To clarify, I added, "For saving my life. Twice, I believe."

"You're welcome. Does it mean you'll lower my rent?"

"Huh? You don't pay any rent, remember?"

"How about some sort of stipend then?" Sam was enjoying my misery way too much.

I gave her a dismissive shake of my head. "How'd you do it? Know the bullet was coming?"

"I felt a slight change in the air pressure."

"Really? You're screwing with me. Right?"

"No. When a bullet comes out of the barrel, there's a mini-explosion of gasses released. This causes a tiny vacuum that displaces the air."

"You're fucking with me. Aren't you?"

"No. Seriously. You're aware I have super sensitive hearing and an exceptional sense of smell?"

"Yeah?"

"I've trained my body to be hyper-aware of outside events, such as a sudden change in my surroundings." I didn't respond and studied her trying to determine if she was being straight with me. When I didn't say anything, it encouraged her to add, "You've heard, a butterfly flaps its wings, it causes a hurricane halfway around the world? It's based on that. Google it when we get back. There're probably a couple dozen people on the planet who have this condition. You must have suspected something like this for a while. No?"

"But…but…a bullet?"

"Why not? You know how people experience pain in a joint when the barometer changes or it's going to rain? Same difference."

"That's incredible!"

Sam laughed so hard she had to pull over to the side of the road to get back under control.

"What? What?" I asked.

With tears streaming her face, she said, "You are so freakin' gullible, Ace. You know how fast a bullet travels?" She didn't wait for me to answer because she knew I didn't have a clue. "Over 1500 miles an hour. That's over 2,250 feet per second. Sound travels at one-fourth that speed. You'd never hear the shot before the bullet hit you, much less feel a change in the air pressure."

"So, you *are* fucking with me?"

"Of course, I am. I'm hyper-aware and hyper-observant, but we were inside a store. We'd never have felt something like that even if we were outside and a few feet away from the rifle."

"Hyper-aware, huh?"

"Technically, situational awareness. I'd sit in class in high school and college, dividing my attention between the lecture and everything else happening around me. Like kids passing notes or guys hitting on girls or events taking place outside on the commons. After a while, it became a part of me."

"How did you know? About the shooter."

"The shooter was using a laser scope. He painted you. When I questioned JJ regarding the tattoo being henna, he moved away from me. It changed my line of sight. In my peripheral vision, I saw the red laser dot resting on the back of your head, and I reacted."

"But why me? I'm the sidekick. Shouldn't the shooter be more concerned with you?"

"I'm sure you're right, but the shooter probably felt he could kill two morons with one stone. You and JJ. The bullet would have passed through the back of your head and, although that thick noggin of yours might have slowed it or even deflected it a little, it'd have most likely gone through JJ, as well. At the angle I calculated, then subtracting the height differential between you and JJ, who was 5' 7 1/4", if it had continued on a relatively straight path, it'd have caught him in the face with enough force to kill him. But who knows for sure?"

"It doesn't answer the question, why us, not you?"

"I suspect I was too far to the side, hidden behind the brick wall. When we were in handcuffs on the couch, I recreated the scene in my head, calculating where the shooter must have been. There are three buildings across the street where our shooter could have fired from the roof. The third building opened his field the most. I eliminated that one, because, you're right, given his or her preference, I should've been the primary target. Although a case can be made, he or she also needed to eliminate JJ. If we, JJ and I, were indeed the intended targets, it'd have made more sense to shoot me first, then JJ."

She stole a quick glance to make sure I'd followed her train of thought. I said, "He shoots you first, JJ freezes. He shoots JJ first, you react and move."

"Exactly. If the shooter were on the roof of the second building, I'd have been partially exposed. But the assassin didn't have a kill shot. The best he or she could have hoped for was to wound me then prayed I bled out. I still believe he or she'd have risked it, shot me first, then JJ. That leaves the first building. From the first building, the shooter's angle was such, I was hidden by the wall. Plus, it's the only one, putting the two of you in a straight line with the path of the bullet. The other rooftops didn't present the same angle."

"Why didn't he...or she...wait until they got a better shot at you?"

"We'd been talking for over five minutes. Which, I suspect, felt like an eternity to our shooter. This person has never played sniper before. To take it one step further, the shooter doesn't have that type of background, and we can rule out anybody with that specific training. More likely, it's someone who is an avid hunter – patient enough to sit in a tree stand and wait for their prey, but not so patient they'll wait until they have a perfect shot, for fear their trophy might slip away. Or, in this case, afraid someone might see them perched atop the building, even though I'm sure they were well hidden."

I stared at her open-mouthed.

"Of course, that's speculation and conjecture on my part. Perhaps he or she was exposed to your childish sense of humor, and you were the target after all."

"So, we're back to my theory the lawyer did it?"

We laughed, but then I started to shake uncontrollably when I grasped how close I'd come to lying side-by-side with JJ on some cold, steel table, in a cold, dark morgue.

FORTY

Based on our conversation, Sam was eager to investigate the backgrounds of the people still on our suspect list to see if any of them possessed the skill level of a trophy hunter or military marksman. She called Adrianna, once more, to tell her whom the five people were she wanted checked out. They were Miles Phillips, Sonny Stokes, Tim Howard, Andres Rosario, and Joe Carroll. She also gave her the partial license plate number of the SUV that followed us up Highway 41, although the way Sam said it to Adrianna, I'd the feeling she had a strong inclination as to who it belonged.

When I questioned Sam why Landrace wasn't on the list, she said, "He'd have hired someone to do something like that. We need to find an inside source to see who he uses as enforcers for his slum houses. We'll have Adrianna uncover the other information to see where it takes us first."

When we arrived at our loft, she went to her bedroom to retrieve a copy of the Muskies' Media Guide for the current season.

"Where'd you find that?" I asked.

"It was lying on Carroll's desk. When he walked out of his office, I slid it under my jacket. I'm not expecting to discover much because these bios are pretty generic, but you never know. Plus, it gives me something to do until we hear back from Adrianna."

Sam sat sideways in my recliner. Her long legs hung over an arm of the chair as she leaned her back against the other one.

"Wouldn't you be more comfortable if you sat in it properly and used the footrest?" I asked.

"I'd be more comfortable if you were someplace else, but you don't see me suggesting it, do you?"

"And that right there is why you don't get invited to many parties."

Sam ignored me. Maybe I *should* start charging her rent. I plopped down on my couch and turned on the TV. I channel surfed but found nothing of interest until I hit the Discovery Channel and a show dealing with the Curse of Oak Island in Nova Scotia. I became engrossed in the search for long lost Templar treasure.

Sam interrupted my viewing. "In both Phillips' and Howard's bios, they mention they're avid hunters. Phillips was a biathlete in college. Sonny's page only recounts his college and pro career stats."

I thought she might add something, but she returned to reading, and I returned to my TV show. I rewound the part I missed and hit play. When the show started again, Sam said, "It says Andres Rosario graduated from the University of Wisconsin-Milwaukee with an MBA when he was twenty-nine." That was it. Nothing else from Ms. Summers.

I rewound the show for the second time. I pressed the play button. She said, "I find it a bit strange. Graduating at that age."

I rewound it for the third time. It played once more. "It either means he was on the John 'Bluto' Blutarsky seven-year plan or he didn't go to college right after high school. Hmm." I stared at Sam, waiting for her to say something else, but she remained silent and read some more.

After a few minutes, I went back to my program, rewinding it for the fourth time. I pushed play.

"It'd have been right around the time of Desert Storm. Maybe he was in the military. Who knows for sure? Perhaps, he was the family's sole source of income. Or his mother was sick, or he was helping raise his siblings."

Again, I waited. Again, nothing more was forthcoming from Sam. I rewound it for the fifth time. I hit play, then quickly the pause button, thinking Sam might say something. I waited a bit, turned back to my program, and started it up.

"You think he was in the army? Had some training with rifles?"

"Goddamn it, Sam. I'm trying to watch this. Either tell me everything at once or with all due respect and the utmost sincerity, shut the fuck up."

"What?" Sam acted confused at my outburst, then laughed. "Sorry," she apologized though she continued to chuckle. "I get squirrely when I've been shot at. Both Phillips and Howard enjoy hunting so they'd own their own rifles. Probably multiple ones if I read them correctly. Phillips most likely possesses the skill to pull off the Little Chute shooting," Sam smiled at what she'd said, then went on as if she'd never stopped, "with him having been a biathlete. I'll bet anything, Rosario was in the service, which explains the gap between high school and college. You have to be smart to earn an MBA. I'm assuming it didn't take him seven years to do so."

"He could have been going part-time," I said.

"True. As a minority, though, he'd be eligible for many different grants and loans, not to mention scholarships. I know someone in the records office at UW-M who owes me a favor. I'll see when he enrolled if Adrianna can't uncover it."

"What about Carroll?" I asked.

"After he left college, he played for six years in the ABL before his knees gave out. He became an assistant coach with the San Antonio team then came to Milwaukee before taking over when Charlie Parks developed health issues. He's been coaching in Milwaukee for three years. It says his hobbies are golf and more golf, and he's an eleven handicap. Which leaves Dr. Foucher, who I have to admit, seems to be a lot more well-meaning than I initially thought, but…"

"But?"

"Let's say I'd be happier if we could establish his whereabouts when Juanita was killed." A second later, her jaw set and her nostrils flared as if I'd said something complimentary about her mother.

"What?" I asked as I shrunk deeper into the couch.

"It bothers me that you're his alibi for Anita's murder." She thought about what she'd said, then let her shoulders slump. "There's no motive. Why kill the golden goose?"

A thought struck me out of nowhere. "Do you believe we were followed to Little Chute, or was the shooter tipped off somehow?"

"Yes."

"Huh?"

"The shooter was tipped off. I don't know by who or when. I'm certain we were followed. At least in the beginning. I noticed the SUV soon after we left the Quiznos' lot. It stayed with us for more than forty miles. After you started to drift, he, or she, shot past us because the person knew we were headed to the tattoo parlor. I suspect they were following you as you searched for the tattoo artist because I'd have noticed if someone was following me. It means we must be close. By the way, we should close the curtains until this guy is caught."

I spun my head so fast to look out my window, I hurt my neck. I sprung off the couch, dropped to the floor, did a bear crawl, reached up, and pulled the curtains closed.

Sam laughed. "I was kidding. Unless he finds a way to open one of the windows in the US Bank building, we're safe."

I left the curtains closed.

It was a side of Sam I rarely saw. I was accustomed to her screwing with me, but this rose to the level of torture. But, she did save my life. We lapsed back into silence. I rewound my show.

I hit the play button for the sixth time. Sam headed for the kitchen. With her back to me, she said, "They don't find the treasure."

FORTY-ONE

Police Head Quarters – Detective Callas

The next day we returned to police headquarters to see Detective Callas. Sam woke that morning determined to find an answer to a question that had plagued her sleep.

"Ms. Summers, I hear you had an exciting day yesterday," Callas remarked as we walked up to his desk.

Sam told me she planned to make nice with Detective Callas. "Yes, it was exhilarating. I find somebody trying to kill me thrilling. And you? How was your day?"

"Same old, same old. You know how it goes." Callas was taking way too much delight in the knowledge someone other than himself wanted Samantha Summers off his case.

"Do you mind if I ask you a question?"

"You just did," Callas said with a hint of a smile.

"Never heard that before," Sam said. "I bet you're the life of the party with your witty banter."

Callas searched for a comeback but failed. "I'm really swamped. Just ask me your question so I can get back to work."

"Sure. I was hoping you might have an idea who could have told someone from the Muskies' organization we discovered Trey's tattoo was a fake?"

"What? What the hell you talkin' 'bout?"

"It's only logical. We told you to check it out. The next thing we knew somebody was on to us, taking potshots while we were questioning the artist about the name of his client."

"Are you insinuating I'd something to do with that?"

"No, not at all. Despite our contemptuous relationship, you're a decent cop. Your attitude sucks, but I checked you out. The people I know vouched for you."

The color rose in Callas' face so fast I thought the top of his head might blow off and steam shoot out of his ears, much like a Looney Tunes' character. "You what?"

"Listen, we got off on the wrong foot. I apologize," Sam said. "Is there someone in the department, a higher-up, who insists you report to them on every new development in this case?"

His eyes narrowed as he considered Sam's implication. "Why?"

"Because whoever that person is, they're sharing info with someone within the Muskie organization."

Callas glanced at a glass-enclosed office then back to us. He lowered his head. "Son of a bitch," he hissed.

Sam concentrated on the office Callas had a moment before. She spun back to Callas. "Is that Captain Harrison?"

Callas didn't answer but grew more and more upset. "Son of a bitch," he said in a low, angry mutter, this time a little louder.

Sam straightened up. "That's right. I've seen him sitting with Landrace courtside at the Muskies' games."

Callas dropped his head and scowled at the floor as if pissed at it for making the soles of his shoes dirty.

"Thanks, Detective. I appreciate this."

"I didn't tell you anything. Understand?"

"Sure. Thanks."

"No problem. Good luck." He sounded sincere. He swiveled back to his computer and stared at his blank screen, his fingers hovered above the keyboard, lost in thought.

We rose to leave. Callas added, "I'll send the 9-1-1 call to your email address."

I asked Sam what'd happened, but she held up a hand to halt my questions. When we climbed back in the car, she said, "Callas has been told to report everything he discovers about this case to his boss, Captain Harrison. Harrison is one of those friends Landrace enjoys taking to games and the locker room afterward. When we told Callas the tattoo was fake, and the shell casing planted, he told Harrison. Harrison told Landrace."

"Is Landrace behind this, after all?"

"Possibly."

"How're we going to know for sure?"

"I have to give it some more thought."

Her phone rang. After saying hello, she listened for close to four minutes, making the appropriate, uh-huh's and yeses and goods, that go along with listening to a one-sided conversation. "Thanks, Adrianna. That's great work."

When she hung up, she said, "Adrianna was able to unearth preliminary backgrounds on our narrowed list of suspects. She's got the results. Let's go to my office so I can read what she found."

FORTY-TWO

Milwaukee – Sam's Office

After warmly greeting Adrianna, we entered Sam's office. It wasn't much larger than a utility closet, but it had a desk, a computer, a filing cabinet, three chairs and a small sofa where Sam sometimes took catnaps when working late on a case. Sam opened the email from Callas. The conversation went like this: "9-1-1, what is your emergency?" No answer from the other end. The operator asked the caller once more, "9-1-1, what…."

Before she finished, Anita's voice came on the line, "Trey Williams…"

I began to speak, but Sam waved me silent. She replayed it. I heard the same thing again. Sam brightened. I asked her what she'd heard. She ignored me, grabbed a pair of headphones – my noise-canceling Beats she'd "borrowed" – and placed them over her ears. Okay, I can take a hint.

I watched her play the 9-1-1 call over and over. After listening to it four times, she removed the headphones and handed them to me. Sam hit the play button. When it finished, I shrugged.

"You didn't hear that?" It was easy to tell her opinion of me had hit an all-time low.

"Hear what?"

"Right at the end?"

"At the end?"

Sam became more frustrated the longer we talked. Before she spouted like Ms. Mount Vesuvius, I said, "Just tell me."

"Right at the end, she says something."

"Huh? I didn't hear anything. It sounded like she said Trey's name, then passed out. All I heard was, 'Ah,' then nothing."

"Exactly!"

I was more confused than ever.

Sam next delved into Adrianna's findings. They didn't contain much more than what we'd either already discovered or was public knowledge. The report listed where everyone grew up, where they went to high school and college, their grades, when they graduated, and some of their better-known associates. The pages also mentioned the personal appearance Dr. Foucher made on the day Juanita was murdered.

The pertinent facts were these: Sonny Stokes attended the University of Arkansas but left after his freshman year for the NBL. No mention was made of any friends or family, other than his two children, a boy and girl by two different mothers. Adrianna could not find where he'd been on the night of either murder. He owned three registered handguns – two 9mm models and a Smith and Wesson revolver. When he went out for personal appearances, he usually hired two bodyguards to accompany him. He attended strip clubs or porno shoots in whatever city the team traveled.

Miles Phillips had zero close friends, a wife, Beth, and no children. He owned five registered handguns: a Magnum .44, a Colt revolver, a 9mm Sig Sauer, and two Springfield XD (M) Competition series. He also owned numerous rifles and shotguns and had received awards for marksmanship as a biathlete.

Joe Carroll and his wife led a swinger lifestyle until they began having kids. That's when she opted out. He didn't. He owned two registered guns – a 9mm Glock 19 and a 38 Special RIA M 200 revolver. His closest friends were two guys he met while at North Carolina State, Mike Elliot and Trevor Brooks.

Tim Howard grew up in Milwaukee. When a Milwaukee ownership group was granted an NBL franchise, he knew someone who knew someone and ended up the go-fer to the first CFO, Jim Huber. He and his wife, Donna, had a son named Zed. He had one close friend, Jon Kwiatkowski. Howard owned one registered handgun – a 9mm Beretta – three hunting rifles and a shotgun.

Andres Rosario grew up on the near Southside of Milwaukee. He reportedly kept the books for one of the local Hispanic gangs. At eighteen, he joined the army. When his penchant for math was discovered, and attaining abysmal marksmanship scores, he became an aide to one of the generals. He was in Kuwait during the First Gulf War but didn't see combat. No firearms were registered in his name. He had few known associates other than his wife, Rosa, their three children, and their maid, Camilla Gonzales. He and a childhood friend, Abdin Valenzuela, had entered the military together in '89.

Dr. Foucher, on the morning of February 16th, the day Juanita Sanchez was murdered, was 90 miles away on the Southside of Chicago doing a promotional event for the Boys and Girls Club. One of the local morning TV shows had broadcast live from the site with Dr. Foucher acting as the guest host.

"Other than establishing another alibi for Dr. Foucher, there's not much there," I said when Sam was done reading the report aloud.

It was evident in Sam's tone she held me in low regard. "There's a lot here. The type of guns Stokes, Howard, Carroll, and Phillips own, Phillips marksmanship abilities, and we know a few more people in their respective circles."

She walked out into the main office and asked Adrianna to do background checks on the acquaintances of Carroll, Stokes, Rosario, and Howard.

When she came back into her office, I asked, "What kind of name is Zed? The kids gonna hate his parents when he grows up."

"It's what the Canadians and English use for Z."

"Huh? What? Use for Z. You did say Z? As in Zorro."

"Yeah. The last letter of the alphabet. We say Z. They say Zed. There's probably some story behind why he named his kid that but…"

"Like he's going to be the last male in the Howard line?"

"Sure, why not."

"He's the end all and be all and will save the world someday?"

"Why do I even bother? Don't make me regret saving your life."

I shrugged. "What's next?"

"We'll wait to see what Adrianna comes up with. Perhaps we'll find a connection between someone or something."

"You think there's something there?"

"Who knows? But the more information I have, the easier it'll be for me to connect any dots. In the meantime, let's go. I'm thinking of buying a new phone. I have an idea I want to explore. Hopefully, it may lead us to our murderer."

We said our goodbyes to Adrianna and drove to the mall.

FORTY-THREE

On the way to the Verizon store, Sam called Shannon. "Hey, it's me. How're you doing?" She waited for the answer. "Good. Listen, can you do me a favor? Look up Trey's phone account and give me the list of calls and their numbers he received the morning of February 16th. I'll hold."

A minute later, Sam became more attentive, listening to Shannon giving her the answer. She committed what she heard to memory, before repeating each of the seven phone numbers back to Shannon. When they finished, she said, "Thanks. Do you have a number for Landrace?" She listened as Shannon rattled off the number. "Is it the only one?" Sam nodded at Shannon's reply. "Hang in there. I'll call you when we have some more questions...or answers. Thanks, again."

I asked her about their conversation, but Sam gave me the one-minute signal and hit a number in her contacts' list. "Hi, Adrianna. I have a phone number I want you to check." After a moment, "Yes, carrier and type of phone." She recited it to her, then said, "It's a priority. Get back to me a.s.a.p. Thanks." She hung up the phone and stared out the window. I'd known her long enough to read her actions as, *keep your mouth shut, I'm thinking.* We didn't speak until we hit the mall and went inside to the Verizon store. As we were about to enter the store, Adrianna called back. Sam stood stark still as she listened to what she'd uncovered.

Once inside the Verizon store, Sam held a nice long talk with one of the sales reps: keeping us captive for over an hour. She purchased two Galaxy S4s. To be more precise, I purchased two Galaxy S4s. Because Sam just wanted the phones and refused to sign a contract or get insurance, it cost us – I mean, me – $1,000. She opted for a basic plan with minimum data for both. When I asked her what was going on, her succinct reply, "It's an experiment."

FORTY-FOUR

Milwaukee Ale House –Ronald Landrace – Muskies' Owner

Sam told me to drive to the Milwaukee Ale House on Water Street. It was too late for lunch and too early for dinner, so I thought we might be headed for happy hour, hopefully, to recreate our experience from a few nights previous. As I drove, Sam played around with the settings on her new phones. Not bothering to look up from what she was doing, she said, "Turn left at the corner, turn around, and park so we can see the building."

"Why are we staking out the Milwaukee Ale House?"

She ignored my question and continued to adjust the settings on both phones, before downloading three apps. I parked the car and waited for her to tell me what we were going to do next.

"We might be here a while," Sam said as she dialed Adrianna using one of her new phones. "Hi, it's me. I have a new phone. Two of them actually. At least for a few more minutes." She laughed at whatever Adrianna told her, before saying, "I want you to login to this account. The one associated with this phone. Here's the number for the second one. Log into that one, too." Sam rattled off the numbers and the passwords for both accounts. She gave me a benign smile while waiting for Adrianna to check. "Good. Now there should be a cloud account associated with each." Another pause. "Great. Let me know if anything comes through either one in the next minute. Call me back on my other phone." Adrianna must have questioned her to make sure of Sam's instructions because Sam told her, "Yes, not either of those. My usual one. Bye."

Sam took my picture with one of the new phones, lowered the window, and casually dropped it on the curb.

"What're you doing?" I screamed. "That cost me $500."

She grabbed the second phone and took a picture of me looking aghast. In one smooth motion, she extended her arm out the window, raised it as high as she could, and spiked the phone against the curb as if she'd scored the winning touchdown in the Super Bowl. She opened the car door, retrieved both phones, and examined the damage. Not satisfied with the carnage, she placed the second phone on the ground and stomped on it.

"God damn it, Sam. That's $1,000 worth of phones you just destroyed."

"Relax. You're lucky I didn't buy the S5. It'd have set you back over $1,300." She pulled out her iPhone and waited. Within seconds it rang. She didn't say hello, but, "Did you get it?" She smiled at the answer, then at me as if I was in on her little "experiment." "Great. Thanks." When she hung up, I started to ask her what the hell was going on, but once more, she gave me the finger – the hold-on-a-minute finger – but I was beginning to feel it held the same significance as if she was using her middle digit.

"Hi, can I talk to Detective Callas, please?" Another pause. "Yes, Samantha Summers." Pause. "Thank you."

I attempted to ask her again what she was up to, but, as before, I received the wait-a-minute finger. I was sorely tempted to reach out and snap it off, but I pride myself on my self-restraint. It wasn't because I didn't want to hurt her. I so wanted to after she destroyed the two new phones. The restraint came from knowing if I made an aggressive move toward her, I'd be the next item lying busted against the curb.

"Hi, Detective Callas. I wanted to tell you, we might have a break in the case." She listened to the other end of the conversation. "I'd prefer not to go into it if it doesn't pan out. Plus, I promised to share it with Attorney Thomas first." … "I suppose you're right. We received a call from somebody who lives down the street from Juanita's house. And…" Callas interrupted her. She listened for a while before speaking again. "A teenager who lives across the street and down a few houses received a brand new phone. He was out the night of the 10th and took a video of the black SUV sitting in front of Juanita's place. We're supposed to swing by tomorrow after he gets home from school to see what he has." … "No, I'm sorry. I want to check it out first. Not that I don't trust you guys, but…"

She moved the phone away from her ear as Callas screamed into the other end. Sam smiled at me. Her eyes lit up, and she gave her eyebrows and shoulders an isn't-this-fun shrug.

When the shouting died down, she said, "We can't today. We're in Little Chute, answering some more questions regarding the shooting from the other day. I'll call you. Bye."

Two seconds later, her phone rang. She hit "ignore." Twenty seconds later, it rang a second time. She turned it off.

"Now, we wait. As I said, we may be here a while. Turn off the car."

"It's freez…" I said, but when she gave me the death stare, I shut it down – both my mouth and the engine.

While we waited, Sam explained her little ruse. She told Callas that bit of fiction hoping he'd pass it on to Captain Harrison. She believed if she pissed Callas off enough, he'd run to his captain to tell him about the kid with the phone. She speculated Harrison would then call Landrace, who occupied the office building we were watching while I froze my ass off.

Sam had determined one of two things were about to take place. "Either Landrace will run out to meet his accomplice, trying to find the imaginary kid with the imaginary video before we can, proving he's part of this or..."

I gave her the finger, the wait-a-minute one. "But why not just call his accomplice or have him come here?"

"Too many eyes and ears. He won't want a record of meeting with this person at his office, especially so soon after being informed of the incriminating evidence. As for a phone call, he, like me, carries two phones. As I said, he doesn't want to risk anyone overhearing what he has to say or who he calls regarding the Trey matter."

"Three. You had three phones, but you just destroyed two of them," I corrected her with a little pissivity in my voice.

"All right, three. I noticed he had two of them when we interviewed him at the Pfister. I suspect one is for business, the other for his personal use. The first phone is an Android. The second appeared to be some type of cheap phone."

"And?" I asked, prompting her to finish her "or" from a few seconds earlier.

"Or, we sit here and freeze because he has nothing to do with this."

"Great," I threw up my hands in exasperation as I tried to remember what my toes once felt like. I wrapped my arms around my chest and stomped my feet. "Sam, this is crazy. I'm going to die of hypothermia. Let me warm it up." I moved my hand toward the ignition.

She slapped it away. "God, you're such a whiner."

"Really? This from a woman who has more problems than a calculus final." Before she could respond, I added, "When we left the loft, you didn't say we were going to be on a stakeout. I'd have dressed for it."

"I remember telling you to grab your coat. I thought for sure you'd wear something a bit warmer. Besides, you don't hear me complaining. Some rough, tough football player you must have been. For the life of me, I can't understand why you never got off the bench?"

Ouch!

"Somebody got up on the wrong side of the cage this morning. Look at me. I've got on loafers and dress slacks, a dress shirt and a sports coat. I wasn't expecting to be sitting in a freezing car for hours. You have on boots, a winter coat, gloves, and a stocking cap. Plus, a wool sweater underneath. Come on. Just five minutes."

"Shush," she pointed toward the street. "There."

A Town Car pulled to the curb. A chauffeur exited and hustled around to the other side. He opened the door as Landrace came out, a phone pressed against his ear. He climbed into the back. The chauffeur closed the door, ran back to the driver's seat, and drove away.

"What're you waiting for?" Sam asked. "Follow him."

With numbed hands, I turned the engine over and pulled away from the curb, leaving behind pieces and parts of my $1,000 phones, and what little was left of my football ego. I stayed a few lengths behind the Town Car as I followed it through the Southside until we reached the St. Francis Brewery. Landrace exited the car and hurried inside.

Sam grabbed me by the arm. "There," she pointed to a Black Ford Escape SUV. "That's Miles Phillips' car." The license plate read, MSK TRNR.

FORTY-FIVE

St. Francis Brewery – Ronald Landrace – Muskies' Owner, and Miles Phillips – Muskies' Trainer

I pulled into the parking lot. Sam got out before I could turn off the car. I hurried after, stopping short of crashing into her when she blocked the doorway as she searched the bar/restaurant for Landrace and Phillips. Feeling my breath on her neck, she looked over her shoulder, annoyed. Don't mess with me sprang from every one of Sam's pores. I apologized and took a cautionary step away, then two more. She found Landrace and Phillips and moved with determination toward a booth near the back where they were seated.

As we walked up to their table, Phillips recoiled. He looked past Sam and saw me, a panicked expression crossed his face. He asked, angst-ridden, "This isn't your investor, is it?"

It took a second for me to grasp what he was yammering about. "Huh? No. Of course not. The committee liked my idea."

"You're shittin' me? Golf shoes?"

I gave him a what-can-I-say shrug.

Landrace turned to see whom Phillips was talking with. Catching sight of Sam, he grew excited. "Have you changed your mind?"

"Yeah. I'm joining a convent later today. I thought I'd have one last fling. I couldn't imagine anyone I'd rather share that with than you."

The sarcasm was hard to miss, but Phillips did. He shifted his attention to Sam. "Can I have your gun? I take it you won't need it where you're going."

"I'll let you chew on the barrel a little later. I'll have to make sure the safety is off." Sam gave what she said deep reflection, and added. "Better yet, maybe I'll give it to your wife."

I could tell by Sam's demeanor the proceedings weren't going as she'd hoped. Landrace slid over and patted the seat next to him. Sam said, "Sorry, I have this phobia about sitting on restaurant benches, especially if I might catch something."

"Hard to get. I like that in a woman."

"That's not the only thing of yours you like in a woman. Your Viagra bill must be staggering." Sam took a deep, cleansing breath. "May I ask what the two of you are doing here?"

"That's hardly any of your business," Phillips said, more than a bit irritated.

Landrace reprimanded him. "Miles, it's no way to talk to a beautiful girl."

"Sorry," he said shamefaced.

While the two men were engaged, Sam moved so she could see the document lying on the table. She got cartoon eyes then shifted her attention between Phillips and Landrace. She finally focused on Landrace. "You're investing in his stupid insole idea?" Sam asked.

"Hey, hey, hey! It's not a stupid idea. It's revolutionary," Phillips said, playing the part of Patrick Henry. As an afterthought, he added, "It's not just an insole. They're orthotics."

Landrace patted the air with both hands ordering Phillips to settle down. He turned his attention back to Sam. "Of course I am, my dear. Miles has agreed to give me eighty-five percent of any profits. As collateral, he will work for the Muskies at a reduced salary for the next fifteen years. So, it's a win/win...at least for me."

"That's it? You're not doing this as payment for something else?"

"Something else?" Landrace said. "I'm not sure I understand."

She asked Phillips, "Where were you on Wednesday, March 4th?"

"Huh? What?"

"Where were you on March 4th? It was a Wednesday. Were you anywhere near Little Chute?"

"What's a little shoot?"

"The city of Little Chute, near Appleton."

"That's the name? Little Shoot? As in shoot a gun?"

"Chute as In C-H-U-T-E. Not shoot, like in S-H-O-O-T."

The longer Sam questioned Phillips, the more confused he became. I knew he wasn't acting. He was baffled by the city's name. He pulled out his phone to check his calendar. "I was getting prepared for our game against Minnesota. Why?"

Sam ignored his question, grabbed the contract, and speed read through the seven-page document. Phillips appeared as if he might go into cardiac arrest as he eyed Sam flipping through the pages. When she finished, her shoulders slumped. She casually tossed the contract back on the table. She addressed

Landrace. "I thought Rosario handled all your money interests?"

"Only the basketball side. Things like this, I prefer to do myself."

Sam looked like a seal pup who couldn't believe someone just clubbed it.

"What's the matter, my dear? You seem disappointed. Come on. Sit. Let me buy you a drink. We can finish this later." He motioned to the document.

I glanced at Phillips. I sensed he was giving strong consideration to reaching across the table to wrestle away Sam's gun to shoot her. He finally had someone who gave a shit about his insole…sorry, orthotics, and Sam was about to flush it down the toilet.

"Sorry, I can't stay," Sam said. "We were passing by and saw the two of you. Chancy wanted to come in to share his news with Miles. Now that Miles knows, we'll be on our way. But first, why don't I give you my phone number?"

Landrace grabbed his pen, holding it poised above the contract waiting for Sam to recite it. Phillips reeled in horror. Sam gave Landrace a coy smile. "Hand me your phone. I'll put it in your contacts list."

Landrace fumbled for his phone and handed it to Sam. She eyed it. "A man of your stature should have a much better phone than this."

"I do." He patted his coat pocket. "That one's for my close, personal contacts." He winked at Sam. She took the phone from him, typed in a number, and returned it.

Landrace eyed the phone with renewed interest as if Sam had handed him a cashier's check for a million dollars. He gave Sam a lecherous smile. "I'll call you."

"Please do." Sam gave him a tiny finger wave before pivoting on her heels and stalking toward the exit.

After we'd buckled ourselves into the car, I said, "So he does have two phones. And one is for his conquests."

"Every name in it was female," Sam said. "Neither Anita's or Juanita's were listed."

"Let me guess. You gave him the STD hotline number?"

"The Milwaukee Chapter of Sex Addicts Anonymous."

"Know it from memory?"

Sam ignored me, lost in thought.

I turned east to take Howard Avenue over to I-794, and stole a quick glance at Sam, "Do you still believe they're part of this?"

Sam glared at me as if I'd blown a fuse, and all my lights had gone out.

FORTY-SIX

On the way back downtown, Sam called Callas to apologize. "Sorry, Detective. It was a false alarm. Some kid was trying to get the reward we're offering for information leading to freeing Trey."

Sam's eyes narrowed while she listened to Callas' response. "Seriously?" Sam said in a shocked voice. After a moment, she added, "It was rhetorical. When?" She listened. "No shit?" Before Callas could say something, she said, "That was rhetorical, too."

Sam listened to the rest of what Callas had to say while turning toward me, bobbing her head. When she caught me watching her a little too long, she snapped her fingers and pointed toward the road. I shifted my eyes on occasion to see if Sam was still on the phone because nothing emanated from her. No yeahs. No uh-huhs. No reallys. Nothing.

I concentrated on the road ahead while my mind somersaulted through some mental gymnastics trying to puzzle out what Callas might be telling her. Her body language said it had nothing to do with him pulling her license, or insisting she come in for questioning.

Ten minutes later, I received my answer. "They found Trey's doppelganger. In Chicago."

"Great! Did he say who hired him?"

"Nah. He's dead."

"Huh?"

"He's dead as in, he's a goner, doornail, the big sleep, the deep blue goodbye."

"How do they know it's him?"

"They found a picture of him and Anita on his person. One of the cops remembered hearing the Milwaukee police were searching for a guy who strongly resembled Trey. They called. Callas confirmed it. The guy was showing the picture around the Southside of Chicago to his buddies. And he was throwing around lots of money. Bragging how he'd been paid for it. They found him in an alley this morning. Said he'd been killed last night after the bars closed. Whoever killed him took whatever money he had on him, but left the photo."

"So it probably wasn't done by someone associated with the case. They'd have taken the picture, don't you think?"

"Definitely. There goes another lead. This day is starting to suck." Sam lapsed into silence. I let her be.

When she stirred, I asked, "Why'd you destroy the new phones?"

She perked up. "Thanks for reminding me." She unlocked her phone and speed-dialed Adrianna. "What's up, woman?" she said by way of greeting. I listened to more, uh-huhs, and waited for the conversation to end. But it didn't. It was still ongoing when I pulled into our underground garage. I navigated the rental car into my assigned, tiny parking spot, and turned off the ignition. I watched as Sam continued to nod.

When Adrianna stopped, Sam told her, "You're the best. Thanks." She smiled at me. "Perhaps today doesn't suck so bad after all." Sam threw open the door and headed for the elevator.

"What? What?" I called after her.

She gave me the finger once more.

FORTY-SEVEN

Sam accessed her emails before she took off her coat and stocking cap. She did remove her gloves, however. Adrianna had sent two files. One was a more in-depth background check on known associates of our potential suspects. The second file was additional information Adrianna uncovered on our suspects themselves.

Sam opened the first file on the known associates. Phillips had no friends, so there was nothing more to report.

As for Carroll's acquaintances, Mike Elliot owned a real estate company in Myrtle Beach and, on occasion, showed up to party with Carroll on the road. Trevor Brooks owned a messenger delivery service in Manhattan. Elliot was arrested twice for soliciting prostitutes, while Brooks impregnated two of his bike-messenger employees. Both men possessed guns, but neither owned a 9mm handgun or a rifle, or at least any that were registered. On the days Anita and Juanita were killed, Brooks was in his office trying to save his business from going bankrupt. Elliot had been traveling on both dates. Adrianna attempted to uncover where but had no luck.

"It appears we have to keep Carroll on our list, for now," Sam said. "Although I'm not sure how much of a viable suspect he is. We'll have to see what more Adrianna can uncover. If I had to guess, I'd say *if* Carroll is behind this, he used Elliot to do his dirty work. Carroll's too recognizable to be out and about, killing people. And that's a pretty drastic step to take just because you don't like the way one of your players approaches the game." Sam thought about it further, then added, "Unless, of course, there's something else going on we haven't uncovered yet."

"Like what?"

Sam thought my question was much less intelligent than usual. "How should I know? Trey could be sleeping with Carroll's wife...or his daughter...or his son...or all three at the same time. I'm not clairvoyant, for god's sake. Just hyper-observant."

"And hypersensitive," I said with an edge to my voice. When she didn't rip out my tongue, I said, "Come on, Sam, you often have insights no one else has."

Sam gave my statement some thought. "That's an excellent point... Sorry, Chance. I get this way when I'm close to solving a case."

She smiled and returned to the report and read the section regarding Howard's close friend Jon Kwiatkowski. She found one part particularly interesting and read it to me. "They aren't close anymore. When Howard went on a rant about how he could do a better job as the COO than their current guy, Kwiatkowski distanced himself from Howard. He's become so entrenched in the game-day ops, his move didn't have an effect on his employment situation. The report indicates the two have become more like North and South Korea."

"That still doesn't let Howard off the hook," I said.

"True," Sam said. She explained Adrianna's report mentioned Howard signed out the van to take the bobbleheads back to Tri-Awards on the day Sam and I were shot at. But there was no record of him making contact with the company or dropping off the statues. It also said he possessed the marksmanship qualities, allowing him to pull off the Little Chute murder. Furthermore, she couldn't establish his whereabouts for either of the Sanchez sisters' deaths.

When she'd finished, I said, "There's all that memorabilia in the warehouse. Some of it has to be worth a lot."

"No, not really. Adrianna's report states anything of value is locked in a vault in Landrace's office building. Not too many people around the organization trust Howard."

"I can see why you say Adrianna's the best."

"Yes. She's able to uncover facts most people couldn't begin to," Sam said.

"What does her report say in regards to Rosario?"

She read the section on Rosario and his associates in silence. I watched her grow more tense and alert.

"What?" I asked.

As usual, when she was engrossed in putting the pieces together, she ignored me. She flipped back to the original report Adrianna had sent a few days earlier.

She slumped back in her chair, her body relaxed. I thought she'd finished. I asked, "Well?"

I didn't think she was going to answer, but then she gave a quick shake of her head. I took it to mean there was nothing there.

"How about Sonny?" I asked. "Does she have anything in there about him?"

"She still can't determine where he was on the night either woman was murdered. She sent pictures she pulled off Facebook from Juanita's account, showing her and Anita with Sonny. It appears to be an outdoor setting. Perhaps they were taken at Trey's barbecue. I'll double-check. The other thing she sent, we already knew, Trey's contract could cost him $14 million in the long run."

I flipped through a series of photos of him hugging the twins. They welcomed the attention. One, in particular, jumped out at me. The twins were kissing him on the cheek while his hands had drifted and rested on their asses. He was smiling the same lecherous smile he favored Sam with in Vegas. "Wow! He's starting to look good for this."

Sam's computer pinged, letting her know she'd received an incoming email message. It was another one from Adrianna, entitled: "Juanita Sanchez's Verizon & Cloud account." Sam stopped reading the report, switched to her email, and opened the attachment. Something caught her eye. She bounded out of her chair.

"What?" I asked a little more fervently.

"Road trip. Dress warmer this time."

FORTY-EIGHT

Sam told me to head to the Muskies' arena. She made two more phone calls along the way – one to Shannon, the other to Callas. She ended her conversation with Callas by saying, "We'll meet you at the security entrance."

We arrived at the same time as Callas and Nunn, and parked behind the arena in the employee parking lot, next to Sonny Stokes' MKX. Sam went to Callas and showed him something on her phone.

"Son of a bitch," Callas said. "I need to call in back-up." He called the dispatcher and asked a couple of squad cars be sent. We waited five minutes until three more units arrived.

As we headed toward the entrance, Sam glanced up at the building. "Oh-oh," is all she said. Callas badged the security guy, who then buzzed us in. We took the elevator to three and walked into Andres Rosario's office.

His secretary yelled at us to stop. "What's going on? You can't barge in here like this."

Rosario's office was empty. Callas asked the secretary, "Where is he?"

"He said he was going to the bathroom."

"How long ago was that?"

"A few seconds before you barged in. Why?"

"Where's the bathroom?" Callas demanded.

The secretary pointed along the hallway to the left. We reversed course and headed in that direction. I turned to say something to Sam, but she was no longer there. In all the excitement, I'd focused my attention on Callas and didn't notice Sam was AWOL. Callas took note of her absence. "Where'd she go?" he asked me.

I shrugged.

"Go find her. She's *your* partner." I thought it might be a bad time to remind we were associates, not partners.

Callas, Nunn, and the four police officers marched toward the restroom to find Rosario. I had a hunch where Sam might be. I pressed the elevator button, but it never moved from its position on the ground floor, so I decided to use the stairs. I opened the door and heard footsteps moving down the concrete stairwell.

I called out, "Sam? Sam? Is that you?" but received no answer.

The footfalls picked up speed. I took the stairs two at a time, trying to catch up to whoever was ahead of me. I turned the corner on the second-floor landing and caught a glimpse of Rosario a step away from the first floor. The door opened, then crash closed. Halfway down the last flight of stairs, I grabbed hold of the railing and leapt over, landing two long strides away from the door. I threw it open and stepped into the hallway. I stopped to catch my bearings, and my breath. The corridor curved, so I'd no idea which way Rosario had gone. My heart raced, and I heard the blood pounding in my ears, drowning out Rosario's footsteps. I made an educated guess and ran toward the parking lot. I turned right and sprinted as if I was at the NFL combine wanting to impress the coaches in my 40-yard time.

As I rounded the curve, Rosario was eighty feet away. He'd reached the exit and glanced over his shoulder. Sensing I was too far to prevent him from getting to his car, he gave me a dismissive smile then ran out the door.

Sam was leaning on his Ford Fiesta with her arms and legs crossed, her butt resting on the driver's door. When Rosario saw her, he quickly weighed his options: fight or flight. He chose poorly. "You need to move away from my car. I'm late for an appointment."

"It's been canceled," Sam said.

He looked over his shoulder again and saw me hurry through the door. Sam pushed off the door and stood to face him. He took five quick steps toward Sam, then raised his hands to shoulder height to push her out of his way.

Two steps away, Sam still hadn't moved. As he extended his arms, Sam did a reverse pivot, grabbed him by his wrists, and yanked him forward. Watching him stumble reminded me of someone who thought they were at the bottom of the stairs, only to find there's one more. As he pitched forward, Sam stuck out her arm and clotheslined him. His feet flew out from under. He landed with a thud on his back.

He rolled onto his stomach and gathered himself. He rose to one knee, pushed off the asphalt like an NFL defensive lineman intent on sacking the quarterback, and charged Sam. She rotated her hips, pulled her left elbow back to add torque as she thrust her right arm forward. She hit Rosario on the tip of his nose with the heel of her hand, pushing up and through upon contact. It was a hell of a stiff arm. Rosario went down once more.

"It would be best if you stayed there," I said. "I've seen this movie. Trust me, it won't end well."

Rosario, blood streaming from his broken nose, scrambled to his feet. He gave his head a quick shake to clear the cobwebs. He crouched in a boxer's stance and waded-in cautiously. Sam brought her hands to waist height, palms up, and gave her fingers a bring-it-on motion. He threw a right-handed jab. She leaned to the side, grabbed his forearm, and pulled him forward, throwing him off balance. He braced his right leg to keep from falling. Sam aimed a kick at the outside of his knee, there was a sickening crack, and it buckled as Rosario screamed in pain. A good thing I hadn't had much to eat, or I would have repeated my Little Chute performance, barfing all over him.

I give him credit. He didn't give up. He gingerly got to one leg. He hobbled toward Sam, his hands in a street fighter's pose. He faked a jab and unleashed a sweeping roundhouse left. Sam leaned back, let his momentum carry him past her, and slid behind him. She threw her arm around his neck, locking in a chokehold. He struggled for a few seconds before his body went limp. Sam let go. He dropped like a puppet whose strings had been cut, like a boulder from the top of a mountain, like an anvil in a Looney Tunes cartoon, like…never mind, you get the picture.

Someone next to me said, "That's one bad motherfucker. Bitch got skills." A smiling Sonny Stokes clapped me on the back, mumbled something along the lines of, "I'm glad that wasn't me," and strutted to his SUV.

Sam pulled plastic flex cuffs from her coat pocket and secured Rosario's hands behind him. When he was restrained, Sam opened her phone and called Callas. She told him where we were, and we'd apprehended Rosario.

My mind flashed to the night Sam and I first met. I said wistfully, "Is that a replay of the night you kicked JB's fat ass?"

She smiled. It reminded me of the one I enjoyed after my tryst with Dana.

When Callas and the others joined us, Rosario was sitting with his back against his car, dazed. Blood ran down his face and into his open mouth, while the overflow dripped off his chin.

Callas smiled at Sam. "How'd you know?"

"He saw us through his office window just as the backups arrived. I figured he'd try to make it to his car."

"Doesn't appear as if he put up much of a fight," Callas said offhandedly. "Nice work, detective."

"Thanks," I said, making Sam laugh. I received a dismissive side-eye from Callas.

Callas said to Rosario, "Andres Rosario, we are placing you under arrest for the murder of Anita and Juanita Sanchez. You have the right to remain silent. Anything you say, can and will be used against you in a court of law." When he finished, he asked, "Do you understand these rights I have told you?"

Rosario, breathing through his mouth, attempted to uncross his eyes. Callas asked him a second time. Rosario nodded in the affirmative. Two police officers marched the one-legged Rosario to their squad car and took him to police headquarters. Callas instructed us to follow so he could debrief Sam before they questioned Rosario.

When we arrived at the police station, we adjourned to a conference room, where Sam laid it out. She started with her call to Shannon. She'd told Sam, when the Williamses' maid told them she was quitting, she suggested they hire Anita and gave them her phone number. During the interview for the job, Anita never mentioned Rosario was her cousin.

"Wait a minute," Callas stopped Sam. "You said their old maid, the one who was quitting, suggested they hire Anita. How is Rosario a part of that?"

"The Williamses' 'old maid' is Camilla Gonzales. She's the Rosarios' current maid. You'll probably find when she left the Williamses' employment at the end of last season, it was suggested by Rosario that she propose Anita as her replacement, and she should give her a glowing recommendation."

Sam further explained the Rosarios were swimming in debt. Their expensive house on Lake Drive had a monthly payment of over $10,000, or $120,000 a year plus taxes. The three kids in University School added another $60,000 annually. In addition to that, Rosario's wife enjoyed an extravagant lifestyle, living well beyond their means.

Callas said, "But Landrace must pay him well."

"He does, sort of. It depends on the bonus. His annual salary is over $250,000 a year. He's made double that in bonuses in four of the last five seasons by staying under the salary cap. Landrace gives him six percent of every dollar he saves when they're under it."

To clarify what Sam said, Callas asked, "With Trey in the position to put the team over the cap, he stood to lose close to a half-million each year?"

"He'd hoped Landrace might sour on Trey when the paternity suit came out, but Landrace couldn't have cared less. So, Rosario played his other card." Sam glanced my way and gave me an impish smile when she used another poker analogy. She said to Callas, "With the paternity test proving the baby was Trey's, Rosario knew Trey would be required to give Anita approximately 10% of his salary for child support. According to NBL insiders, Trey was set to receive a five-year, eighty-million-dollar contract extension. He'd average sixteen-million-dollars a year. That's one-point-six million on average, per year, in child support. If she and Rosario split it, it would easily make up for what he'd lose with the team over the cap."

"What about the pictures?" I asked.

"I believe those were meant to be used to ensure Trey didn't fight the paternity scheme. When Rosario had Anita killed, he decided to use them to blackmail Trey instead. He was desperate."

"But Rosario has a rock-solid alibi for the night Anita was killed," I said.

"That's where his old friend, Abdin Valenzuela, comes in. I recognized him from a picture Adrianna sent me. He was the guy we saw coming out of Rosario's office the day we interviewed him. They joined the army together. Adrianna's report stated he received exceptionally high marksmanship scores in boot camp. The car that passed us on our way to Little Chute was his. His license plate is MR DTALR."

"We have officers picking him up," Callas said. "We'll play one against the other to get them to talk."

"So, he was the guy who took potshots at us in Little Chute?" I asked.

"When Detective Callas obtains a search warrant for Valenzuela's home, car, and work area, I'm sure it will turn up a high-powered rifle with a laser scope. The police will have no trouble matching the bullets from the rifle to the shooting at the tattoo parlor. And, unless he threw it away, they'll also find the gun that killed Juanita, although it won't be necessary to find it."

"Which explains the shell casing found at Juanita's," I said.

"I can't say for sure it's why Rosario went to the gun safety class, but somewhere along the line, he saw an opportunity to frame Trey in case his original plan didn't work. He pocketed one or more of the shells he knew Trey had handled when he reloaded his gun. It'd have been easy for him to pick up the ejected shells that rolled behind Trey. With all the commotion, and the other players milling around, no one noticed."

We turned our attention to Detective Callas. "You were right. The casing matched the one you brought in from the gun club. Excellent work."

"Thanks," Sam said, offering him her best smile.

"I'm still confused," I said. "Can't Rosario blame everything on his buddy? It's most likely his gun and rifle. Plus, Rosario has an alibi for the night Anita was killed. And why kill her in the first place?"

"Remember, Anita and Juanita were twins. It's been my experience most twins share everything. Maria Alvarez mentioned she'd heard the sisters arguing constantly. I believe Juanita was disgusted with what her sister was doing. Anita then told Rosario she was thinking of backing out of the deal. Rosario sent Valenzuela to threaten her. He ended up killing her instead." Sam gave her head a mini shake trying to loosen an elusive thought.

"But why Juanita, too?" I asked as I studied Sam's body language.

"When she found the pictures of Anita and Trey together, she called Trey to tell them she had them. She probably assumed he already knew of their existence. She didn't call to blackmail him. She called to tell him she'd found them, and he could have them back. Her English was so poor, though, Trey didn't understand what she was trying to say."

Sam focused on me, "Do you remember Trey telling us she kept calling him 'darling you?' "

"What of it?"

"She wasn't saying 'darling you.' She was saying, 'Dartelo.' 'Give it to you.' "

I found the revelation such an eye-opener I repeated, "She wanted to *give* them to him. She wasn't blackmailing him, she was offering him the pictures."

"Si. Rosario confronted her. When she refused to give him the pictures, he killed her. He planted the shell casing and did a quick search for the photos. Something scared him off – possibly us coming up the front stairs – or he felt he'd been there too long, or decided the photos weren't at her place after all. He left without finding them."

Callas informed us the police had found them hidden in a recessed panel in the back of Juanita's closet the second time they searched the house. They also found a picture of Trey and his tattoo on Rosario's phone. "He must have snapped it while Trey was getting ready for practice. It was mainly from the side and captured the first five letters of the tat. The O and last N were missing, and it's the reason they didn't add the two dots in the fake tattoo."

I was still unsure what made Sam and Callas so confident Rosario was behind the murders. I asked, "What's this proof you have that shows he's the killer."

Sam pointed to Callas' computer. "May I?"

"Knock yourself out."

Sam logged into her email site and brought up her account. She opened the last email from Adrianna and the attachment. She scrolled down until I could see the top of a photo. She said, "Most smartphones require you *manually* send pictures from your camera to either the cloud or your home computer."

"So?" I asked, trying to understand where Sam was headed.

"But not all. The Galaxy S4 automatically sends the photos taken as soon as the camera on the phone is triggered. The picture I'm going to show you, came from Juanita's smartphone camera seconds before Rosario killed her." She addressed her last statement to me. She'd already shared it with Callas in the parking lot. It was the reason he was so quick to arrest Rosario. The photo showed Andres Rosario reaching for a throw pillow with one hand while holding a 9mm gun in the other.

"He knew she'd taken his picture, but he didn't know about the automatic download. He thought he could take care of the problem by smashing the phone to bits. If Juanita had just dropped hers, at best, it'd have cracked the screen, and the contents of the phone could have been recovered – much like the first phone I dropped out of the window of your car while we waited for Landrace. Rosario must have felt it was safer destroying the phone than taking it with him and possibly have somebody track him through the GPS. He thought he'd made everything inside it 'useless,' as Detective Callas told us earlier. It's why I not only spiked the second one, I also needed to destroy it to see if the picture still came through."

She said to Callas, "Your little leak problem was indeed Captain Harrison. When you told him what we'd uncovered, he called Landrace. He, in turn, told Rosario. From the way he reacted to our questions, I knew Landrace was unaware he was giving information to the killer."

Sam turned to me for confirmation. I searched my memory banks and nodded. She went on to explain her theory to us. "When Rosario discovered we knew about the doppelganger and the tattoo being fake, he sent Valenzuela to follow and kill us and JJ."

Callas, who'd been leaning forward in his chair, hanging on every word, slumped back when he understood how well everything fit. As if someone had explained the meaning of life to him, he said, "Son. Of. A. Bitch."

"One of my operatives also uncovered on the day we were at the Muskies' training facility, Rosario signed out the team's van and drove there. Here I'm speculating, but Landrace must have told him we were investigating people within the organization, and he was on our list. When we called from Connecticut to set up interviews with him and Carroll, he saw it as an opportunity to get rid of us. He loosened Ace's lug nuts, hoping to put an end to our investigation before we could get around to questioning him."

Callas looked at Sam with unadulterated awe, acknowledging Sam did an exceptional job of cracking the case.

I slapped him on the back. "I'm glad I could solve this for you, Detective. If you ever need my assistant and me again, don't hesitate to call."

Sam did her patented eye-roll and said, "Forgive him, Dominic. His mom and dad are also his aunt and uncle."

FORTY-NINE

We made reservations to dine at Mo's Steak House to celebrate. On the way, Sam remained quiet. I kept talking to her, but the few times she responded, it was with, "Uh-huh." She stared out the window, but I sensed she wasn't gazing at the scenery but something inside her mind.

I'd picked up my Tesla after we'd left the police station. It felt nice to drive it again. The body shop did a remarkable job making it look brand new, although the realignment needed to be checked one more time.

"Pretty sweet," I said, trying to draw Sam out of her reverie.

"Uh-huh."

"Feels brand new."

Nothing.

"I don't know about you, but I'm hungry."

"Uh-huh."

"What are you going to eat?"

I heard crickets chirping.

"I think I'll have the twenty-ounce New York Strip."

"Uh-huh."

"With a side order of garlic mashed potatoes."

"Uh-huh."

"After we're done, I'm going to call my parents to tell them I'm coming out."

"Uh-huh."

"Then, I'm going to cruise the gay bars to see if I can find Mr. Right."

"It's too bad Charles Manson died, I hear he was up for parole," Sam said. "Why don't you hold off, on the whole, coming out thing until the next Jeffery Dahmer comes along?"

"She's back," I sang. "What's got you so discombobulated?"

She ignored my question and continued to stare out the window. She said, "Something's off. It's there, but I'm not..." She didn't finish her statement.

"Like what? Everything fits. The way you laid it out for Callas makes perfect sense."

"Not quite. It'll come to me."

It didn't. At least not that night. It may have been the most boring evening I'd ever spent with Samantha Summers. I'd have been better off staying home, watching reruns of "The Big Bang Theory."

After dinner, we walked to Houlihan's, where three guys and two women hit on Sam. Not at the same time, mind you, but still... Instead of her usual witty put-offs, she said, "Sorry, not tonight."

The next morning Callas called to tell Sam they'd searched Valenzuela's home and workspace but found no rifle or handgun. They also examined Valenzuela's financial records and discovered no large sum of money posted to any of his accounts.

When the police interrogated Valenzuela, he said Rosario had asked him to get a gun for him, which he did. He swore he didn't know he was going to use it to murder someone. Rosario told him it was for his home defense. He denied killing Anita Sanchez and insisted he didn't know who'd killed her, and Rosario never mentioned having a hand in her murder.

Rosario, despite the overwhelming evidence, continued to deny he'd played any part in the whole affair – the picture of him holding Valenzuela's gun being by far the most damning. He refused to talk. His lawyer let it be known they'd use the "other man" defense theory – meaning Abdin Valenzuela. The evidence against Rosario, however, was overwhelming. His financial records showed a payoff to a couple of people at a fertility clinic who inseminated Anita Sanchez with Trey's sperm, and a large withdrawal of $100,000 made out to "cash." The police continued to look into any banks that had a recent deposit for that amount. The belief was Rosario used the money to hire someone to kill Anita Sanchez, Justin "JJ" Case, Sam, and me. The best criminal lawyers in the world couldn't explain everything away. He'd spend the rest of his life in the big house, con college, the gray bar hotel... Sorry. As I said, too many cop shows.

When the police asked Rosario why he ran away, he claimed he remembered an urgent errand he needed to do for his wife. He insisted he was set up, and it must have been Valenzuela acting alone because Rosario hadn't come through with the job he'd promised.

This led to Callas dropping a bombshell. Sam took the news impassively. Until they were able to hang Anita's murder on Rosario, the DA refused to drop those charges against Trey.

"Thanks for the update." Sam hung up the phone. I watched her go into another funk.

"What?" I asked. "What's up with you? You should be happy."

She told me about the DA. The way she reacted mystified me. She didn't seem disappointed. She seemed consternated, like someone searching for the right word, and it was there, on the tip of her brain. The harder she tried to dislodge it, the more elusive it became. Her mind worked so hard I thought I could hear her synapses firing.

"What? You're still sure something's off."

She stared out the window, gazing over the lake.

I grabbed her by the hands and pulled her out of the chair. "Come on, we're going to Ma Fisher's for breakfast." I patted her on the rear end. "Go get dressed. You'll figure this out."

Their lot was full, so we parked across the street. The young lady at the hostess station showed us to a table for two and told us our waitress would be right with us. Sam stared out the window again. I was beginning to take it personally.

I ordered the large stack of pancakes, a thick slice of ham and hash browns. Sam ordered two eggs over easy with whole-wheat toast. Something was wrong.

"Why don't we discuss it?" I said. "Perhaps verbalizing it will unlock something in that magnificent brain of yours? We could brainstorm?"

Sam pursed her lips, gave me a tiny shake of her head, and said, "I'd need more than the brief drizzle you'd bring." It wasn't much, but it was a start. I'd get her to talk to me yet. She watched the traffic flow by our window.

After the waitress delivered our food, I dove into mine like I hadn't eaten since the start of the New

Year. Sam didn't touch hers, at least not with her mouth. She slid the eggs around on her plate and acted as if the toast had been used to make penicillin. I cut into the stack of pancakes drenched – as in swimming – in syrup and speared a section with my fork. As I talked to Sam, I waved the fork back and forth. "Listen, I'm telling you, we need to talk…"

The wedge of pancakes flew off my fork, hitting Sam squarely in the face. "Oh shit! I'm sorry, I'm sorry, I'm sorry. It was an accident. I didn't mean to do that."

I was sure Sam was about to take out her gun and kneecap me. Then I thought no, she'll aim a bit higher. Instead, she said, "That's it." Not, "that's it," in the sense she'd had her fill of me, and she was going to come across the table to throttle me from the restaurant to the mysterious Oak Island and back. It was, "that's it," as in, she had a revelation, a Eureka moment. "Let's go, there's something I want to check out."

I gestured to my plate of uneaten food. "Let me get a doggie bag."

She extracted her wallet, threw a twenty and a ten on the table, grabbed me by the arm, and hauled me out of the restaurant. I was shocked. I couldn't remember the last time Sam picked up a check. She marched me out to the car. "Home, Chancy." Not Ace, Chancy. Something was definitely up.

She ran the five flights of stairs, reread the crime scene report, and smiled. She delved further into Adrianna's reports. I watched fascinated as she moved from one piece of information to the other. Along the way, there was an occasional nod, or I heard her say something like, "Yes, that makes sense." She stayed at it for over an hour before she got a second email from Adrianna. She stared wide-eyed at her monitor, then called me over and pointed at a picture on the screen. "Who does this remind you of?"

She didn't wait for me to answer. My mouth hung open so far it'd have come out more unintelligible than usual.

She grabbed her phone and called Adrianna again. "What's up, woman?" she said again. "I want you to check out someone else for me. ... His name is Walter Davis. Traditional spelling for both. He died in Flint in 1989. He was murdered. That should help narrow it. I want everything you can find on him." She waited while Adrianna repeated the info, then asked, "How long do you think it'll take?" ... "Thanks, we'll be waiting."

Sam refused to say anymore. I was still hungry, so I fixed myself some bacon and eggs and flipped on the TV. Sam spent the next two hours doing research. *I* spent the next two hours channel surfing. Springsteen was right, 57 channels and nothing on. In my case, it was closer to 5700 channels and nothing on.

Sam's phone buzzed. She answered it before it could ring, "Talk to me... Thanks as I said, you're the best."

She opened the new email from Adrianna and the attachment. She leaned in closer to the computer as if the proximity might help her better understand what the report held. She returned to the prior report, printed out the picture she'd shown me earlier, jumped out of the chair, and said, "Let's go."

On the way to my car, Sam called Shannon. "Hey, hi. We discovered something. Do you mind if we come by?" Shannon must have said it was okay because Sam said, "Thanks, we'll be there in thirty minutes. Do you..." Shannon interrupted Sam's question. After a moment, Sam said, "That's even better. Perfect."

I asked her what was going on, again, but, again, she held up her one-minute finger. I can't begin to express my sincere loathing for that gesture.

"Hi, I'd like to speak to Detective Callas, please." She gave her name and waited. "Hi, Detective Callas, we're headed to Trey and Shannon's. You may want to be there for this." He said something to her, but she answered with, "I think it'd be better if I explained it to you there. Trust me, it'll be well worth your time." She didn't wait for an answer and hung up. She was none too forthcoming with me either as we drove. Before I could inquire further, she shut me down. "You'll see."

We pulled into the circular drive, stopping behind a purple and green Cadillac Escalade SUV. We rang the bell, and Shannon let us in. We joined Dr. Foucher in Trey's den. As we entered, he jumped out of his seat. "I hear you did great. You proved Trey's innocent. I never did trust Rosario. Imagine killing someone over money."

Sam didn't acknowledge what he'd said, walked past him, and took her place on the loveseat. I parked myself next to her.

"What is it you wanted to tell me?" Shannon asked a bit on edge.

"I'll explain when Detective Callas arrives. It shouldn't be long."

"Detective Callas is coming here? Does this concern Trey?" Shannon asked. "Is he okay? You are going to be able to prove he didn't do this. Right?"

"Yes, I'm positive. But let's wait until Callas gets here."

While we waited, Shannon fidgeted with the items on Trey's desk. She straightened the papers and set the pens in a row. She squared off the tray and placed the stapler and letter opener parallel to one another. The doorbell rang. Shannon rushed to stand, but Sam stopped her. "Chancy, why don't you go get it?"

I led Callas and Nunn back to the office. They chose to stand. "This better be good," Callas said. "The reason I agreed to this was because you helped us find Juanita Sanchez's killer. ... Oh, and don't ever hang up on me again."

"Or what? You'll ground me? Take away my phone privileges? Relax." Sam smiled to let him know she was teasing him. "Trust me, Detective, you'll find this both educational and illuminating."

Despite Sam's effort to placate him, Callas wasn't too pleased to be talked to in such a manner, especially in front of two relative strangers, but he kept his mouth shut and motioned as if to say, "Go ahead. It's your show."

"I did some research this morning after we talked. Jeff Tomlin of West Allis Shooter's Supply deposited $100,000 in an offshore account in Belize. From there, the money was transferred once more, but I couldn't find out where. I ran into a dead-end."

When Callas opened his mouth to ask a question, Sam added, "Tomlin is way overextended in his finances. He's made contact with a law firm, specializing in bankruptcy."

"How...?" Callas started to ask.

Sam waved him quiet, which pissed him off, all over again. "I checked his phone logs." She turned to me and added, "As soon as we left Cream City Shooter's, he called Rosario. It got me thinking, so I researched the last owner and the sale of the range. The cameras *were* working that night of the Muskies' gun safety lesson. It was in the contract Tomlin and the last owner signed, the cameras were fully functional. My guess is Tomlin must have seen Rosario pick up some of Trey's cartridges and pocketed them. When I asked him about someone picking up cartridges that night, Tomlin put two and two together and realized Rosario had framed Trey. I suspect Tomlin called to blackmail him. There were subsequent calls between the two over the next few days. At some point, I'm guessing Rosario brought up the possibility of hiring him to kill us...well me. The $100,000 cashier's check was taken out of Rosario's account after their third phone conversation. There was also a call from Tomlin to Rosario at the same time we were headed to Little Chute. That's when Rosario must have told him about the tattoo parlor and to take out Justin Case as well."

"But why would Tomlin agree to kill someone?" I asked.

"His shooting range is woefully lacking clients. A large number of people posted on his website that they wouldn't patronize a gun club that catered to clientele like 'those people' who made up the Milwaukee Muskies. The same day of the Little Chute shooting," Sam paused and smiled at what she'd said, "Rosario got a second cashier's check for $30,000, although, there's no record of it being cashed."

Sam turned her attention to Callas. "Tomlin enlisted in the Marines where he earned expert marksmanship scores. He drives a Ford Escape, its license is M SHOOTR."

Callas called the information into the Department and asked Tomlin be picked up and questioned.

When he hung up, he said, "You couldn't have told me over the phone. You dragged us all the way out here…"

Sam said, "It gets better."

FIFTY

Sam pulled out the picture she'd showed me on the computer and handed it to Shannon. "Who does this remind you of?"

"Why, it looks like Trey, kind of. But it appears to be an old picture."

Detectives Callas and Nunn moved toward the desk and viewed the photo. Dr. Foucher didn't move. He stared at the ceiling while scratching his left hand.

"Aren't you curious, Doctor?" Sam asked.

"Uh-uh. I know who it is. I thought you might get 'round to finding it."

"Is this you?" Shannon asked.

"Forty-two years and eighty pounds lighter. It's my high school graduation picture."

"What does this mean?" Shannon asked, confused. "Are you Trey's uncle or something?"

Before Foucher could open his mouth, Sam said, "Grandfather. It's why he treats Trey differently than the rest of his clients. Blood is thicker than money, in his case."

"Why didn't you say anything?" Shannon asked Foucher.

We studied Foucher, who gathered his thoughts before answering. "I couldn't bring myself to do it. I wanted to when I first met Trey and his mama, but..." He lapsed into momentary silence. "I was sixteen and got my girlfriend pregnant. Her name was Regina Davis. I offered to marry her, but her parents said no. They even insisted on giving the baby their last name. I lost track of the family when I went off to college and tried for years to make the NBL.

"But one day I read an article in the paper of a Walter Davis being killed. He was the right age. I checked into it and found out it was the son I'd never known. I got hold of Regina before she died. She told me how our son raped a young woman and was killed by the girl's mama. She said the girl's name was Adelphia Williams, she'd had his baby. Using that, I tracked down Trey's mama and discovered her son was a McDonald's All-American Basketball Star. But..." He returned inside his head and became silent.

I'd my own Eureka moment. "That's why you knew Adelphia had 'been through too much in her life.' That's right. She said the only person she'd ever told was her therapist." I gave myself a mental head slap for not coming to that realization sooner.

Not having been privy to Foucher and my conversation, Sam still caught the gist of what I'd said. She remained focused on Foucher and continued my revelation. "Once you found them – and after you'd come to understand Adelphia was still in therapy because of the rape – you didn't want to be reminded of the grief your son, Walter Davis, caused the family whenever they looked at you, even if you had nothing to do with the way he was raised. Better to play the benevolent agent than to be thrown from the life of your newfound grandson. Especially when Trey was close to making it. You saw it as an opportunity to stay close."

Foucher dropped his chin to his chest.

"This is all so touching, Summers, but what does that have to do with anything?" Callas asked.

Sam explained, "I reread the police report on Anita's murder. Two sets of fingerprints were on the statue – Trey and Anita's. Which makes sense because Trey handled it when it was presented to him, and Anita, when she dusted it, then stole it. Whether she took it for sentimental reasons, or because she saw it as a fitting punishment for Trey fighting the child support, we'll never know. We do know she stole other items from the house, though. The fingerprints on the statue were right side up as if someone was holding it to show other people."

To demonstrate, Sam took one of the statues off the shelf, gripped it as if it was an Oscar, and held it out toward Callas. She turned it over and grasped it by the top. "This is the way it was held to kill Anita. No fingerprint pattern similar to that was discovered on the statue. That's because the person who wielded it wore gloves. When we talked to Theresa Garza, she told us she remembered the man she saw, wore gloves."

Callas interrupted her. "Anyone could have worn gloves, including Trey."

"Yes, but a few other details must be considered. Before I get to those, let me ask you this. The first time you took us to the crime scene, you knocked on the door. Why?"

"Whaddaya mean?"

"Why didn't you ring the bell? Why did you knock instead?"

"The doorbell didn't work?" Callas sounded as if he was trying to guess the correct answer to Sam's question.

"Exactly. Theresa Garza mentioned the person walked up the stairs and knocked. He didn't try to ring the bell."

"And?"

"It means the person had been there before and knew it wasn't working. Trey told us he'd never been there. He'd asked Dr. Foucher to pick up Anita to take her to the clinic to have the blood work done for the paternity test. Dr. Foucher knew from his earlier visit the bell didn't work. Just like you knew it didn't work."

Callas nodded his understanding.

"Second, the door was unlocked, so everyone reasoned she knew her assailant. She knew Dr. Foucher from that day at the clinic if not before, through Trey."

"What's the third thing?"

"Remember the footprint found in the hallway? It's too small to be Trey's." She pointed to Dr. Foucher's feet. "It was a size twelve and a half. Trey wears a fifteen."

Foucher slid his feet under his chair when everyone swung their attention to his shoes.

"Theresa Garza described the person she saw as not young but not old either." She said to Dr. Foucher. "Other than your weight, you've kept yourself in decent shape. You don't move like a sixty-year-old. I watched the video of you hosting the event at the Boys and Girls Club the same day Juanita died. You still move up and down the court fairly well with some of those youngsters."

Sam returned to explaining her theory to Callas. "There's also the 9-1-1 call. When Anita spoke, she said Trey's name followed by what sounded like, 'Ah.' She was trying to tell the operator it was Trey Williams' agent."

"But 'agent' doesn't sound like 'ah'?" Callas asked, confused.

"It does in Spanish." To prove her point, Sam said with perfect Spanish diction, "Agente."

We watched Foucher. He remained resolute, not giving away anything by his body language.

Callas asked Sam. "What's his motive?"

"He didn't go there to kill her. Ace accidentally hit me with a fork full of pancakes this morning and spent the next five minutes apologizing, saying it was an accident."

Callas was still bewildered.

"The two murders were different. One an act of passion, the other premeditated. If Valenzuela committed Anita's murder, he'd have used a gun. The statue was an instrument of convenience. It may have been something which sent Foucher into even more of a rage when he knew she'd stolen it from his client/grandson."

She turned her attention to Foucher. "Did you go to talk to her? Offer her some money to make it go away?"

Foucher stared at Sam for a long time, debating if he should confess or ask for his lawyer. His face grew placid. He said to Shannon, "I was trying to protect Trey. I was sure he didn't get her pregnant. He loves you way too much. I thought if I talked to her, I could convince her to tell the truth – get her to admit the baby was somebody else's. She stuck to her story, insisting it was Trey's. I offered her money, but she laughed in my face. She screamed Trey was going to be paying for years, and what I was offering didn't begin to come close to that.

"Her laughter became maniacal. She ordered me to leave. Summers is right, when I saw the trophy, it pissed me off even more. Before I knew it, she was lying at my feet, blood pooling beneath her head. I panicked and ran out."

"But not before you reset her watch ahead twenty minutes and smashed it against the hardwood floor. Twice," Sam said. "It must not have shattered the first time. You used much more force the second. If it broke upon the impact of a natural fall, there'd have been glass in both indentations, not just the second, more pronounced hit."

Everyone turned to Sam, wondering how she knew that bit of information. Foucher gave his head a shake of disbelief. "How...?"

"Two separate marks were on the floor where the watch hit. The first was barely perceptible. The second gouged the floor. Plus, tiny, minute bits of glass were embedded in the second mark and none in the first. You needed to swing her arm twice to break it. The autopsy photos showed slight trauma to Anita's knuckles."

The silence hung heavy in the room. Everyone focused on Foucher. I ended it. "That's why I was able to alibi him out. She was attacked earlier than the 7:10 of the broken watch."

"Yes. When we talked to Maria Alvarez, the clock on her microwave was seven minutes ahead of time. Do you remember when we interviewed Maria and Theresa? It took us three minutes thirty-two seconds to reach the end of 16th Street viaduct across from the casino after we'd left Theresa's. I calculated it'd have taken us another minute, forty-four seconds to drive down the ramp and up to the casino valet. Less than seven minutes. It allowed Dr. Foucher plenty of time to establish an alibi if the police jumped to the conclusion the watch broke at the same time as her murder."

I said to Foucher, my voice tinged with disgust, "Yet, you played cards that night?"

He shrugged. "I didn't want Trey to become suspicious. I drove straight to the game, trying to make sure I arrived before him. Little did I know you'd show up three minutes after I did. On the way, I convinced myself the best thing to do was to act as if nothing had happened. I rationalized Trey was finally going to be free of her and her lies. His reputation intact. I never dreamt they'd accuse him of her murder." He turned to me. "I'm a much better poker player than you saw."

"Obviously," I said without a hint of sarcasm. "Most people don't have the ability to appear as calm as you did, knowing they'd killed someone."

"Most people don't grow up in the inner city either. Violence and death were realities we dealt with every day. Most of my friends were dead before they could legally drink."

Callas told Foucher to stand and cuffed him. He read him his rights, although I was sure they'd have no trouble getting a conviction with what he shared voluntarily.

I asked, "How come you let Trey take the rap for this?"

"If it'd gone to trial," Foucher said, "I'd have come forward." He glanced over his shoulder at Sam. "In hindsight, I'd have been better off not suggesting Trey hire you to investigate whether Shannon was having an affair. When the two of them insisted on keeping you on the case, I suspected it'd come to this. When you fingered Rosario, I thought maybe I'd gotten away with it."

Callas received a call from one of his officers. When he hung up, he said, "Tomlin's nowhere to be found. His assistant at the gun club said he hasn't seen him in two days. Tomlin told him he had to go out of town on business. Hasn't talked to him since. We'll put out an APB for him, but with a two-day head start, he could be any place. We'll flag the flight manifests, but..." Callas shrugged, then nodded at Nunn, and they led Foucher out.

After the door closed, I thought of something else. "What about his car?"

"I'm sure you can buy it cheap," Sam said with a knowing smile.

"No, I mean, it's purple and green, not black."

"Not in the dark, it isn't. Without light reflecting off it, it appears to be black. It's in the light it changes from one color to the other. Theresa told us it was noche. She also said the streetlight wasn't working. Remember?" Sam quoted Theresa, " 'The streetlight not so good.' She couldn't tell he wore gloves until he was on the porch because the porch light was on, which means there wasn't enough light coming from the street."

"How did you figure it was Foucher and not either Rosario or Tomlin?"

"Maria Alvarez said on the night Anita was murdered, she thought the sisters were going to start arguing again until she recognized it was a man's voice."

"And?"

"That's the other thing that bothered me. I knew something was there, but I couldn't dislodge it from my brain. I was stuck on the idea *one* person was behind both murders. You hitting me with the pancakes and apologizing, moved me in the right direction."

"You're welcome," I said. She ignored me.

"Anita's was a spur of the moment murder, not premeditated. At Ma Fisher's, it dawned on me I had it back-assward. I recalled what Maria said when we talked to her, what she remembered hearing. The two sisters fought for weeks. If Juanita had been able to convince Anita what she was doing was wrong, they wouldn't have been fighting anymore. The fact Maria thought they were going to begin fighting again, spoke volumes. That's when I realized Anita was still going through with the plan. There'd have been no reason for Rosario to want her dead. Somebody else was behind it – Dr. Foucher."

"All that from pancakes smacking you in the face. Admit it, I'm a great asset."

"You're off by two letters."

Shannon interrupted our banter. "Will they release Trey?"

"Most definitely. It'll take an hour or so to fill out the paperwork, but he'll probably be out in time for you two to have lunch."

"I don't know how to thank you two."

Shannon gave me a chaste hug. Then she and Sam embraced. It lasted so long, I thought I would have to drive straight to church and confess my impure thoughts.

When they let go, they bussed each other's cheeks with European kisses. Sam asked, "Are you going to be okay?"

"Eventually," I said.

Shannon laughed. "Yes. I will. I feel terrible I ever doubted Trey, but hopefully, he'll forgive me, and we'll move forward. Thank you, again. I don't know if I'll ever be able to repay you."

Sam waved it away as if Shannon was too magnanimous. "You take care of yourself? And Chancy and I'd love to go to a game once in a while."

The two women gave one another loving smiles. Sam said to me. "Speaking of lunch, I'm starving. Come on, your turn to buy. I got breakfast, remember?"

"You mean, the one I never got to finish?"

She patted my stomach. "It's not as if you needed it."

EPILOGUE

Three days later, we found ourselves in the law offices of John Anthony Thomas to meet with him, Trey, and Shannon. The five of us were positioned around a table in one of the smaller conference rooms.

"Thank you for your help in this matter," Attorney Thomas said after Trey, Shannon, Sam, and I talked and laughed for a few minutes. "Ms. Summers, I take it you brought your expense report for me?" Sam slid a manila envelope across the table to him. "I'm going to run this over to our accounting department. I'll be right back."

When he left, I said to Sam. "He's going to freak out when he sees the Vegas trip."

"I didn't put that in there."

"What? It cost me a small fortune."

Sam shook her head. "Trey got us the rooms. We were comped the tickets to the show. All you paid for were the plane tickets and the dinners."

"And the cabs."

"How much did you take home, Ace?"

"Oh, yeah."

I must have appeared duly chastised because both Shannon and Trey laughed. "We can't thank you two enough," Trey said. "This whole thing has been bittersweet. Shannon and I have a renewed commitment to our marriage. And, I found out I have a grandfather. Unfortunately, he'll be in jail for a long time. I've hired Attorney Thomas to defend him. We're hoping to get the charge reduced to manslaughter."

He shifted his attention to Shannon. "Do you want to tell them, or should I?" She gestured for him to go ahead. "We're going to keep the baby. I've had time to reflect on how selfish and irrational I was being. We'll give her a beautiful home. I'm sure we'll make great parents. Shannon will, for sure." She leaned into him. He gave her a firm one-armed squeeze. "Who knows? Perhaps we'll even have some more."

"That's great," I said. "What're you going to name her?"

Shannon smiled at Sam. "Samantha Adelphia Williams. We'd like you two to be the godparents."

Sam and Shannon embraced once more. Not as long as they did in Trey's den, but long enough, I was headed to the confessional again. I reached over and shook Trey's hand.

"Thanks, that's a great honor," Sam said with a catch in her voice when the two women let go.

"Trey's mom is going to come live with us to help take care of the baby." Trey and Shannon moved together, placing their arms around one another. I don't know if I've ever seen two happier people.

To stop from crying, Sam said to me. "Pretty neat, right, Ace?"

I smiled at her discomfort.

Trey asked, "Why do you call Chancy, Ace?"

"His full name is, Aaron Chancellor Evans. A. C. E."

"Sam calls me Ace whenever she thinks I'm being a dick." Before Sam could say anything, I added, "She uses it a lot."

Everyone had a nice laugh, so I continued to explain. "My mom's Irish. She wanted to name me Erin with an E because she thought I was going to be a girl. She's still pissed I'm not. My mom refused to let anyone cut my hair, and she dressed me in tights and skirts. My dad called me Chancy to deflect the 'what a beautiful little girl' comments. Before I entered kindergarten, my dad took me to a barber and got me my first haircut. He also bought me jeans and a little man golf shirt. My mom didn't speak to him for a year. My dad was the happiest man alive."

Trey and Shannon couldn't stop laughing.

Thomas returned. The room went quiet. The discomfort grew until: "One day little Billy's teacher asks him what his dad does for a living."

"I've heard this."

"Little Billy proudly announces, 'My dad is a piano player in a whorehouse.' "

"I've heard this."

"The teacher quickly changes the subject, but later, calls Little Billy's mother, and says to her, 'Your son told the class your husband is a piano player in a whorehouse.' The mother says to the teacher. 'Actually, he's a lawyer, but how do you explain something like that to a seven-year-old.' "

When Attorney John Anthony Thomas finished telling his joke, he laughed harder than the other three. I deadpanned, "I've heard this," then joined in.

When we exited the elevator on our way back to my car, I said, "You seem pensive again. What's bothering you?"

"I don't know. Seeing the two of them so happy, makes me wonder if I'll ever find someone to love that much."

"You'll always have me. I'd go to the ends of the earth for you."

"I know, but would you stay there." She placed her arm inside of mine and laid her head on my shoulder.

Please leave a review on Amazon

GNMBooks.com
Robert G. Peterson
http://www.GNMbooks.com

Stacking The Deck)Samantha Summers Book 2
Doubling Down (Samantha Summers Book 3)
Cashed In (Samantha Summers Book 4)
Tapped Out (Samantha Summers Book 5)
Hedging A Bet (Samantha Summers Book 6)

Hoop Dweebs

(Young Adult Series)

The 8ᵀʰ Mayan Prophecy (Series)
Wind Walkers
Fire Keepers
The Minoan Legacy

Short stories: (Available as E-Books)
Dreamcatcher
AJ
The Tepal

Contact: RGP@GNMBooks.com
Find us on Facebook @ GNM Books

Made in the USA
Monee, IL
20 July 2021

74011424R00197